THE COUNTRY HOUSE MURDERS

A 1930s MURDER MYSTERY

Kel Richards

Marylebone House

Originally published in Australia in 2014
as *C. S. Lewis and the Country House Murders*
by Strand Publishing

First published in Great Britain in 2015

Marylebone House
36 Causton Street
London SW1P 4ST
www.marylebonehousebooks.co.uk

British Library Cataloguing-in-Publication Data
A catalogue record for this book is available from the British Library

ISBN 978–1–910674–19–2
eBook ISBN 978–1–910674–20–8

Manufacture managed by Jellyfish
First printed in Great Britain by CPI
Subsequently digitally printed in Great Britain

eBook by Midland Typesetters, Australia

Produced on paper from sustainable forests

THE TIME: The spring of 1934; during the short spring break between Hilary and Trinity terms at Oxford.

THE PLACE: Plumwood Hall, a stately home on the outskirts of the small village of Plumwood.

ONE

~

'Dear Jack,' I wrote, 'I think I'm about to be arrested and charged with murder.'

As I leaned back in my chair I looked at the sentence I had written. The words captured my rising sense of panic. No, panic is too strong a word. Perhaps the best word for how I felt at that moment, at that stage of the investigation, was: apprehensive. Or, as Mr Roget would have put it in one of his lighter moments: apprehensive, anxious, uneasy, worried, fearful, hesitant, nervous, disquieted, concerned, angst-ridden and twitchy.

As I picked up my pen to continue the letter, a gust of wind flapped the curtain and rattled the window pane. The wind was blowing in from the coast and carried a hint of salt spray—a suggestion of waves shattering on rocks above a green and grim-looking sea. The wind made me shiver, as if someone had just walked over my grave. I leaned over the small writing table and pulled the window closed.

It had not been windy like this three days ago when it all began—the day of the murder.

Although it was only March, three days ago spring had burst upon us full of vim and vigour, hustle and bustle and determined to do business. Under sunny skies it scattered butterflies and rosebuds like a tipsy millionaire scattering bank notes to the hoi polloi. The spring that arrived that day looked like a promissory note in firm handwriting guaranteeing a hot summer ahead.

It was because of the delightful weather that Lady Pamela suggested tea on the terrace.

The marble-topped table was set up on the lawn just beyond the flagstones of the terrace. As the lady of the house, the wife of my employer, Sir William Dyer, Lady Pamela presided at the teapot, saying to each of us in turn, 'One lump or two? Lemon or cream?'

And responding in turn, seated around the table in cane chairs, were most of the members of the household. Next to me was Lady Pamela's cousin Connie, and next to her was Uncle Teddy, muttering something quietly to himself behind his floppy brown moustache. Then on the other side of Lady Pamela came her sons, Will and Douglas, and Douglas's friend Stephanie Basset, known as Stiffy. The only person missing, in fact, was Sir William himself. He had excused himself on the grounds of work to do. Looking up I could see him in his study on the first floor. He'd opened the study windows to let in the warmth, the sunshine and the birdsong of that early spring day.

In the middle of the table, on a cake plate, was one of Mrs Buckingham's rich, moist dark fruit cakes.

The butler and one of the maids stood behind Lady Pamela's chair, ensuring that everything was to madam's satisfaction. With the tea poured Lady Pamela nodded and said, 'That will be all, Keggs.'

'Very good, madam,' he replied, and his massive form turned slowly and gracefully around and glided back into the house, rather like a stately ocean liner steaming into port. The small kitchen maid trotted behind him like a tug boat bobbing along in the wake of the great steamship.

Douglas and Stiffy had their heads together, whispering and giggling, and young Will was staring greedily at the fruit cake, so I turned towards Uncle Teddy. Leaning across Connie, I said, 'What are you working on at the moment, Uncle Teddy?' (Everyone in the house being under instructions to address this dotty old duffer as 'Uncle'.)

'Eh? What? Working on? Oh, ah, yes, well . . . I'm trying to invent a way we could bake biscuits with chocolate inside them . . . how about that, eh? What do you think of that, Connie? Biscuits with chocolate inside them? Eh?'

Connie turned one of her famous icy stares on Uncle Teddy.

Constance Worth had only been staying at the house for a few weeks, but young Will had already nicknamed her the 'Ice Queen' and I'd overheard Douglas and Stiffy referring to her as the 'Black Widow'. On the rare occasions I had dared to disagree with her, she had given me a look that would have sent uncomfortable shivers down the spine of any passing penguin. In fact, the penguin would probably have turned to the polar bear beside him and jabbed it in the ribs to alert it to the arrival of an unexpected cold snap.

'The cake looks nice, Uncle Teddy,' I offered, ignoring Connie's arctic silence. 'One of Mrs Buckingham's masterpieces, I dare say.'

'Eh? What? The cake? Oh, yes, the cake. Yes, yes, yes, yes— wonderful woman, Cook. A wonderful woman. We exchange recipes, you know.' Uncle Teddy lowered his voice and leaned over Connie to whisper, 'The science of food, you see . . . she understands . . . it's really organic chemistry . . . it's all chemistry, you see.'

'Uncle Teddy,' said Lady Pamela in her clipped voice, 'are you talking nonsense again? Here, have a slice of fruit cake.'

Uncle Teddy accepted the offered plate and gave the cake the single-minded attention it richly deserved. Connie was served next, and I was served last of all.

My place in the household was slightly anomalous. I was there cataloguing the library of Plumwood Hall—a task I was close to completing. That made me not a family member or a guest exactly, but not a servant either. Not sure how I should be regarded, I had been, early in my stay, admitted to the family table as the scholar in their midst.

'Are you close to finishing your work, Mr Morris?' said Lady Pamela. Sir William had purchased Plumwood Hall from Lord Bosham, an impoverished nobleman, including the fittings and fixtures, the paintings and the contents of the library. And while this latter had belonged to generations of Lord Boshams, it had never been catalogued. That was the task I had begun many months earlier, and now the end was in sight.

'Very close,' I replied. 'There are a handful of volumes that are difficult to identify or classify. I've been putting them off until most of the task is completed. It now is. So all I need do is solve a few puzzles and tidy up some lose ends.'

Lady Pamela sniffed by way of reply, making it clear she wasn't really interested and had now made as much effort in the direction of polite conversation as she could be bothered with. I turned my attention to Mrs Buckingham's dark fruit cake.

I had just taken my first bite when I noticed that Connie beside me was acting strangely. Her eyes were wide open as if in panic, and she seemed to be having difficulty breathing.

'Mrs Worth?' I said. 'Are you all right?'

Her face was flushed a bright pink. She staggered to her feet, clutching the back of her chair and started to sway.

'Here,' I said, reaching out a hand. 'You'd better sit back down again. You don't look at all well.'

'Connie? Connie?' demanded Lady Pamela sharply. 'Are you ill?'

Connie opened her mouth to reply, but what came out were not words. She suddenly leaned forward and vomited onto the grass. I leaped up to avoid the fountain, then reached out to steady her as she swayed back and forth on her chair. Suddenly she slumped forward, her head coming down hard on the marble table. Uncle Teddy stood up and backed away, his crumpled old face looking fearful and confused. Lady Pamela rushed forward.

'Connie! Connie! What's wrong with her?' she demanded looking at me.

I leaned over her then replied, 'She's unconscious, but she's still breathing. You'd better get a doctor—quickly.'

'Yes, yes, of course. Douglas—go and telephone for Dr Henderson. Tell him it's an emergency.'

Henderson's small black Austin came rattling up the driveway fifteen minutes later. But by then it was too late. By then Constance Worth was dead.

TWO

~

'Dear Jack,' I wrote, 'I think I'm about to be arrested and charged with murder. Inspector Hyde seems to think I murdered a woman I barely know.' I paused and looked up again, across the small writing table and out of my bedroom window, before continuing. 'She is, or *was* I suppose, Constance Worth—known around the house as Connie. She was Lady Pamela's cousin, and was fairly universally disliked—so why I've been chosen to play the role of First Murderer in this little melodrama I'm not entirely sure.

'Inspector Hyde is the man we both met last year. Do you remember him? He has a face like a weasel, but not just any weasel—a weasel with a grudge against the world and a bad case of indigestion. Leaping to conclusions seems to be his favourite form of exercise. His policy appears to be: pick your chosen villain first and examine the evidence afterwards. He's like those boys in mathematics classes who don't want to understand the formula, they just want to know the answer.

'What possible motive could I have to murder Connie? My murdering Connie Worth is about as likely as my trekking to the North Pole—naked, while chatting to a polar bear and whistling "Old Lang Syne". And I don't even like the songs of Robbie Burns! In fact, I'd be more likely to murder Robbie Burns than Connie Worth.

'The man is a complete idiot. Inspector Hyde, I mean, not Robbie Burns. However, to be fair, I understand his problem. It's a question of who put the cyanide in the cake and how they did it.

'The problem is that we each one of us around that table ate a slice of Mrs Buckingham's delicious dark fruit cake, and only Connie died. So the question is: how? How did a massive, fatal dose of cyanide get into the slice of cake she ate when there wasn't a trace of cyanide in the rest of the cake?'

I kept scribbling away, describing the situation that afternoon three days earlier: seven of us sitting around the small, marble-topped table; each of us eating a piece of dark fruit cake; six people showing no symptoms while the seventh was dead within minutes of taking a bite.

'The village doctor (I wrote) is Dr George Henderson—a fussy, careful little man. As he checked for Connie's pulse and breathing and pronounced her dead, he had Lady Pamela hovering by his side squawking like a pirate's parrot during a storm at sea. She bleated about poor Connie having died from a sudden heart attack or a sudden stroke . . . or from a sudden something.

'Henderson actually pulled a pad out of his Gladstone bag to write out a death certificate and then thought better of it. It took him a long time to get Lady Pamela to accept that in cases of sudden death it was important to be certain and not to jump to conclusions. Of course, a conclusion was exactly what Lady Pamela wanted jumped at—preferably jumped at, hurdled and quickly left behind. Connie was only staying in the house thanks to the family's sense of obligation, as Lady Pamela's cousin. No one particularly liked her, and Lady Pamela just wanted her death cleared away and forgotten about—like a mess the dog has made on the drawing-room floor.

'Dr Henderson asked me how quickly death had occurred after the first symptoms appeared. I guessed about five or ten minutes. He looked at the pink flush on Connie's face and even smelled the vomit on the lawn. Then he took Lady Pamela to one side and quietly explained that he would have to inform the police of the death. At that point I thought there might be a second murder—that Lady Pamela might attack Dr Henderson with the nearest available blunt instrument. However, he survived her horrified reaction and made the phone call.

'That was when the fun and games began. Inspector Hyde arrived with the local village bobby in tow to take notes—a nice chap named Charlie Nile. Hyde questioned everyone, made a diagram of the seating plan at the afternoon tea table and confiscated the rest of the fruit cake.'

At that point I lay down my pen and looked up out of the window facing the little writing table in my bedroom. Three days earlier the sky had been sunny; now it was filled with menacing clouds. The rolling, thick, purple-grey thunderheads seemed to express my own gloomy frame of mind. It was late in the day and the sun was close to the western horizon. The blood-red glow of sunset, with scattered splashes of gold, reflected from the underside of the clouds, making them look like a city hanging upside down in the sky.

As I watched, the heaviest clouds rolled apart to reveal clear sky filled with the red-tinted golden glow of the setting sun. An omen, I told myself—a sign that there was light at the end of the gloomy tunnel of storms.

'The day after Connie's death (I wrote) we were told that she'd died from a massive dose of cyanide. Then yesterday Inspector Hyde rolled up with the news that the only cyanide was in the slice of fruit cake Connie had bitten into, while the rest of the cake was completely clear of contamination. Even his slow-working brain had deduced that this must mean the cyanide had been added after the cake had been cut. So who had tampered with Connie's slice of cake? We were all questioned and no one admitted to touching Connie's cake, which is hardly surprising. But, in addition, no one had seen anyone else touch the cake on Connie's plate.

'That's when Inspector Hyde turned his attention to me. Since I was sitting beside Connie, he reasoned, I must have, by some sleight of hand, slipped a fatal dose of cyanide into her cake while no one was looking. I pointed out that while I was on Connie's left hand, Uncle Teddy was seated at her right hand and had as much opportunity as I did. This was dismissed out of hand. Uncle Teddy is well known in the district as a harmless old eccentric so absent-minded and muddled he must have been dropped on his head as a baby.

'So, reasoned the rodent-like inspector, I must be a homicidal maniac who murdered a woman I hardly knew, for absolutely no reason, employing a method not unknown to medical science—but, still, it must be me. He is ignoring every other possible aspect of his investigation and pestering me day and night. When he's not asking me questions, he stands in the distance eyeing me suspiciously or asking everyone else in the household about me.

'Which brings me to the rest of the household. Quite frankly I am as puzzled as Inspector Hyde—since none of the family had reasons I know of for wanting Connie dead, and I can't imagine any of them committing murder.

'Lady Pamela is the matriarch who runs the house. I was once told she was a grocer's daughter before she married Billy Dyer. But then Billy Dyer turned his father's small biscuit factory into a mass production masterpiece churning out *Dyer's Digestive Biscuits*. The inclination of the citizens of these islands to want a digestive biscuit with every cup of tea has turned Dyer into a self-made millionaire, and a generous donor to political parties and fashionable charities. The result was that he collected a knighthood in the King's Birthday honours list some years ago. That made the former grocer's daughter into Lady William Dyer. She instantly became a bigger snob than if she had been the daughter of a long line of earls going back to William the Conqueror. But I still can't see her as a murderer.

'She and Sir William have two sons. Douglas is up at Oxford in his first year. He turned up a few days ago, as soon as Hilary Term ended, with a girl in tow. This is Stephanie Basset. My own theory is that when she looks at the rather pimply and unattractive Douglas, all she sees is the beautiful money he'll inherit one day. The younger son, Will, is rather more likable. He's also back here from his school for the term break. I can't conceive of any rhyme or reason for these youngsters to commit murder.

'The Uncle Teddy who has featured prominently in this correspondence is an interesting old bird. Strictly speaking he's only Sir William's uncle, but everyone is instructed to address him as uncle as he likes the title. He was the younger brother of Sir William's father, and he thinks of himself as an inventor—especially of new ways of making biscuits. Biscuit obsession seems to run in the family. Part of the stable block has been converted for his use. He calls it his "laboratory" and spends his days there conducting experiments he imagines will become new products for the giant biscuit factory Sir William manages. None of his experiments, it seems, ever produces anything practical. And Sir William is careful to keep him well away from the factory, and from having anything to do with real biscuit making.

'You would have to agree, Jack, it's a pretty dud cast of suspects. Which is why Inspector Hyde has fastened upon me as the most likely of the lot. I expect him to produce the hand-cuffs and lead me away in irons any day now.'

THREE

~

Jack's telegram was a delightful surprise: 'Arriving two o'clock train. Meet me at station.' So as the slow local train wheezed and clanked its way into the Plumwood railway station, I was standing on the small platform. A bundle of afternoon newspapers was thrown onto the platform from the guard's van at the rear, and a door opened on the passenger carriage.

Only one passenger alighted—a man dressed like a moderately successful farmer: old grey Harris Tweed jacket, with leather patches in the elbows; trousers of thickish grey flannel, uncreased and very out at the knees; stout brown walking boots; and an old grey felt hat. Underneath the hat was a round, ruddy, cheerful face. It was my old Oxford tutor, C. S. Lewis, known to all his friends as 'Jack'. He was carrying a single, battered suitcase.

He grinned broadly as he shook my hand. 'Morris, you old chump, what mess have you managed to get yourself into this time?' Then he laughed heartily and added, 'Nothing that can't be sorted out in short order, I warrant.'

We fell into step side by side as we walked out of the station and down the main street of the small village. 'Thanks for coming, Jack,' I said.

'Had no choice,' he boomed, in his robust voice. 'How would

it look for me if one of my former pupils became a convict in irons?'

I laughed at his pretence of having come entirely out of self-interest, but added, 'This is a case of murder, Jack. It's not the prison cell and the leg irons that loom but the hangman's noose.'

'Don't be so gloomy, Morris. The hempen rope and the sudden drop are not in your future, I assure you.'

'It's Inspector Hyde you need to assure, not me. He's the one who's refusing to look at any aspect of the case except the Tom Morris angle.'

'I do recall Hyde as a man inclined to adopt the narrow view.'

By now we were standing in front of *The Cricketers' Arms*, the only pub in Plumwood.

'I told Alfred Rose you were coming, so he'll have a room ready.'

No sooner had I said these words than the publican appeared at the front door—like the cuckoo popping out of the little door in the cuckoo clock at precisely the right time.

'Mr Lewis,' he beamed, 'welcome back. Nice to see you again, sir. And how is your brother?'

Rose had a remarkable memory for customers, even those he had not seen for the better part of a year.

'Warnie is doing very nicely,' said Jack, handing his suitcase over to the publican. 'And he sends his regards to you, Morris. He instructed me to get you swiftly and smartly untangled from whatever web you've fallen into.'

Warnie was Jack's brother, Major Warren Lewis, now retired from the British Army and living with Jack at their cottage, *The Kilns*, in Oxford.

'Dreadful business, this murder up at the hall, Mr Lewis,' said the publican. Then as we all stepped into the public bar he bellowed, 'Ronnie—come and take this gentleman's suitcase up to his room.' Ronnie Fish, barman and general dogsbody, emerged from the cellar, blinking in the daylight like a startled mouse, and took charge of Jack's suitcase.

As he disappeared up the stairs with this modest item of luggage, Alfred Rose said, 'Now, gentlemen—some refreshments before you settle in?'

He had stepped behind the bar as he uttered these words, but Jack turned down the implied offer of a pint and asked instead for a cup of tea—a large cup of tea.

Jack and I sank into the armchairs by the fireplace at one end of the bar. It was such an unseasonably warm day for March the fire had not been lit, but the chairs were the most comfortable in the room.

'Now then, Mr Lewis,' said the publican as he returned carrying a tea tray, with a teapot under a knitted cosy and cups and saucers, 'who slipped the cyanide into Mrs Worth's cake?'

Jack chuckled and said, 'I assume the murder is the only topic of conversation in the village?'

Rose nodded in vigorous agreement. 'Most exciting thing to happen in this village since the Great Plague of 1665. So, Mr Lewis, who's your hot tip as the most likely suspect?'

Pouring his cup of tea, Jack said, 'Solving a murder is not like solving a crossword—it's not done in minutes. You must at least give me time to examine the cryptic clues first.'

When the publican had wandered off and left us alone, Jack asked me for the latest news.

'Inspector Hyde still thinks of nothing but how to get me facing a charge of murder at the next assizes.'

'Narrow minded, as I said. He's rather like a small boy looking through a gap in the paling fence around a playing field: he doesn't see much of the game. Well, we must find a way to get him thinking in other directions. The stumbling block, I take it, is still the puzzle of how the poison got into the cake.'

'Mrs Buckingham, the splendid cook up at Plumwood Hall, has been in tears over the matter. Her kitchen has been searched by the police from top to bottom. They failed to find a single trace of cyanide, but of course that was always going to be a hopeless search since the cake, fresh from the oven, was completely uncontaminated—except for that one slice.'

'So, freshly baked and perfectly fit for human consumption?'

'Except for a single slice which, Dr Henderson told me, contained enough potassium cyanide to kill a horse—and a fairly robust horse in training for a major racing event at that. There was not even a hint of cyanide in the remainder of the cake.'

Jack finished his tea and said, 'That puzzle must wait until we know more. In the meantime, any chance that I might inspect the scene of the crime and meet the cast of this village melodrama?'

'Come on,' I replied, swallowing the last of my tea and rising from my armchair, 'we'll walk up to the hall—it's not far, just on the outskirts of the village.'

We stepped out into the sunshine, Jack paused to light his pipe, and then we started down the village street. Just ahead of us my employer, Sir William Dyer, appeared, coming out of the village post office and about to duck into the village chemist's shop. But when he saw me he stopped and walked over.

'Morning, young Tom. Glorious day.'

I took the hint that he wanted to be introduced to the visitor beside me.

'Sir William, this is my old Oxford tutor, C. S. Lewis.'

'Delighted to meet you, Mr Lewis. You here to give aid and comfort to young Tom in his hour of need?'

'Something along those lines.'

'Shocking murder, of course—shocking, shocking. Dreadful business. But I think Hyde is an idiot. He's making it clear to everyone that Tom is his main suspect. His only suspect. Rubbish. Complete rubbish. This young man's a scholar, not a killer. I've told Hyde that too. But he won't listen. Man's an idiot. You have my full support, Tom, and complete confidence.'

'Thank you, Sir William,' I muttered.

'You taking Mr Lewis up to the hall for a look around?'

'That's the idea,' I agreed.

'And you must come to dinner at the hall one night, Mr Lewis,' said Sir William affably, 'while you're in the district. Our son Douglas is up at Oxford; I'm sure he'd be delighted to meet you.'

Then Sir William wandered off, slapping me on the shoulder while assuring me I should dismiss all concerns that I might soon be facing a capital charge.

As my employer disappeared into the chemist's shop, Jack chuckled quietly and said, 'Odd way of cheering you up—by reminding you of the dark clouds.'

'Yes, he's a bit like the old friend you meet who greets you by telling you how ill you look,' I agreed. 'Eeyore would recognise in Sir William a kindred soul.'

FOUR

~

Just beyond the last row of cottages, at one end of the village street, stood two stone pedestals topped with carved lions. These flanked the driveway leading onto the grounds of Plumwood Hall.

The broad gravel drive was lined with poplars and wove around a grove of elm trees.

'Remarkable weather for March,' said Jack as we strode through the dappled sunlight. 'Reminds me of a pupil who once argued that every country has a climate except for England. England, he said, only has *weather*.' He paused to look up at the sky, then added, 'So today we suffer with this warmth and sunshine. I much prefer the cold.'

Just then a figure came crashing out of the undergrowth to our left and stumbled onto the road. It was Uncle Teddy, looking wilder than ever, his clothes untidy and twigs caught in his hair.

He looked at me and blinked. I could see the slow process of recognition and identification going on behind his grey eyes.

'Eh? Ah, oh it's you, young Thomas.'

'Well spotted, Uncle Teddy. And this is my friend, Mr Lewis.'

Jack extended a hand in greeting. Uncle Teddy finally decided to shake it after examining it for some moments as if it were a doubtful specimen under a microscope. Teddy was always rather slow to take to visitors. So after shaking Jack's hand he turned to me, as a familiar face, and simply pretended Jack wasn't there.

'What do you think of these, Tom? Eh? Eh?'

He opened his clenched right fist to reveal half a dozen very small, very bright red berries.

'They're . . .' I began, trying to work out what kind of response might be appropriate. But Uncle Teddy wasn't waiting for my answer.

'Highly acidic. Very good food acid, these. Should have a clarifying effect on the formula.'

And with that cryptic statement he simply stopped talking. So I asked, 'What formula, Uncle Teddy?'

'Eh? Eh? Formula? Oh, yes, yes, I have a new formula I'm working on. It's all organic chemistry, you know . . . all chemistry.'

'May I ask you a question, sir?' boomed Jack, in that lecture room voice that couldn't be ignored.

Uncle Teddy spun around, startled by this reminder that there was someone else present. He squinted suspiciously and then said, 'What question? What, what, what?'

'About the murder,' continued Jack. 'You were there when it happened. In fact, as I understand it you were sitting beside the victim. So should my friend Morris here have done anything suspicious, such as sprinkling a large quantity of poison on the victim's cake, you would have noticed. So did you?'

'Did I what?'

'Did you notice anything suspicious? Did you see Morris tampering with the victim's slice of cake?'

'No,' said Uncle Teddy, shaking his head vigorously. 'No, no, no, no. Nothing like that happened. Nothing at all. I told that policeman the same thing.'

'Good for you, Uncle Teddy,' I said. 'Inspector Hyde insists on regarding me as guilty despite your testimony. But thank you anyway.'

'Huh,' grunted Teddy, 'that policeman wouldn't listen to me. I told him it was all chemistry . . . organic chemistry. I told him to investigate the chemistry. He didn't seem interested.'

Jack intervened again to ask, 'So, who do you regard as the most likely guilty party, sir? Do you have a favoured suspect?'

A cunning look passed over Uncle Teddy's face, like a cloud passing over the face of the sun. For a moment the cheerful, dotty old man disappeared and was replaced by a cunning, calculating schemer with wild eyes.

'Douglas,' hissed Teddy. 'Look closely at Douglas. That's my answer.'

'And why is that?' asked Jack.

'I don't like him,' replied Teddy, the dark look again shadowing his face. 'Never have done. Plays tricks on me. Even when he was a small boy he was nasty. This will be one of Douglas's practical jokes gone wrong.'

I couldn't imagine any practical joke that would involve potassium cyanide. At the same time Uncle Teddy's words brought back a memory—of Douglas and Stiffy with their heads together giggling as the cake was served.

For a moment I was back on the day of the murder, reliving the nightmare. When I pulled myself together and returned to the present moment, Uncle Teddy had fallen silent and was staring down at the small red berries in his hand—as if surprised to find them there.

'More,' said Teddy at length. 'I shall need some more.' And with those words he walked rapidly off the gravel drive and plunged once more into the undergrowth. For a while we could hear him thrashing about, then the sights and sounds faded away.

We continued up the drive, following its slow, graceful curves, until the trees around us were replaced by rolling, manicured lawns, and there, ahead of us, was the house itself.

The main part of the building was said to be Elizabethan, with Georgian extensions and stables at the back, and late Victorian refurbishments and plumbing inside. The gravel drive now became a broad circle that swept up to the front door.

Just as we reached the house the door flew open and Inspector Hyde bounced down the steps like an impatient rubber ball. When he saw me standing on the drive he almost skidded to a halt on the gravel.

There was a slightly uncomfortable silence, an aggressive silence on his part, an apprehensive one on mine. Then he said, 'Good, good, you're here.'

'Where did you expect me to be?'

He narrowed his eyes, bared his teeth and breathed heavily. His impersonation of a weasel was becoming more uncanny by the minute. I'm sure any passing stoat would have cheerfully hailed him, calling out, 'Hey cousin! Nice to see you again. And keep all those non-weasels in line.'

'I ordered you not to leave the district,' he said, if heavy breathing counts as speaking, 'and I'm pleased to see you're obeying orders.'

'Inspector Hyde, may I introduce my friend, Mr Lewis. He's—'

But Hyde interrupted me. 'I've met Mr Lewis before. He

interfered in a murder inquiry and hampered police in the course of their duties.'

'And he solved the murder,' I pointed out.

'I'm delighted to see you again,' said Jack, his round face beaming and his voice at its heartiest and cheeriest.

Hyde ground his teeth in silence for a moment and then growled, 'Just see you don't do it again. Don't stick your oar into an official police investigation. Your theorising is all very well in Oxford, but it's not welcome here.'

Time to give this pompous man a jab in the ribs, I thought, so I cheerfully asked, 'So how is the investigation going then?'

The inspector took a few rapid paces down the drive and then turned, spinning in the gravel, and snapped, 'Scotland Yard is being called in. The Chief Constable has called them in. There was no need. I was on top of the case. I *am* on top of the case. I have my suspect and I'm collecting my evidence. But if Colonel Weatherly wants to call in Scotland Yard that's . . . well, that's his prerogative.'

He became quite red in the face during this short speech. Having delivered it, he strode purposefully down the drive and disappeared from view.

'My guess, young Morris,' chortled Jack as Hyde vanished around the curve of the drive, 'is that the Chief Constable has been urging him to call in Scotland Yard since day one. Our friend Hyde is a man for writing rosters and organising traffic duty, not solving puzzles. Now, shall we examine the scene of the crime?'

FIVE

~

I led Jack around the corner of the house to the south wing. There, just outside the French windows leading into the drawing room, was the paved terrace and the spreading lawn where we had that fateful tea on the day of the murder. The small marble-topped table was still there, but someone, the gardener presumably, had put the cane chairs away— probably in a garden shed out of the weather.

Jack walked over to the table on the lawn and stood looking down on it for a moment.

'Now, young Morris, talk me through the seating arrangements.'

So I stood in each of the places around the table where the chairs had been arranged that afternoon, saying such things as 'I was here' and (shuffling to my right) 'Connie was here' and so on, until I had, Magellan-like, circumnavigated that small world.

'And the cake was where exactly?'

'Right in the middle of the table.'

'Who cut it?'

'Lady Pamela.'

'So it came to the table uncut?'

'It arrived whole. In fact, it was still slightly warm so it can't have been long out of the oven.'

'How, exactly, did this cutting proceed?'

'Well, it was a log-shaped cake so Lady Pamela cut across one end. The end slice can be a bit dry so she put that to one side, then proceeded to cut one slice at a time, and pass it, on a small plate with a cake fork, to the intended recipient.'

'In what order?'

'Douglas's girlfriend got the first slice. Stephanie Bassett, known to one and all as Stiffy, has genuine blue blood, unlike the nouveau riche Lady Pamela. I think the Dyers are quite keen on a match between her and their son, so she is always favoured with attention. Douglas was served next, and then Will—mainly because Will was loudly demanding his slice of the cake, as growing boys are wont to do. Then Lady Pamela served Uncle Teddy, Connie, herself and me last of all. I am only the scholar in residence—not a servant, but not really a proper guest either, so my place is at the end of queue.'

'Hard to see how a fatal dose of cyanide could get into one slice—a slice freshly cut off the cake—and be totally absent from all the others. What do we know about the cyanide in the slice the victim ate? Was it spread evenly throughout the slice? Or in concentrated clumps?'

'I've heard nothing,' I admitted.

'Well perhaps,' said Jack, filling his pipe, 'if we ask nicely, this local GP chappie . . .'

'Dr Henderson.'

'. . . yes, will tell us.'

Just behind where the table stood was an ancient oak. When in full leaf it provided welcome shade from the summer sun. March was too early for the tree to have begun shooting, so above us were only bare, gnarled and twisted branches.

As we stood there, Jack smoking and thinking and me waiting for his flash of insight, an arrow whistled between us and thudded into the grey trunk of the ancient tree.

To say that Jack and I were startled would be an understatement. In the words of the great Wodehouse, we were as startled as the man who, while bending over to pick flowers beside the railway line, was struck in the small of the back by the Cornwall Express.

As I looked around for the source of this attack, and for other possible flying missiles, Will emerged from the French windows with a sheepish grin on his young face and a bow in his hand.

'I say . . . sorry, Tom . . . sorry, sir,' he said as he walked across the terrace, trying not to look too pleased. 'But my aim's jolly good, isn't it? I got it right between the two of you and into the tree trunk.'

'You should be scalped, young Will,' I said, trying to look stern. Will responded by grinning more broadly.

'We haven't been introduced,' said Jack.

'This scoundrel is Will Dyer, and this gentleman, Will, is my old Oxford tutor, C. S. Lewis.'

'How do you do, sir? I'm very pleased to meet you.'

Jack was amused by Will's cheeky charm and responded, 'So how did you learn such deadly skill with the bow and arrow?'

'My Uncle Edmund taught me. He knew about these things.'

'That's someone I've not met, Will,' I said, 'although I've heard him occasionally mentioned. Who is Uncle Edmund?'

'He's dead,' replied the boy, with the cold indifference of youth. 'He was mama's younger brother. He was an explorer.'

'And whereabouts did he do his exploring?' asked Jack.

'Mostly in South America. In the jungles, you know. He brought back jolly interesting things—native weapons, that sort of thing.'

'And he taught you how to shoot?' I asked.

'We used to aim at targets here on the terrace. Uncle Edmund taught me and the Pater to use a slingshot too, and a blowpipe. The slingshot was used by gauchos—it came from Argentina, and the blowpipe came from Brazil. And we're deadly accurate with all of them. Sometimes Edmund and I would lean out of the window of my bedroom up there, and fire at targets down here on the terrace.'

'How did he die?' I asked.

'One of those tropical diseases,' said Will with a shrug of the shoulders.

'Your practice sessions must have made the terrace a rather dangerous spot to be,' said Jack with a laugh, 'what with arrows and darts and slingshot pellets raining down on the place.'

'Of course not!' responded Will, deeply offended. 'Me and Uncle Edmund were both very accurate—we never hit anyone we didn't aim at.'

'Very comforting words, young Will,' I said, with the merest hint of sarcasm. And turning to Jack I said, 'All this talk of objects raining down on the terrace reminds me of *Young Men in Spats*.'

'Remarkable,' said Jack. 'Why, exactly, should the dangers of walking on the terrace remind you of an article of clothing?'

'No, no,' I hurried to explain, '*Young Men in Spats* is a book I've just been reading by P. G. Wodehouse. In it he tells the story of Freddy Widgeon, who was staying in a house much like this when, to his great horror, he saw a tortoiseshell cat attacking the dress shirt he'd laid out to wear for dinner. Uttering a hoarse cry, Freddie scooped up the offending animal and flung it out of the window. Unfortunately, walking on the terrace, and directly in the path of the projectile cat, was his host, Sir Mortimer Prenderby—whose daughter Freddy was hoping to marry. Suffice it to say, having biffed his prospective father-in-law with a flying feline, things did not end well for Freddie.'

Will, having no interest in my literary ramblings, asked, 'Does that policeman still suspect you of the murder, Tom?'

'He appears to,' I replied. 'In fact, he seems to be obsessed by the notion.'

'Then he's stupid,' Will said firmly.

'Most encouraging,' said Jack. 'You appear to be quite convinced of Mr Morris's innocence.'

'I am.'

'On what grounds?'

'On the grounds that anyone with a cricket blue from Oxford couldn't possibly be a murderer.'

'I see,' said Jack thoughtfully, 'this is clearly a line of reasoning the police are yet to explore.'

'You're not a bad cricketer yourself, young Will,' I said. 'You bowl a very fast swing ball.'

Will grinned broadly as he explained, 'The last time we played, Mr Lewis, Tom wasn't quick enough getting out of the way of my demon ball. I hit him right on the hand, near the thumb. It was all purple and swollen after the game. He couldn't write with it for a week.'

'Fascinating as these sporting accomplishments are, it's a different topic I want to hear your opinion on, Will,' said Jack. 'Since you are so certain of my friend's innocence, who do you think is the guilty party? Who committed the murder?'

'My poisonous brother Douglas, of course, and his equally poisonous girlfriend, Stiffy. It's just the sort of thing they would do.'

These words made me stop and think. They appeared to be nothing more than fraternal friction—but this was the second time that day we had heard Douglas named as the killer. Why were both Uncle Teddy and young Will accusing Douglas? Were both comments blind prejudice? Or were they seeing something in Douglas's character that we should be looking into?

SIX

~

Thoughts of Douglas as a murderer—either with or without the aid of Stiffy, his girlfriend or fiancée (I wasn't sure which)—continued to occupy my mind as I led Jack into the house to show him the library and the work that had occupied me for most of the past year.

The library of Plumwood Hall was a long, narrow room, with tall, narrow windows overlooking the front drive on one side and floor-to-ceiling bookcases on the other. All the bookcases were protected by leaded-glass doors, so even the most ancient of bibliographic memorabilia—or "books" for the slow boy at the back of the class—were in remarkably good condition.

'Anything of interest in the collection?' Jack asked.

'A complete bound set of Addison and Steele's *Spectator*. First editions of Richardson's *Pamela* and Fielding's *Tom Jones*. The original pamphlet edition of Johnson's *Vanity of Human Wishes*. There's a large number of old legal texts in heavy leather bindings. All the standard classical authors—some looking as though they were purchased by an early Lord Bosham because the spines would look good on his shelves. I've found uncut pages in a number of them.'

'And?' asked Jack with a twinkle in his eye. 'What is the

gem of the collection? I can tell from your manner, Morris, that there is some delight here you've not yet told me about.'

'You always could see through me, Jack,' I said. 'Only a fortnight ago, digging into a remote shelf in a corner of the room, I found a 1597 quarto of *Romeo and Juliet*.'

'Have you told your employer of this remarkable find?'

'Not yet. I wanted to verify it first. In fact, while you're here I'd like you to take a look at it. And I've written to Sotheby's asking for an estimate of what its value might be. I'm still waiting for their reply. I'll tell Sir William when I can lay out all the facts and impress him a little.'

Jack wandered slowly down the long length of the room, glancing at the spines that packed the shelves. When he got to the far end he paused, turned around and, looking me straight in the eye, said, 'And what about you, Morris? How are you coping with all of this?'

Jack always was very direct. It was one of the things I most admired about him, although some saw it as a character defect.

'I feel like a chap,' I said slowly, 'out on a country walk who sees a dark thundercloud form rapidly, and rain begin falling in heavy sheets on the next hillside. He sees the storm moving towards him—but he has nowhere to run. There's no shelter, no protection from the rapidly advancing downpour of freezing rain.'

After a silence I added quietly, 'I find myself thinking about death rather a lot.'

Jack just looked at me, with that round, open, honest, caring face of his, so I continued, 'Well, I was there—right beside her—when Connie's life was just snuffed out. One moment she was a vibrant personality, a living mind, even if a rather unpleasant one, and the next she had abruptly cancelled all her magazine subscriptions.'

I pictured the moment as I said, 'It was like seeing the lights go out and the shutters being nailed up over a house that's just been vacated by its occupant.'

'There's always a sense of theft about death,' said Jack, 'a sense of a life stolen.'

'And it's not just Connie's death I'm thinking about,' I continued, determined to spill the beans while I had the courage. 'It's also my own.'

'What!' snorted Jack. 'You look perfectly hale and hearty to me, young Morris. Why such morbid thoughts?'

'If the odious Hyde has his way, my haleness and heartiness won't help when I'm being led to the gallows by the hangman. Having a spring in my step as I walk to the noose is little comfort,' I said anxiously. 'I'm not ready to be annihilated yet.'

'Is that what you think death is? Annihilation?'

'That's what I'm facing—annihilation . . . snuffed out like a flickering flame.'

'Annihilation?' he asked again.

'Jack, be realistic. It must be. Science has told us enough to know that our minds are just electrical impulses running around the synapses in our brains. When the blood supply is turned off and the synapses stop firing, all those electrical impulses cease to be—they are annihilated. That means *we* are annihilated. It must mean that.'

Jack threw back his head and roared with laughter. 'You really must stop reading those popular science articles in the newspapers, young Morris.'

I said nothing, but I raised my eyebrows, so Jack continued, 'It's possible to be scientific without being a materialist. You can be as scientific as you like and still be convinced that materialism is only half the story.'

Somewhere, in the deep recesses of the dark cave where my

feelings were hiding, a small, warm candle flame of hope flickered into life.

'Go on,' I said.

'Materialism—the belief that matter is everything, that there is nothing but matter—is a creed, like any other creed. And it must be defended logically, just like any other creed. However, I don't think it can be. In the end materialism is illogical—so then we have to ask: what is beyond the physical, what is beyond the material? For in that realm lies life after death, and since death is a certainty for all of us, that's a realm worth exploring.'

'Hold on, hold on,' I said, waving my hands and pacing across the room. 'You're going much too fast for me. Are you saying that death is not being snuffed out like a candle? That death is not annihilation? That the life, the personality, the memories and all the rest of it of an individual can continue beyond physical death?'

'That's exactly what I'm saying.'

'Then Connie, the Connie I knew, the "Ice Queen", as young Will called her, still exists? That personality is still intact somewhere? Or somehow? Or in some form?'

'That's certainly what I believe. That's certainly what the creeds of the church have taught for the past two thousand years.'

'But in the age of science . . .' I began.

'Come now, Morris,' said Jack. 'We've discussed these things before. We've agreed that all that science can study is the physical. So if there is anything beyond the physical we need to turn to something other than science to discover it. And I believe there are strong arguments that make it clear to any open mind that the world consists of more than just the material, more than just the physical.'

'Such as?'

We'd been walking slowly down the full length of the library, and at this point Jack stopped suddenly, flung open the glass door on one of the bookcases and pulled out a volume his eye had spotted.

'Here we are,' he chortled with glee, 'Wordsworth. Now open this little book up to any page and examine whatever poem you find there.'

'Examine? How?'

'Ah! That's exactly the point!' As he spoke Jack was thumbing through the book until he found 'Lines Composed above Tintern Abbey'. 'Now, how would you go about analysing this?' he said as he thrust the book into my hand.

'Well . . .' I said cautiously, suspecting one of Jack's famous logical traps, '. . . just as we did in tutorials. I'd look at the images, at the language, at the flow of ideas . . .'

'Stop!' cried Jack. 'That's just what I would expect you to do. Now analyse the poem as a materialist.'

'I don't follow.'

'Analyse that poem as if matter is all that exists, and that there is nothing other than matter.'

'In that case . . .' I began slowly, for I was starting to see Jack's point, '. . . the only matter that exists here for me to analyse is black marks on white paper.'

'But,' said Jack, with a gleeful grin on his face, 'the marks on paper are not the poem. They record the poem. They print the poem. But they are not the poem itself.'

'Go on,' I said hesitantly, suspecting Jack was about to launch into one of those rigorous logical arguments of his that would make my brain ache.

'Wordsworth's poem can be materially, physically manifested, as it is in this book, as black marks on white paper. Or if someone reads it aloud it would be materially, physically manifested as sound vibrations in the air. Or if somebody memorised it, it would exist materially, physically as those electrical impulses in the brain you spoke of earlier.'

'So far so good,' I said cautiously. 'A poem can have different forms of material existence—as marks on paper, or vibrations in the air, or impulses in the brain. Yes, I can see that.'

'But what is it that's expressed in those different physical forms? What is the "it" that they record? What is the thing each of those expressions has in common? What is the poem itself? The marks on paper are not the poem—they just record it. The vibrations in the air when the poem is read aloud are not the poem—they're just the sound of the poem. The impulses in the brain when the poem is memorised are not the poem—they're just the brain's recording of the poem. So what is the "it" they record or express? What is the poem itself?'

My brain was starting to ache as predicted, so I just nodded.

'You see there are four things here, not three: the ink marks on paper, the sound vibrations in the air, the electrical impulses in the brain plus that fourth thing that is the cause of the other three: the poem itself. The real thing, the poem itself, is a non-material entity—it's not a physical thing at all. It can be physically expressed or recorded, but the thing itself is not its physical recordings or expressions—it's something else. And it's that "something else" that is recorded or expressed. Are you with me so far?'

'I think so.'

'The example of the poem demonstrates that there exists at least one thing that is a non-material, non-physical entity—namely, the blend of ideas, feelings, words and images that make up this poem. Ideas are non-physical and the unique blend of ideas that comprises this particular poem is a non-physical entity. In other words: non-physical entities exist. Consequently, it's clear that the world consists of more than just the material, more than just the physical.'

Jack grinned broadly as he slapped me on the shoulder and continued, 'The poem is more than—it exists independently of—marks or vibrations or impulses. In just the same way, the human personality is expressed in physical matter but is something much more than physical matter. Your personality, Morris, your being—the real you—is, just like the poem, a non-material, non-physical entity.'

Jack lowered his booming voice and said more warmly and intimately, 'The real Tom Morris, the "you" inside you, doesn't need a lump of damp, squashy brain tissue to exist. The poem is something other than the paper just as the human personality, the human mind, is something other than the brain. The poem can survive the destruction of the paper, and the human personality can survive the dissolution of the body.'

Silently I absorbed the enormous idea he had just sketched out, as Jack continued, 'Life after death, Morris—life after death!'

When I remained silent he added, 'At least consider the possibility.'

I was about to reply when the library door was flung open and Lady Pamela stood framed in the doorway. As she advanced towards us, Jack turned to me and said quietly, 'We shall resume this discussion another time. Agreed?'

'Agreed.'

SEVEN

~

Lady Pamela's face was grim as she walked the length of that long room towards us.

'Ah, Mr Morris, here you are,' she said coldly. 'I see you've brought a friend of yours into our house.'

'Lady Pamela, may I introduce my old Oxford tutor, C. S. Lewis.'

'How do you do, Mr Lewis? And what is the purpose of your visit?'

She was shorter than both Jack and me yet somehow she contrived to look down on us. Some sort of optical illusion, I suppose.

'I'm here,' said Jack affably, 'because of the recent tragedy in your house, and the shadow this may cast over my young friend, Mr Morris.'

Lady Pamela sniffed audibly and said, 'I'm quite sure the police are perfectly capable of conducting their own affairs without assistance from members of the public.'

She somehow managed to make 'members of the public' sound like an unsavoury group to belong to—as if it consisted mainly of garbage collectors, street sweepers and pickpockets.

'Actually,' I began defensively, 'on a previous occasion Jack was able to help—'

'Oh, I'm sure,' she interrupted, 'that on rare occasions rank amateurs will have something to contribute. But I suggest that for the time being we leave this to the professionals.'

She made me feel as if I was twelve years old and had been caught flicking ink balls at my little sister. I went pink and began to stutter as I explained, 'We did meet Sir William down in the village and he encouraged Mr Lewis to visit.'

She glared at me. She had a glare that could kill a charging bull elephant at fifty paces. Her glare had been known to penetrate stone walls and cause solid objects to spontaneously burst into flames. It was a glare Attila the Hun might have been able to withstand, but only when surrounded by most of his army.

Jack smiled warmly and said, 'If I am in the way or underfoot, Lady Pamela, please just bid me depart and I shall leave at once.'

Lady Pamela dismissed this attempt at affable humility with one wave of her hand as she muttered coldly, 'If my husband said you can be here, then, of course, you must.'

'It seems,' said Jack enthusiastically, 'that the police have settled on the foolish notion that Morris here might be guilty of murder. I know Morris well, and I'm here to defend his character by showing how any circumstances that might count against him are not as black as they first appear.'

'You must, of course, do whatever you think is best for your friend.'

I thought Lady Pamela was about to turn and leave the library, but she was stopped by a question from Jack: 'What about yourself, Lady Pamela? Are you as confident of Tom Morris's innocence as your husband appears to be?'

'I'm sure I really couldn't say,' she replied, looking me up and down as if I were a streak of mildew staining the wallpaper. 'He's always struck me as a nice enough young man and seems to be a competent scholar at this business' (she dismissed the whole library with a sweeping gesture of her right hand) 'but of course one can never really know with people, can one?'

This was clearly Lady Pamela the grocer's daughter working hard at giving the performance she imagined an earl's daughter might give.

Jack ignored the performance and pursued the questions he wanted answered. 'Could you tell me something about your cousin, Lady Pamela—the murder victim, Mrs Constance Worth. What was she like? Did she have enemies?'

'I don't care to discuss Connie outside of the family.'

'But she wasn't popular, was she?' I said, trying to push her towards an answer.

She focussed her high voltage glare on me again before replying, 'She was family. And family is family.'

'Often the key to unravelling a murder,' said Jack, entirely undeterred, 'is understanding the victim. One must presume she was not chosen at random. So who chose her? And why? Was she, as young Morris suggests, generally unpopular?'

Instead of focussing her death ray glare on Jack, Lady Pamela took a deep breath, and in the manner of someone explaining a simple fact to a slow child, said, 'Poor Connie was a widow. At least she was presumed to be widow.'

'Presumed?' asked Jack.

'Her husband disappeared just over a year ago. Connie and Charles were visiting us here when Charles went out for a walk. He loved walking and generally walked alone. He never came back, and his body was never discovered. The police traced his steps as far as they could, which wasn't very far. Finally they presumed that he'd walked across towards the coast. Some of the clifftops there are very dangerous. If he'd fallen, his body could have been carried out to sea.'

'That must have put your cousin in quite an awkward position,' Jack suggested.

'Oh, I suppose so,' Lady Pamela replied irritably. 'It was certainly awkward financially. It was Charles who had all the money. With no body, his will, leaving all his money and all his property to Connie, couldn't go through probate, so poor Connie was rather dependent on the charity of family.'

'Which is why she was here?'

Lady Pamela did not say anything but there was a slight nod.

Again she turned to leave and again Jack stopped her with a question. 'On the subject of family, we were talking to your son Will a short time ago—or, rather, he was talking to us—about your late brother Edmund.'

I chimed in and said, 'I was rather surprised—I've never heard much about Edmund.'

'There's no reason why you should,' she snapped. 'You are here as a visiting scholar—you are not actually a member of the family.'

Both Jack and I waited to see if she would add anything, but her lips remained firmly and grimly closed.

'Will said that Edmund is dead . . .' I began, after a long silence.

'There is no reason why I should discuss any members of my family with you,' she repeated.

At this point Jack boomed in with his hearty voice to say, 'Uncle Teddy seems like a delightful old chap.'

Lady Pamela actually smiled. 'Poor old Uncle Teddy,' she said. 'He's harmless. We like to indulge him.'

'Do his experiments at inventing ever come to anything?' asked Jack.

'Of course not! He's just playing around. He has the mind of a child. He never does anyone any harm.'

Jack opened his mouth to ask another question, but before he could speak Lady Pamela said, 'I have household affairs I must be about. Nice to have met you, Mr Lewis. And I trust, Mr Morris, that your work in our library is close to being concluded.'

She didn't wait for a response but turned on her heel and stalked out of the room.

When she was gone I turned to Jack and asked, 'Anything useful there?'

'Quite a bit. We need to find out more about the history of Connie Worth. Do you think some of the younger members of the family might tell us?'

'Possibly. Will would certainly tell whatever he knows, but it might not be much.'

'Second,' Jack resumed, 'did you notice how quickly she dropped the topic of her late brother Edmund? Whatever happened to him she certainly doesn't want to talk about it. And third, it was striking that she twice in the space of two sentences told us that Uncle Teddy was "harmless". Did she think we needed to hear that? Is she afraid that Uncle Teddy's dottiness might take a homicidal turn? Why this stress on how "harmless" he is?'

EIGHT

~

'A more practical question now,' said Jack, abruptly changing the topic. 'The question of how the poison got into the cake.'

'What do you suggest?' I asked.

'Tracing the progress of the cake from the oven to the table.'

So I led Jack out of the library, down the corridor and through the green baize door that led to the servants' part of Plumwood Hall. Here, towards the back of the house, was the huge kitchen presided over by the cook, Mrs Buckingham.

She was a small, bossy woman—no more than five foot tall. In fact, she was probably about five foot in every direction, a round bun of a woman—but an unbaked bun. She had the pale grey, puffy look of unbaked dough—and the sprinkling of flour that always covered her person added to this impression.

I introduced her to Jack, who sniffed the kitchen aromas appreciatively and said, 'There is nothing nicer than the smell of baking bread.'

Mrs Buckingham beamed so brightly she resembled the Cheshire cat in Alice—all smile, and almost nothing but smile.

'Mrs B's bread is magical, Jack,' I said. 'Golden crust on the outside, soft and warm on the inside.'

'May I make a confession to you, Mrs Buckingham?' said Jack. 'When I was a small boy my brother Warren and I would sometimes sneak into the kitchen and break open a freshly baked loaf to eat the soft, warm bread out of the middle.'

The cook wagged an admonitory finger at him and said, 'Just like all small boys. And if you'd tried that in my kitchen you'd have got a good walloping with a wooden spoon.'

Jack roared with laughter as he said, 'And thoroughly deserved it would have been too. As all small boys know, the trick is not to get caught. Now, Mrs Buckingham, the problem we face at the moment is that there is every likelihood the murderer of Mrs Worth will also not be caught. So would you mind if I asked you a few questions about that day?'

The cook trembled slightly, like a lump of dough on a tray being shaken. 'I get goosebumps on my goosebumps just thinking about that day. Whoever that person was—that awful murdering person—how dare he use one of my cakes to commit his crime! How dare he!'

A crimson flush of outrage swept over her face, like pink icing on a bun, as she said, 'If I can help you, sir, I certainly will. That man, or woman, or whoever it was, must be made to pay for using my cake—my beautiful cake—to kill somebody.' Then she added so quietly that it was almost under her breath, 'Even Mrs Worth.'

'She was not very popular, was she?' asked Jack, his acute hearing having picked up the last three words.'

'Mrs Worth, you mean? No, not what you might call popular. At least not with the servants.'

Jack encouraged her to tell us more, so she continued, 'Well . . . she was . . . there was a word I read the other day in one of them romantic novels by Rosie M. Banks. And when I read it I said myself, "Gladys," I said, "that sums up that Mrs Worth exactly." Now what was it? Ah yes, I remember—imperious.'

She said the word slowly, sounding out the syllables.

'Rosie M. Banks used it to describe a cavalry officer who was always ordering people about. I had to look it up in the little dictionary I keep on my bedside table. And it describes exactly how Mrs Worth was. She spoke to servants like a master of hounds giving orders to his pack of dogs. She thought she was so far above us. But what I've heard is she came from quite a modest family. The only money she had she'd married. At least that's what I'd been told.'

Jack put his hands behind his back and paced slowly around the big working table that filled the middle of that huge kitchen.

'Now,' he said as he paced, 'the practical question: just how did the poison get into the slice of cake eaten by Mrs Worth? And only that one slice of cake, without a trace in any in the rest of the cake?'

Mrs Buckingham folded her arms across her ample chest and drew herself up to her full diminutive height as she replied, 'That did not happen in this kitchen, sir.'

'Are you quite sure?' I asked.

'Positively certain,' said the cook firmly. 'I prepared it. I put it in the oven. I took it out myself. No one else even so much as touched it.'

'None of the family or guests?' asked Jack.

'None of them even came into the kitchen that afternoon.'

At that moment a young woman in a maid's uniform entered. When she saw us in conversation, she turned and was about to leave, but Mrs Buckingham called to her. 'Jane . . . Jane, come over here a minute. Now, Mr Lewis, this is Jane—she worked with me that afternoon and she took the cake out to the terrace, didn't you, Jane?'

'Yes, cook,' she said. Jane was a pert and pretty young village girl, still, I would have guessed, in her teens.

'Where did you first see the cake?' Jack asked.

'Right here on this table,' Jane replied. 'I was here when cook brought it out of the oven and stood it on the table to cool. And a lovely smell it had too. I remember thinking to myself that if any of that cake came back from the afternoon tea on the terrace I would sneak a bit for myself. I'm sorry, cook, but I did.'

'That's all right, dearie,' said Mrs Buckingham. 'Everyone loves my cake.'

'So who, apart from you and Mrs B,' I asked, 'touched the cake?'

'No one,' Jane insisted. 'I put it on a cake plate and carried it outside and laid it on the table on the terrace. The first person to touch it was Lady Pamela when she started to cut it. I stayed out there for a little while, just in case I were needed like. And in all that time Lady Pamela was the only one who touched the cake.'

'It's impossible!' I said, turning to Jack. 'There's no way a fatal dose of poison could have got into one slice of cake leaving all the rest without a trace. It can't be done. Unless Lady Pamela is the killer?'

Jack rubbed his chin thoughtfully. 'Now, Jane,' he said turning back to the housemaid, 'tell us about the members of the household.'

'They're nice enough, I suppose. Uncle Teddy is daft. Will is a cheeky boy. Douglas and his girlfriend think they're very high and mighty.'

'What about the master and mistress?'

'Lady Pamela's all right . . . once you get used to her manner.'

'And Sir William?'

'We don't see a lot of him. He's often away at the factory.'

She stopped abruptly. Jack prompted her, suggesting that she was about to add something to her description of Sir William.

'Well . . .' she said with an expression on her face I couldn't quite read. 'Well . . . he is a bit of a flirt.'

'He's worse than that,' said a voice from the doorway. 'He's a letch. He's almost a dirty old man.' The speaker was another young woman in a maid's uniform.

'Lizzie Havershot!' cried Mrs Buckingham. 'How dare you speak of the master like that!'

'I will,' said the maid defiantly, 'and I don't care who hears me. I still think the reason poor Ruth was sacked was because Lady Pamela caught Sir William carrying on with her.'

Mrs Buckingham threw her hands in the air in disgust. 'These girls today. They get ideas in their heads, and they insist on speaking their minds. It wouldn't have happened when I was young, I can tell you that for nothing.'

'It's not just an idea in my head,' said Lizzie stubbornly. 'I knows what I knows.'

NINE

~

Jack and I were chased out of the kitchen by Mrs Buckingham on the excuse that she had to start on the dinner. But I had the feeling she was more concerned to stop the maids from telling us anything more.

As we made our way out of the house and into the sprawling grounds, Jack asked, 'Would there be any cyanide on the property, Morris? Is there any use for cyanide other than poisoning unwanted guests?'

Yes, I thought to myself, cyanide did have some common uses, but what were they? Not far from where we were standing was the wall that enclosed the kitchen garden, beyond which was an orchard. Thinking of the garden and the orchard started a train of thought.

'Wasps,' I said. 'Cyanide is sometimes used to poison wasps' nests.'

'Meaning,' said Jack, 'that any supplies of cyanide close at hand will be found in the gardener's shed. Where might we find the gardener?'

'We could start with his shed.'

'That's what I had in mind, Morris, or was I being too subtle?'

We both grinned. Jack's working life as an Oxford tutor tended to make his conversations into a battle of wits—a gentle and well-intentioned battle of wits, but a battle nonetheless.

I led the way around what had once been the stable block and was now a garage for the cars and the home of Uncle Teddy's 'laboratory' towards the back of the kitchen garden. There stood the garden shed, and sitting on a wooden bench in front it, smoking a foul-looking pipe, was Franklin the gardener.

'Good afternoon, Mr Franklin,' I said as we approached.

'Afternoon, young Tom,' he said with a grin, displaying an alarming lack of teeth in his mouth, and the few that were there were stained a deep brown—roughly the colour of aged oak. Clearly the dentist who had been waiting for Franklin's patronage had long since hung up the 'Bankrupt—gone fishing' sign.

'You've not been arrested yet I see,' he muttered through pursed lips that held tightly to his old pipe.

'Are you expecting me to be?'

'It's only you that Inspector Hyde ever asks me about. He has his eye on you, young Tom.'

Ignoring this leering banter, I said, 'Mr Franklin, may I introduce a friend of mine, my old Oxford tutor, C. S. Lewis.'

'Pleased to meet you, Mr Lewis. You here to help Tom escape the hangman?'

'Something like that. Can I ask you about cyanide, Mr Franklin?'

'You can—and you'd not be the first.'

'That weasel-faced Hyde,' I grumbled. 'That odious rodent has been asking you about cyanide?'

Franklin gave a big grin, displaying his three remaining teeth in all their glory, and nodded cheerfully.

'Now you can't have it both ways, Morris,' boomed Jack. 'Inspector Hyde is either a weasel or a rodent, but he can hardly be both. The weasel, I believe, is a member of the mustelid family and is not related to rodents.'

'Poetic licence,' I muttered with a foolish grin.

'The Department of Licensing will withdraw your poetic licence unless you exercise it more carefully,' lectured Jack with mock severity. 'Now, Mr Franklin, may we see your supply of cyanide?'

Franklin rose from his bench, tapped out his pipe on the heel of his boot and invited us to follow him.

He led us into a dark, and surprisingly cavernous, garden shed. Stacked against one wall were the cane chairs we had been using on the day of the murder. The gardener wended his way through a tangle of mowers, rakes and other equipment to the back wall. Here, on a high shelf, was a locked metal box—the sort often used as a cash box. This was a rather battered and ancient example of its kind. He dug deep into one pocket of his grimy cardigan and produced a key.

'Behold, gentlemen,' he said with the air of a showman presenting his star attraction, 'my current supply of cyanide.'

He unlocked the box and flipped open the lid. Inside was a very small brown paper bag, tightly rolled up and held in place with a rubber band.

'That's my total supply of cyanide. That's the amount I had at the end of last summer when the wasps were bad, and none of it's gone missing. That's what I told the inspector, and that's what I'm telling you.'

After a dramatic pause, filled only with his loud wheezing, he continued.

'And let me add,' he said, tapping the side of his nose to indicate that he was about to impart a deeper truth (probably the sort of gesture Socrates used every day as he enlightened his students in ancient Athens), 'this here is the only key, and

I always has it about my person. And the box has not been forced open—anyone can see that.'

'Then the cyanide that killed Connie didn't come from here?' I said quietly.

'Ah hah!' cried Franklin. 'With your lightning fast Oxford-educated brain, young sir, you've reached exactly the same conclusion as the rather slower official brain of Inspector Hyde.'

Jack and I thanked Franklin and wandered slowly away from the garden shed speculating on where the cyanide might have come from if not from the gardener's supplies.

Jack asked if Franklin might be part of the murder plot—might have agreed to supply cyanide to the killer. But knowing the household as I did, I could see no motive for him to act as poison dispenser to anyone at any time. He was a cantankerous old man, I explained, very jealous of his privileges as head gardener and inclined, out of habit, to be as unhelpful as possible to all people at all times.

Rounding the corner of the old stable block we saw Uncle Teddy heading towards his laboratory.

'Uncle Teddy,' boomed Jack.

In response the old duffer turned around quickly, startled by the salutation. He stood still blinking in our direction as if trying to work out exactly who we were. The furrowed look on his brow suggested he had deep doubts about us. Then the mental wheels clicked into place, he recognised us and his brow cleared.

'Oh, ah, yes . . . young Tom . . . and Tom's friend.'

'I wonder if you might like to give us a guided tour of your laboratory, Uncle Teddy?' Jack asked.

The old man's moustache quivered with pleasure as he broke into a broad grin. He waved us towards the building. 'Come on, come on . . . let me show you what I'm working on . . .'

He urged us ahead, following behind like a sheepdog rounding up a few strays. Perhaps he wanted to get us into his workroom before we lost interest.

We passed the Daimler and the Rover sitting in the large, open garage, nodded to the chauffer who had the bonnet of the Daimler open and was wiping his hands on an oily rag, and reached the door set into the walled-off end of the old stable block. Uncle Teddy patted all of his pockets in turn, several times, until he located a large, rusty key. With this he unlocked the door, stepped inside, turned on the electric light switch and ushered us in.

It was a high-ceilinged room, painted white, with cupboards along one wall and a long bench around most of the remaining three. Scattered randomly over this bench were assorted pieces of laboratory equipment—test tubes in racks, retorts, Bunsen burners, Petri dishes and pieces of rubber hosing. Most were covered in dust. Incongruously, there were also cooking trays, mixers and various cooking utensils mingled in with the chemistry set.

'Oh, ah, yes . . . ,' said Teddy, looking around the room as if trying work out what sort of commentary should accompany this guided tour. 'Food, you see, food is . . . organic chemistry. It's all organic chemistry. If you . . . oh, ah . . . get the chemistry right, you get the food production right.'

Sitting on one end of the bench was a pile of old copies of *Boy's Own Paper*—some of them open. These, I suspected, occupied more of Uncle Teddy's time than any experiments he might ever succeed in conducting.

'So, you have chemicals on hand then?' asked Jack.

'Ah, yes, yes . . . quite so. But in food chemistry we call them . . . "ingredients".'

'Any dangerous chemicals?'

Teddy shook his head as if making a sad admission. 'No dangerous chemicals. My nephew won't trust me with anything . . . says I'm too absent minded . . . everything here is edible.'

'So then,' said Jack, fixing Uncle Teddy with a penetrating stare, 'if someone wanted to include cyanide as an ingredient in a cake mix, this is the last place they'd come?'

Teddy looked startled, as if the idea that anyone might connect him with the murder of Connie had not occurred to him before. Then his look slowly turned to one of alarm.

'No, no, no, no . . . not at all. Nothing dangerous here at all. Wherever that dreadful stuff came from, it wasn't from here.'

TEN

~

Leaving Uncle Teddy's laboratory, and Plumwood Hall, behind us, Jack and I set out to walk back to the village. As we walked I turned to talk to Jack but thought better of it. He had stuck his pipe in his mouth and was fiddling with his matches. In his eye was a faraway gleam as if studying a distant horizon. I knew that look of old; it meant that his mind was at work. So I kept my peace and left him to his thinking.

In the village we made our way back to *The Cricketers' Arms*. In the saloon bar we each ordered a pint of bitter, still occupied with our own thoughts. Or, at least, Jack's brain still seemed to be steaming ahead at full speed and I remained disinclined to interrupt its progress.

Sitting in a nook at the far end of the room I saw Sir William's son Douglas and his girlfriend Stiffy. As I watched, the young man rose and walked to the bar to order fresh drinks.

'Same again, Mr Rose,' he said to the publican, 'two G and Ts.'

Then he glanced sideways at me and said, 'How does it feel to be a convict-in-waiting, Tom?'

'Well, since I'm innocent . . .' I began.

'Good luck in persuading the police of that,' sneered Douglas. 'They've got you bang to rights, old son. If I were you, I wouldn't start making any long-term plans for the future.'

'Morris!' exploded Jack, emerging from his reverie. 'Introduce me to your friend.'

'Jack, this is Douglas—Sir William's older son. Douglas, this is my old Oxford tutor, C. S. Lewis.'

'Actually, I recognise you, sir,' Douglas responded, sneer disappearing under a layer of obsequiousness for the moment. 'You were pointed out to me in Oxford. Everyone knows you. My tutor wants me to attend your lectures on medieval and renaissance literature.'

'And which college are you at, young Douglas?' asked Jack genially.

Instantly the superior tone and expression returned as he replied, 'Balliol.'

'Good tutors at Balliol. What are you reading?'

'History.'

'Not English? Then why were my lectures recommended?'

'I was told they would be good for my understanding of the period.'

'And so they would be,' Jack responded warmly. 'Do you a power of good. My lectures should be made compulsory for every student in every course.' Jack grinned broadly at the joke he'd made at his own expense. Douglas just looked confused. He clearly didn't know what to make of this larger-than-life Oxford don whose wit included self-mockery.

At this point Alfred Rose delivered two gin and tonics. As Douglas picked these up and started to walk away, he glanced over his shoulder and said to me, 'If I were you, Tom, I'd visit my tailor to be measured for a pair of handcuffs.'

Then he hurried off to the corner booth where Stiffy was waiting. In a moment they had their heads together, giggling—no doubt at Douglas's retelling of his joke at my expense.

I turned to Jack and said quietly, 'Not an entirely likeable young man.'

'How is he doing in his studies?' asked Jack. 'Do you know?'

I thought for a moment, and then replied, 'From something Sir William let slip a few months ago, I gather he's loafing somewhat. It seems that he'd be happy with a poor second. All he wants to do is to graduate and take his place as a senior executive with Dyer's Digestive Biscuits. And take the handsome salary that would, undoubtedly, come with it.'

Jack's voice dropped to what he fondly imagined was a confidential whisper as he asked, 'And would he have a motive to murder Connie Worth?'

'Well, he and his girlfriend were in the habit of referring to her as "the Black Widow"—although why, I'm not sure.'

'We understand the "widow" part now,' Jack said, 'after what Lady Dyer told us. Whether the adjective was intended simply to mock her cold lack of emotion or had a somewhat more sinister import we shall have to see as our investigations continue.'

We finished our pints, then Jack said, 'Come along, let's stretch our legs, young Morris—you know that my brain works best when my feet are in action.'

For the next ten minutes we paced the length of the village street and back. Again Jack was quiet and thoughtful, but at least twice he mumbled that the police—or Inspector Hyde, at least—must have evidence of my guilt that he so far hadn't revealed.

'Even Hyde,' muttered Jack, 'with the IQ of an elm tree, wouldn't be so narrowly focussed on you unless he had something more than the opportunity you had to administer the poison from sitting next to Connie Worth. There must be something more.'

We were still discussing what that might be when we drew level once more with *The Cricketers' Arms*. As we did so, two figures disappeared around the side of the pub into the shadows.

'Furtive activity,' said Jack. 'Worth investigating?'

I nodded.

We walked to the pub wall and then edged down it in single file, with me in the lead. At the end of the wall I cautiously peered around the corner into the pub's backyard. This was bathed in dark shadows, and that crepuscular dimness was empty except for two figures—a young man and a young woman—entwined in each other's arms in passionate embrace. The young woman was Stephanie Basset, known as Stiffy—and, interestingly, the other party was most certainly *not* Douglas Dyer, the young man she was, either officially or unofficially, engaged to.

I edged back from the corner and gestured to Jack to take my place. He did so. When he returned to my side he whispered, 'I recognise the young man. He's a barman in Oxford at the Bird and Baby—the *Eagle and Child*.'

'Our pub!'

'As you say, our pub.'

Now voices could be heard coming from the backyard. Jack and I ceased our whispered colloquy and listened.

Stiffy was promising herself, in the most passionate language, to the young barman—'even,' she said, 'when I'm married to Douglas. That won't stop us seeing each other and doing whatever we like with each other.' These last words were accompanied by a salacious giggle. 'I'll have Douglas for the money,' she continued, 'and you for the fun. And don't worry, sweetheart, you'll get your share of whatever part of the Dyer millions I can get my hands on.'

As Jack and I made our way, with quiet footsteps, to the front of the pub, Jack was shaking his head. 'It's sad, Morris, the damage that people inflict on themselves, on each other and on their relationships when they choose to plunge into immorality.'

'You think she's heading for unhappiness then?'

'I think they all are. It will all end in tears.'

'Do you know much about the barman?' I asked.

'Very little,' said Jack, still shaking his head sadly at human folly. 'His name is Evans, I believe. My impression is that he's a bit of a local Lothario in Oxford. I doubt that he is any more faithful to her than she is to Douglas. Young people do seem to be able to get their lives into a tangled, unhappy mess.'

'Could this be connected to the murder?'

'Ah, that's the question, young Morris. Once people have secrets they may well have a motive for murder. We must press on and find out more.'

ELEVEN

~

The publican, Alfred Rose, emerged from the doorway of the pub, wiping his hands on his large white apron.

On his face was a contented smile, like a bookmaker just after a race in which the favourite has run last. He said, 'To tell you the truth, Mr Lewis, this murder is good for business.'

Jack asked him in what way, and Rose replied, 'Well, first I got your custom out of it, and now I get a telegram telling me to get rooms ready for two Scotland Yard men who are coming on the late afternoon train.'

And that late afternoon train, it appeared, was due to arrive in around ten minutes.

'We shall meet it then!' cried Jack heartily. 'Let the experts from Scotland Yard meet their chief suspect the moment they step off the train.'

With that he set off with long strides in the direction of the Plumwood railway station. A few minutes later we were waiting on the platform, peering down the track in the direction of Market Plumpton, looking for the first puff of smoke that would herald the arrival of the late train.

As we waited we talked about the people in the case: Sir William and Lady Pamela Dyer, Douglas and Stiffy, Uncle Teddy, young Will Dyer, Keggs the butler, Mrs Buckingham the cook, the maids Jane and Lizzie, and even Franklin the gardener. Which of these people, if any of them, could have had a motive to murder Connie Worth? She was not a likeable person, a cold fish of a personality (the 'Ice Queen' according to Will, the 'Black Widow' according to Douglas and Stiffy)—but people are not murdered just because of their lack of table manners.

Our discussion of possible motives, methods and opportunities was ended by the sound of a distant train whistle wailing like the sad hoot of an aged owl whose children have all turned out to be disappointments in life. Some minutes later the small locomotive, with its few carriages, steamed, chugged, wheezed and clanked to a halt at the platform.

Only two passengers alighted—and to our surprise they turned out to be familiar faces: Inspector Gideon Crispin and Sergeant Henry Merrivale of Scotland Yard.

Crispin, who still looked like a well-tailored city banker, recognised us almost as quickly as we recognised him. He strode up the platform and offered his hand in greeting.

'A pleasure to see you again, I'm sure, gentlemen—although we could, perhaps, wish for pleasanter circumstances.'

The silent Sergeant Merrivale nodded in recognition. He could not offer to shake hands as he was carrying all the bags.

'You don't seem surprised to see us, inspector,' said Jack.

'I read the case notes on the train journey, so Mr Morris's role in this affair I was familiar with. And it did occur to me, Mr Lewis, that you might have come to Mr Morris's aid, given that the local police have cast him under some shadow of suspicion.'

We fell into step beside the two detectives and walked with them down the village street in the direction of the pub.

'And do you share Inspector Hyde's suspicion that Morris here is some sort of homicidal maniac?' asked Jack.

'Early days, Mr Lewis, early days,' replied Crispin. 'I find it pays not to leap to conclusions too quickly.'

At *The Cricketers' Arms* Alfred Rose warmly welcomed his latest pair of murder tourists, and bellowed for Ronnie Fish to carry their bags up to their rooms.

Then he said, 'As it happens, gentlemen, you already have a visitor. Someone is waiting for you in the snug.'

With an air of gleeful mystery the publican led the way to the small private back bar, and there we found, waiting for the Scotland Yard officers, Dr Henderson.

Mine host made the introductions and then left. The small, bustling local GP rose to his feet to shake everyone's hand. He pulled a sheaf of papers out of his medical bag. Then he hesitated.

'The final toxicology report,' he began, and then paused, looking at Jack and me. 'But I'm not sure if . . .'

'Undoubtedly,' said Inspector Crispin calmly as he pulled up a chair, 'the contents of that report will be around the village by tomorrow morning, so there's no harm in these gentlemen hearing them now.'

'If you say so,' muttered the doctor doubtfully.

'I do say so,' said the Scotland Yard man. 'I know these small villages. And I know their gossip networks tend to be as quick and efficient as anything invented by Mr Marconi. So, go ahead, doctor.'

Henderson cleared his throat and, still looking at us doubtfully, resumed. 'To be on the safe side I sent the stomach contents to the home office pathologist in London. Case of murder, you know. Don't see many of those myself. Best to be scientifically precise.'

'And what did the home office pathologist say?' prompted Inspector Crispin when Dr Henderson came to a halt, perhaps overawed by his own efficiency in the face of murder.

'Say? Oh, yes. Well, he confirmed my finding of death by cyanide. But that was never really in doubt. The interesting thing was his finding that the cyanide had been ingested in a solid lump by the deceased. The full technical account you'll find here in his report.'

With this he handed over the sheaf of papers.

As Crispin glanced at the pages he asked, 'Was the cyanide administered in liquid or powder form?'

'Powder . . . definitely powder.'

Inspector Crispin turned the pages of the report silently and slowly. When he had finished he puffed out his cheeks and looked puzzled.

'It says nothing here,' he said, tapping the pages, 'about how such a large dose of cyanide could be in one slice of the cake without a single trace elsewhere.'

'Yes, yes,' burbled the local GP excitedly. 'I noticed the same thing myself. Which does nothing to point us towards the solution to the most baffling part of the mystery: how did the cyanide get into the cake at all?'

'Well, thank you, doctor,' murmured the Scotland Yard man. 'We won't keep you any longer.'

Dr Henderson rose somewhat reluctantly, muttering about 'getting back to my patients', but my impression was that he would have happily stayed for the next hour talking murder with the experts from London.

Alfred Rose returned to offer us tea. The offer was accepted, then Crispin turned to me and said, 'Now, Mr Morris, in your role as chief suspect I suppose I should begin by interviewing you.'

As I agreed wearily, Sergeant Merrivale pulled out a notebook, huffing and puffing loudly like the faithful bulldog he was.

'Were you watching as the cake was delivered to the table, cut and served?' asked the inspector.

I assured him that I was.

'And during that process, what opportunity was there for someone around the table to tamper with just one slice of cake—tamper in the sense of inserting cyanide?'

None, I said, unless Lady Pamela did so as she cut and served each slice. 'Even then,' I said, 'she must have been performing some sort of conjurer's trick in which the hand is faster than the eye. But aren't you going to ask me about my relationship with the deceased? Look for a motive for murder?'

'If you want me to I shall,' said Crispin with an amiable smile. 'So tell me, Mr Morris, how did you get on with Mrs Worth?'

'Much the same as everyone else, to be honest.' I went on to explain that I saw very little of her, that I'd only had one clash with her—and that was over her wanting to take one of the rare and valuable books from the library to her room. But apart from that, I said, I'd had almost no dealings with her.

'After all,' I added, 'I'm not a member of the family . . . just the scholar in residence.'

'Are you satisfied now, Mr Morris? Have I asked you the questions about motive that you wanted me to ask?'

I looked at him blankly, surprised by his not taking his chief suspect more seriously.

'And what about you, sergeant?' Crispin continued. 'Have I cross-examined this gentleman closely enough?'

Merrivale snapped closed his notebook and gave an

unpleasant smile. 'For the time being,' he said. Ah, I thought to myself, he speaks! The silent sergeant has a voice after all.

'Now,' the inspector resumed, 'I'll turn my attention to the matter that really interests me—the source of the cyanide.'

TWELVE

~

It turned out that Inspector Crispin had made some preliminary inquiries before leaving London, and had decided that the local chemist's shop was the most likely source of the poison. That was where he wanted his real investigation to begin. He even invited Jack and me to go with him. As we left the pub and started down the street, I had no idea that things were about to get much darker for me.

The village chemist shop had a large flask of coloured water and an ancient ceramic mortar and pestle in its tiny window. In an arc over the top of the window, in fading gold paint and in the style of an earlier age of lettering, was the word 'Dispensary'.

The front door to the tiny shop opened with the tinkle of a small bell that hung from a spring on the top of the door.

Recalling that bell later made me think of a 'Had-I-But-Known' detective novel by Mary Roberts Rinehart I once read. The heroine kept hinting to the reader of dreadful deeds by saying 'Had I but known what lay ahead . . .' Well, Had-I-But-Known what was about to be revealed, I would have heard that tinkling bell as tolling my doom.

Behind the small counter, and in front of shelves displaying multi-coloured packets of patent medicines, stood a village girl.

Inspector Crispin introduced himself and produced his warrant card to establish his authority. She nodded dumbly, looking somewhat frightened by this important figure from Scotland Yard.

'And your name is . . . ?' asked Crispin.

'Ruth Eggleston,' she replied in a voice little more than a frightened whisper.

'And your role here is . . . ?' continued the inspector.

'I work for Mr Williamson. This is his shop. I serve in the shop and he does the dispensing.' As she spoke she glanced over her shoulder to the shop's interior.

'Now, Miss Eggleston—I'd like to see your poisons book,' said Crispin.

The young woman froze into immobility, like a rabbit staring blankly into the headlights of an approaching motor car—a rabbit wishing it had never left the comfort of its nice, warm burrow; a rabbit wishing it had listened to its mother ('Avoid Mr McGregor's garden and busy roads on dark nights,' she'd said).

'You do keep a poisons book, don't you?' Crispin continued. 'Every chemist is required by law to keep a poisons book, so I presume you have one?'

'Oh yes, sir,' she said quickly, suddenly finding her voice again. 'Mr Williamson says everything must be done properly.'

'Then please produce your poisons book, Miss Eggleston,' Crispin said patiently.

Once again she gave her impersonation of the rabbit in the headlights—this time with eyes as wide as saucers staring at the headlights getting closer.

Suddenly Sergeant Merrivale barked, in his gruff bulldog voice, 'The poisons book please, miss . . . now!'

She jumped, as if the rabbit had heard a blaring horn emanating from behind the headlights, then reached under the counter and extracted a large, leather-covered book. It looked very old. It was possibly the same poisons book that had been kept in that shop since the early childhood of Queen Victoria.

'Here it is, sir,' she said in her small, trembling voice as she laid it on the counter.

Inspector Crispin spun it around so that it was facing him and slowly turned over the pages. He kept turning until he came to the most recent entries. He stared for a moment at the small, neat writing, then turned and stared at me, and then returned his gaze to the book.

'Your name is in the book, Mr Morris,' Crispin said.

'It can't be,' I protested.

'But it is—see for yourself.'

Crispin stood to one side and I stepped up to the counter. There, in small, neatly curved handwriting, was a notation saying that the most recent purchase of poisons was half a gram of potassium cyanide and the purchaser was . . . 'T. Morris'.

'But I didn't . . . that's not possible . . . why would I ever . . . I didn't . . .'

The Scotland Yard man shook his head and said quietly, 'That's what it says, Mr Morris.'

Sergeant Merrivale reached over and picked up the poisons book. He closely examined the page, with Jack looking on over his shoulder.

Crispin looked back at the nervous young woman behind the counter. 'Now, Miss Eggleston,' he said, 'according to this book Mr Morris here purchased half a gram of potassium cyanide in this shop two weeks ago. Is that correct?'

In a voice so close to a whisper as to be almost inaudible, she said, 'Yes, sir.'

'Did he tell you what is was for?'

'He said he was buying it for . . .' and here her faint voice died away and the words became impossible to hear.

'Speak up, girl!' barked Sergeant Merrivale. 'Who or what did he say he was buying it for?'

She swallowed hard and then said, 'For Hugo Franklin . . . Mr Franklin, that is . . . the head gardener at the Hall.'

'And why would he do that, miss?' asked Inspector Crispin. 'Did he say why Mr Franklin didn't come into the shop and make the purchase for himself?'

'He said that he was walking into the village to post a letter and Mr Franklin had asked him to . . .' Again her voice faded away to nothing. She was like a chiming clock with a faulty mechanism—every chime becoming steadily fainter than the one before.

Crispin suddenly spun and around and confronted me. 'Is this true, Mr Morris? Have you suddenly remembered making this purchase? Had it slipped your mind until now?'

'Of course not!' I protested loudly. 'I made no such purchase. I've never purchased potassium cyanide in my life—not two weeks ago, not ever. And certainly not for Franklin. He has a supply of cyanide in his garden shed. He showed it to Jack and me earlier today. And anyway, the Hall is not far from the village and he's perfectly capable of walking here himself and making his own purchases.'

'My dear Morris,' interrupted Jack, 'that's not what's being implied here, is it? The suggestion is that any reference to Franklin was a blind, and that you were making the poison purchase for yourself for your own nefarious purposes.'

'But . . . but . . . but . . .' I started to splutter like a single-cylinder motorcycle trying to climb a steep hill while misfiring at every stroke.

Suddenly Sergeant Merrivale's heavy hand was clamped on my shoulder as he said to Ruth Eggleston, 'Is this the man, miss? Is this the man who purchased the cyanide? The man referred to in that there entry in your poisons book?'

She nodded dumbly, blinking back tears from her eyes.

Crispin pushed the book along the counter in my direction.

'The law requires every purchaser of poisons to sign the book,' he said. 'Is this your signature, Mr Morris?'

I looked down at the book and felt a sudden wave of relief.

'No,' I announced cheerfully. 'That's not my signature. That's nothing like my signature. Look at any example of my writing and you'll see at once that this is not my signature.'

'How do you explain that, miss?' asked Crispin, turning back to the shop girl.

She swallowed hard three or four times and then said, 'His hand was hurt. It was bandaged up. So he couldn't write with it. He asked me to write his name for him.'

'Well, Mr Morris?' Crispin raised his eyebrows as he asked me the question.

'I did hurt my hand a week or so back. A cricket injury. I copped young Will's fast ball on my wrist. It was bruised and sprained, that was all.'

'And bandaged?'

'Yes.'

'And you were unable to write with it for a while?'

'For a couple of days, yes. But I still wasn't here and I didn't—'

Sergeant Merrivale interrupted my explanation like a bulldog lunging forward to seize a bone. 'So that explains why it's not your signature that's in the book, doesn't it, sir? This young lady says she remembers you making the purchase, so you must have done—is that correct, sir? Do you remember it now, sir?'

'She's lying!' I said loudly. Ruth Eggleston started to sob, and I regretted my outburst. 'Or . . . or mistaken . . . or she just doesn't remember . . . or something,' I added lamely.

'Let's ask the chemist himself,' said Inspector Crispin. Without waiting for an invitation, he picked up the poisons book, lifted the flap in the counter and walked through the open doorway to the back room. The rest of us followed.

There, bending over a small, hand-operated pill making machine was a man in a white coat—a man so elderly that he would have regarded Methuselah as a noisy youngster.

He looked up from his work bench, blinking at us through thick glasses.

'Eh?' he grunted. 'Hello? Who are you?'

'You are the owner of this shop?' asked the Scotland Yard man.

'Indeed I am, sir. I am Arthur Williamson—and I repeat my question: who are you?'

Crispin identified himself and Sergeant Merrivale, and explained who Jack and I were. He then outlined the purpose of our visit to his shop, and produced the poisons book, saying, 'According to this, Mr Morris here purchased a small amount of potassium cyanide a little over a week ago—which Mr Morris denies having done. Were you a witness to the transaction? Can you tell us if this record is correct?'

Mr Williamson accepted the offered book from Crispin and squinted near-sightedly at the open page.

'I have no idea,' he said. 'I leave the shop to Ruth. She runs the shop. I never see who comes and goes. In my experience young Ruth is a reliable girl. If she says this entry in the book is accurate then no doubt it is.'

Both Crispin and Merrivale cross-questioned the old chemist for a further five minutes, but he had nothing to add. Finally he became annoyed and insisted on getting back to his work. He turned his back on us and resumed operating his pill press—stamping some sort of white powder into small, hard tablets.

We left him to his work and walked back out into the village street, Crispin impounding the poisons book on the way.

'Are you about to arrest me?' I challenged Crispin.

He smiled and said, 'I doubt that you're a flight risk, Mr Morris. I have been in this village for less than an hour and I intend to take no precipitate action. I shall continue my investigations and consult with Inspector Hyde and you will hear from me in due course.'

With those words the two Scotland Yard detectives walked back up the hill towards the pub.

Turning to my old tutor and friend beside me I said in despair, 'What is going on, Jack . . . what is going on?'

He clapped me on the shoulder and in his warmest, friendliest tone said, 'Come along—let's take a walk and talk this over.'

THIRTEEN

~

In silence we walked down the narrow, winding road out of the village. After some minutes we left the roadway, climbing over a stile at a break in the high hedge at the roadside, and headed off across the moors. We continued to walk in silence until we were well away from any habitation and striding across the purple heather-covered expanse of the moorland.

All the while my thoughts were swirling turbulently in my brain. Finally I said, 'She's lying. She must be lying.'

'Of course she is,' said Jack complacently. 'It was obvious to anyone listening to her voice or watching her nervous manner that she was lying. And not very well, either.'

'Why didn't you say something? You pretty much left me to my own devices back in that shop,' I protested.

Jack turned towards me and smiled as he pulled his pipe out of his pocket.

'I was busy, young Morris,' he said as he protected the match flame from the wind to light his pipe, 'busy listening to that girl's voice and watching her nervous manner.'

'But you let Inspector Crispin believe . . .' I was spluttering again.

'Crispin is no fool,' Jack responded. 'I'm confident he reached exactly the same conclusion I did. Of course, if Inspector Hyde had been there you would be behind bars by now. Fortunately, he wasn't. But be assured that Crispin no more believed her story than I did. And, also like me, he is now puzzling over what it means.'

A chill wind had sprung up and the sun was close to the western horizon. I did up all the buttons on my jacket and from some deep inner pocket Jack produced a scarf which he wound around his neck.

'Now let's walk,' he said. 'Let this breeze blow away the cobwebs as we work out what's behind that's girl's peculiar actions.'

For a while we tossed back and forth possible explanations for the girl's lies. I was wondering who might have put her up to it, while Jack speculated as to why.

'Clearly you have been selected to play the role of scapegoat in this melodrama. And if the real murderer feels in need of such a distraction then the real murderer fears exposure. Why? What discovery are the police close to that might point towards the real killer? And why select you as the red herring?'

'And what's Ruth Eggelston's role in this?' I asked. 'How was she persuaded to falsify the poisons book and then lie about it?'

Jack turned towards me with a wide grin and said, 'Fascinating puzzle, isn't it?'

'Not the word I'd use,' I growled.

Eventually Jack decided that we needed more information before we could reach a rational conclusion, and insisted that we drop the topic in the meantime.

I sank into a glum silence—sulking, I suppose. Jack responded by setting out to cheer me up.

'Come along, Morris, let's talk about something else entirely—something that will oil the wheels of your brain and get you thinking vigorously of something other than the coils of this plot you seem to be caught in.'

'If you wish,' I replied, a little reluctantly.

'What were we debating back in the library? Oh yes, death. Or rather, immortality: the probability of post-mortem survival.'

I could see what he was doing—engaging me in a philosophical debate to stop me worrying about my immediate predicament. Clearly he meant well, so I went along with him.

'Yes, that's right,' I said. 'And I suppose I have no difficulty accepting that the physical world around us is not the whole of reality. But even so . . . is it likely, is it *probable*, that this visible body of mine is, let's say, an instrument being used by an invisible soul, an invisible person within? After all, I seem very dependent on this material, visible body.'

'Similarly,' Jack responded with enthusiasm, 'a scientist may be dependent—in fact, completely and totally dependent—on his instruments. A scientist can see, know and manipulate the microscopic world only through his scientific instruments. The scientist *uses* his instruments, but it's not true that he *is* his instruments.'

'Are you suggesting that the real me within is *using* my body the same way a scientist uses his instruments? But surely appearances are against that,' I suggested, struggling with the whole line of his argument. 'Surely ordinary appearances are against your claim that the real Tom Morris is an invisible something—mind, soul, whatever—that is operating inside my brain, inside my body.'

Jack puffed his pipe thoughtfully and then said, 'Yes, I agree that appearances *are* against it. But then appearances are against the idea that infection is spread by invisible bacteria, that fatal disease can be spread by a virus invisible to the naked eye. The best physicians and surgeons of earlier centuries laughed at the idea that the greatest risks to human health were invisible to them. Nevertheless, it's the truth.'

'But can we be certain that the mind and the brain are not identical? That inside me are two things: the visible brain the surgeon can see when he cuts into my skull *and* the invisible mind that is operating the brain like a mechanic operating a piece of machinery?'

'Well, think of the facts. The people with the biggest and best minds don't have the biggest brains. Sherlock Holmes, I seem to recall, was impressed by the size of Professor Moriarty's forehead and from that deduced that the evil professor must have a large brain—and that was the cause of his powerful mind. All such ideas have now been discarded. This Einstein chap we read about in the newspapers clearly has an extremely powerful mind, but his physical brain is exactly the same size as others with half his thinking capacity. Ergo, the mind and brain are not the same thing.'

'That's a point, I suppose.'

'And Dr Havard was telling me quite recently about a paper he read in *The Lancet* which apparently demonstrates that destruction of part of the brain does not necessarily mean destruction of part of the mind. He tells me that some sufferers from a stroke recover fully, and medical science now knows this happens because another part of the brain takes over the functions of the damaged part. This could not happen if the mind and brain were the same thing. Damage to the grey matter, the "little grey cells" your friend Poirot talks about, is just damage to the machinery. The operator of the machinery, the mind, the soul, remains intact and, in some cases, able to carry on working through a different part of the machine.'

'Don't blame Poirot on me! It's your brother Warnie who reads all the detective novels.'

'Stop trying to dodge the issue, Morris,' hooted Jack good-naturedly. 'Do you grant my point?'

'Yes, I suppose I do,' I admitted reluctantly. 'But even so, surely the mind or soul or whatever you call it *needs* the brain—so that when the brain dies, the mind, the soul, must cease to exist.'

'Does the mechanic cease to exist when the machinery breaks down? The very idea is illogical. Think of the caterpillar in its cocoon. Once it's completed its transformation into a butterfly it discards the cocoon—it no longer needs it. When the chicken emerges from the egg, it discards the empty shell as no longer needed. There is a pattern in nature telling us that the life within continues, indeed thrives, after it discards the shell, the cocoon, in which it began.'

'What about evolution?'

'Evolution does not present a single difficulty in the way of seeing the self as separate from the body. The physical body may well be the product of an evolutionary process, but the self is from the metaphysical realm, from the realm beyond nature. One thing we can be sure of is that evolutionary theory has no relevance to the non-physical—what Socrates called "the higher part of man".'

I didn't reply immediately as I needed my breath to climb over a break in a dry-stone wall. Then I reached out to help Jack over. We stood at the bottom of a slope of heather-covered moorland. Above us, at the top of the slope, stood the crumbling remains of an old stone tower.

I was puffing as we clambered up the slope, but I managed to ask, 'Well, what is the relationship between the two—between the physical body and "the higher part of man", to use Socrates' phrase?'

'Let me give you the answer Socrates would have given,' said Jack, pausing to catch his breath. 'In his Athenian death cell, waiting for the fatal cup of hemlock, this question was discussed. Some of the old philosopher's friends compared man to a harp and man's mental life to the melody played on the strings of the harp. The physical body, they said, is the instrument that gives voice to the music of the mind. And the music, they said, cannot outlast the destruction of the harp. But Socrates insisted that man is neither the harp nor the tune played on the harp. Rather, he said, man is the harpist who plays the tune upon the strings. The harpist depends on the harp to make music, but not for his existence, since the player may leave one instrument and find another. A good image of life after death, young Morris.'

At this point he ran out of breath, and I didn't try to reply as we both puffed up the last, and steepest, part of the slope.

This brought us to the foot of the crumbling stone tower. I flopped down on a large block of stone and leaned back against the tower wall. Jack, now flushed and warm from walking, unwound his scarf and tapped the ashes out of his pipe.

'What is this place?' he asked when he'd caught his breath.

'The locals call it "Bosham's Folly". Although I've heard the more superstitious among them call it the "Black Tower".'

'It's made from a darkish basalt rock so "Black Tower" I understand. But why "Bosham's Folly"?'

'It was built by an earlier Lord Bosham. I think about a hundred and fifty years ago, more or less. The family call it the Hunting Tower because that was its original purpose—to serve as a base for parties from Plumwood Hall when they were grouse shooting on the moors. But it hasn't been used for years.'

I rose from where I was seated and walked slowly around the base of the tower.

'Jack . . . around here,' I called out from the far side. 'Look— a door,' I said when he joined me. 'The view of the landscape from the top of this tower would, I think, be quite wonderful. It should be possible to see as far as the coast.'

With these words I tried the heavy wooden door but found it securely locked. I shook it and it rattled in its doorframe but refused to open. I remarked that it was unfortunate that the tower was locked up, and offered to ask at the house for a key, to give us a goal for our next walk on the moors.

Then, with dusk drawing in around us, we retraced our steps and headed back towards the village.

FOURTEEN

~

By the time we had regained the road to the village a dim, purple twilight had fallen. The cries of night birds had begun, and in the distance an owl hooted. As we rounded a bend in the road I saw that an early moon had crept over the horizon, adding a dim, silver shine among the purple shadows. The wind had died and the night was still and calm, but wisps of cloud were drifting blackly over the face of the moon, and as I scanned the dark blue of the evening sky I saw a threatening bank of clouds beginning to build.

'Might be rain in those,' I muttered. 'We should hurry along.'

Hedges towered on either side of the road, and behind the hedges tall trees reached out their crooked, clawed arms like threatening giants.

The brisk walking had warmed us up, and I unbuttoned my jacket. In the dying evening light my cheek brushed against the twigs of an overhanging branch, and I flinched and pulled back—as if it were the legs of a large, black spider that I had felt so briefly.

A dull, red glow was coming from Jack's pipe and he was puffing contentedly. I was pleased to have his rugged good sense and robust honesty beside me, for—whether from our earlier conversation about the fate of the dead or not—a sense of the uncanny had crept upon me.

When some mole or badger rustled in the undergrowth, I turned rapidly to look at the source of the sound. Somehow the slow dying of the light focussed my mind on the darkness of death—and the ghost stories of my childhood came creeping out of my memory: tales about the restless dead that made us huddle closer to the nursery fire. Now, remembered in the darkness of a deepening twilight, those tales seemed even stranger—and strangely real.

I gave an involuntary shiver, patted my pockets for cigarettes and then remembered that I'd given up smoking.

The only sounds were the soft clop of our shoes on the road, the distant cries of the night birds and the soft sighing of a gentle breeze as it circled around the bare, black tree branches overhead.

I opened my mouth to make some remark, any remark, just to break the eerie silence when I was stopped by a sound that drifted towards us from around the next bend. It was the sound of two voices arguing.

Instinctively we slowed down and walked more quietly.

As we neared the bend the voices became a little clearer. They were both male. There was one dominant voice—a quietly threatening, belligerent, growling, aggressive voice. It carried most of the conversation. When it paused there were briefer, more submissive responses from the second voice.

Just before the turn in the road we came to a complete halt. I'm sure Jack felt as I did, that to approach any closer would be to invade a private dispute.

Although the tone of the voices was clear it was hard to pick out any words. Once or twice I thought I heard the word 'money'—spoken loudly, as if to give it special emphasis.

I took a few quiet steps forward until I stood at the bend in the road and peered ahead into the darkness. Underneath one of the tall, dark, leafless trees were two black silhouettes, barely visible against the silvery-purple darkness of the moonlit road. One of the figures was large, tall and broad. It towered over the smaller man in a clearly threatening posture. Judging from the gestures that I could vaguely make out, the larger man was jabbing the smaller one in the chest.

Suddenly Jack grabbed my arm and escorted me forward, taking long, brisk steps. As he did so he spoke in his booming voice, 'Hello, you two. We didn't expect to see anyone else out on the road at this hour of the evening.'

The argument, if that's what it was, abruptly halted. As we drew near, the larger figure turned towards us. We caught a brief but clear glimpse of his face outlined by fugitive moonbeams. For a moment I thought he was going to turn his aggression towards us. But he seemed to think better of this, spun on his heels and marched off briskly down the road. This left the smaller man still standing, trembling, by the side of the road.

As we drew closer I was astonished to discover who this smaller man was—Douglas Dyer.

'Hello, Douglas,' I said tentatively. 'We're on our way back into the village. Care to walk with us?'

He said nothing, but fell into step beside us. My guess was that he felt our presence afforded him some protection against the thug who had been threatening him.

'Your friend didn't seem at all happy,' prompted Jack. 'If there's a problem . . .'

'If there's a problem,' interrupted Douglas, 'it's my problem and none of your business.'

'That's perfectly true,' agreed Jack. 'I am not a proctor and this is not the university. However, when I was a younger don I *was* a proctor for a period, and from that time I recognised our friend. When I had to make my nightly rounds scooping undergraduates out of pubs, he often put in an appearance.'

Douglas sulked silently, so Jack continued, 'I have no idea what his Christian name is since he only ever seemed to have one name: Sutcliffe. He's well known to all the proctors as a debt collector for one of the shadier Oxford bookmakers.'

'As you said,' snarled Douglas, 'this is not Oxford and you are not a proctor, so it's none of your business.'

'Perfectly correct,' said Jack soothingly. 'However, we are both members of the university and I offer you the hand of friendship if there's anything I can do to help.'

This time there was no snarl, only a long silence, so Jack resumed, 'Sutcliffe is usually only put on the trail when gambling debts start to mount up—and when they remain unpaid for a longish period of time. Does your father know about your little problem?'

'No!' squeaked Douglas in alarm. 'No, he doesn't . . . and I don't want him to . . . he would explode . . . I can deal with it . . .'

'If you're quite sure. We are, as I said, members of the same university—albeit of different colleges. If I can help you myself, or if I can speak to your moral tutor on your behalf, I'm happy to do so.'

After a lengthy silence Douglas said, 'I realise you mean well, Mr Lewis, and I appreciate it. I really do. But I have resources. I can deal with this problem, trust me.'

'If you say so,' my friend replied. 'So then, let's speak of something else instead—this tragic murder that has come upon your family. The local police seem determined to show my friend Morris here as the guilty party. I'm hoping that the arrival of Scotland Yard will put an end to all such nonsense. And I'm here to do my best to see that it does.'

'I've never heard of a don who played Sherlock Holmes,' said Douglas.

'Lewis has done it once before,' I said. 'Last year, over at Market Plumpton.'

'However,' Jack intervened, 'this time I'm puzzled, and perhaps you can help me, young Douglas.'

'I will if I can . . .'

'My puzzle concerns the motive. Why would anyone want to murder Mrs Worth?'

Douglas laughed cynically and said, 'How long have you got? Aunt Connie was not a likable person, and sooner or later she crossed swords with everyone.'

'But people are not murdered,' Jack objected, 'simply because they're irritating or unlikable. There must be something much more powerful behind this death.'

'You just don't know how detestable the Black Widow was,' snapped Douglas, a deep bitterness in his voice. A moment later he seemed to regret this outburst and said more quietly, 'Anyway, I wish you well in your detecting, Mr Lewis. And I hope you escape the noose, Tom. Now, I've got to get back— Stiffy is waiting for me.'

With that he took off at a rapid trot and soon disappeared into the darkness.

We stood there while Jack lit his pipe. The wind was rising again, so this took several minutes. As Jack fiddled with tobacco and matches, turning his back to the wind, I looked up at the black clouds rapidly rolling across the face of the moon.

That's when the first heavy drop of rain fell.

FIFTEEN

~

A moment later the rain was coming down in torrents. Lightning flashed somewhere in the distance. Then, after a long wait, came the thunder—crashing and rolling across the sky.

'We'll get soaked if we stay here in the middle of the road,' I said, pointing out the obvious. 'We need to find shelter.'

The lightning came to our rescue. The next flash showed a break in the hedge close to where we stood, and beyond, in a field, a large, spreading evergreen tree heavy with leaves.

'That tree,' I said, pointing. 'The lightning's far enough away. The tree should be safe.'

Jack didn't argue, but joined me in pushing through the hedge and running across the field. We sloshed through wet grass and splashed through shallow puddles, unseen in the darkness, until we reached the shelter of the tree.

Its wide arc of thickly leafed arms created a dry circle in the midst of the storm. We caught our breath, shook the rain off our clothes, stamped the mud off our shoes and looked around.

The damp made me feel chilly, so I buttoned up my coat again as I asked, 'What kind of tree is this?'

'The very welcome kind,' chuckled Jack, who always seemed indifferent to bad weather or physical discomfort. He ran his hand over the trunk, then reached up over his head and plucked a leaf.

'I claim no expertise as an arborist,' he said, 'but I suspect this is a box tree.'

'Can't be! The box is a dwarf; they grow them as hedges. This thing is—what? Twenty-five feet tall?'

'What you say is usually true. But that's only because they're trimmed to keep them as dwarves and shaped into hedges. Left untrimmed, to grow wild in the middle of a field as this one has been, they grow to a considerable height. Our gardener at Little Lea gave me a lecture on the common box when I was about ten years old. Bits of it stuck. See this leaf—small, stiff and leathery: that's the leaf of the common box. And the leaves grow close together, very thickly over the whole branch. That's what makes them such good hedges, and, in our case, such a perfectly efficient umbrella from the rain.'

'What on earth was a ten-year-old boy doing talking to a gardener about box trees?'

'I think I must have asked him—perhaps because of a fantasy world Warnie and I invented when we were young. It was a place called Boxen, and at one stage I thought it should be thickly covered with box trees. So I asked about them, you see.'

I kept learning surprising things about Jack.

'What kind of a place was Boxen?' I asked.

'It started out as a sort of medieval animal-land,' replied Jack, and then added with a warm smile of fond remembrance, 'then Warnie added trains and steamships. It was a delightful place for a child's imagination to roam around in.'

The lightning and thunder were receding further into the distance. I pointed this out to Jack and commented that this was a good thing, since the usual advice was not to be under a large tree during a thunderstorm as trees can become lightning rods.

Jack agreed, but pointed out that while the thunder and lightning were less, the rain was heavier than ever.

'We may be trapped here for some time,' he remarked. And it was true that the darkness around us was filled with the smell of rain and the sound of the torrential downpour.

Jack relit his pipe, and by the dim glow of the match I saw his round face looking positively cheerful. It was almost as if he relished English weather at its worst.

'So now, let's fill our time waiting for the rain to stop with good conversation, young Morris,' he boomed at me. 'Where were we up to in our debate on death?'

'I have reached the point,' I admitted, 'where I will grant that there is that in us that can pass on to another kind of existence when the body dies—the part Socrates called "the higher part of man". I think I am persuaded that "Tom Morris, the person" will in some way, in some form, survive death.'

'All to the good,' chortled Jack. 'We make progress.'

'But . . . but . . .' I interrupted, 'the whole question is in which way, in which form, will the inner person who is the real Tom Morris survive death?'

'And I take it you are about to suggest an answer?'

'I am—reincarnation.'

'Metempsychosis is, I believe, the technical term—the transmigration of the soul from one body to another.'

'Exactly. Do you remember Vishal? He didn't read English with you, but he was an undergraduate at Magdalen at the same time as I was. He was reading PPE, I think. We used to say that he was the son of a Rajah. I don't know if that was true or not.'

'I believe he was some sort of Indian prince. But how does he come into your story of metempsychosis?'

'Several of us went to tea in his rooms one afternoon and he explained the Hindu concept of reincarnation. It all sounded jolly strange. But now, well . . . '

'Hence your suggestion that it might be the best way to survive death?'

'Exactly. It solves the problem of the disembodied survival of the soul, or mind, since it goes from one body to another. At least I think that's how Vishal explained it. Have you come across the notion? Have you ever looked at it at all?'

'I had to, I had no choice. I had to understand the whole concept—and what's wrong with it—in order to survive my Great War with Barfield.'

'Owen Barfield? The man I met in your rooms once?'

'That's the chap. A thoroughly delightful man. Pity you never got to know him; you would have liked him. By the time you'd arrived he'd moved to London and become a solicitor. I learned a lot from Barfield about the depth and richness of words and language; about how poetry shapes words as much as words shape poetry. Tollers says the same—shaken to the roots he was by Barfield's insights.'

'So what kind of a "Great War" did you have with him?'

'The kind of war I'm having with you right now, old chap— a war of words and ideas.'

'And this involved reincarnation?'

'It did, among many others things. Barfield became an Anthroposophist—a follower of a German chap named Rudolf Steiner. This meant that Barfield rattled on about the reincarnation of the human spirit. The human being, he said, passes between stages of existence, in an earthly body living on earth, then leaving that body behind and entering into the spiritual world before returning to a new life on earth.'

'That's the sort of thing Vishal talked about over that afternoon tea in his rooms—more or less.'

'And you find the idea persuasive?'

'Well, it strikes me there are good reasons for taking reincarnation seriously.'

'List them for me, young Morris. Let me hear them.'

'First: it allows for the human soul, or mind, to be immortal—not to be extinguished with the death of one body. That fits in with Socrates and Plato as well as your Christianity. Secondly: Vishal claimed that there was psychological evidence—the loves and fears of early childhood, he said, reflect our previous life or lives. And I read an article in one of the Sunday papers last year about people who remembered past lives under hypnosis. Thirdly: it makes the universe a just place. People carry a load of what Vishal called *karma*, meaning the good and bad deeds they've done in this life, and the form of their rebirth either rewards or punishes those deeds. That metes out justice in the universe, and catches even the criminal who escaped the law during his lifetime. There you are—there's a list of three.'

'None of which, I'm afraid, stands up. First: the immortality of the soul, or mind, could operate in any number of ways—disembodied existence, for example, as the Spiritualists believe; or resurrection in a new, perfected body in the New Heavens and the New Earth, as Christians believe. Immortality does not, of itself, logically imply reincarnation.'

'That's probably fair enough. My second point?'

'The psychological evidence is remarkably weak. Infant fears, such as fear of the dark, fear of separation from its parent or fear of sudden loud noises, simply come from being human, not from being reincarnated. And a great many so call "recovered memories" have been exposed as false. Investigation has revealed many to have been implanted or suggested by the hypnotherapist. There was that housewife in Brighton a few years ago who claimed to remember living in London during the Great Plague. It turned out that she was just recycling stories told to her in the nursery by her aunt. No, the psychological evidence is feeble.'

'So what about justice? Doesn't reincarnation make the universe a fair and just place?'

'In fact it makes the whole problem worse. Reincarnation wants us to believe that when the innocent suffer they deserve it—they are being punished for something they've done in a previous life. Someone who is born with a serious disability is assumed to have been especially wicked in their last life. The result is disabled beggars on the streets of India. I hope I don't sound too harsh when I say that it's Christians, not Hindus, who found hospitals and charities because Christians believe we are our brother's keeper and we must love our neighbour as ourselves.'

'Still . . .'

'My dear Morris, reincarnation is, in the end, profoundly anti-humanitarian because there is no room for forgiveness. There is no grace in *karma*, simply relentless, unforgiving punishment. I heard Christmas Humphreys speak at the Oxford Union on Buddhism once. What was interesting was what happened afterwards.'

'Afterwards?'

'As I came out of the Sheldonian, I saw your friend Vishal on the corner being cross-examined by a group of students. Under their questioning he said that anyone who helps a person born with a disability heaps bad *karma* on themselves and on the person they're helping. God's grace is better by far than the cold, unforgiving *karma* of reincarnation.'

I didn't like where this argument was heading, so I said, 'I think the rain is starting to ease.'

'Before I let you off the hook entirely, young Morris,' Jack responded with a deep-throated chuckle at my manoeuvre, 'here's one more thing to think about. The basic idea of a cycle of one rebirth after another is that human beings learn from each life cycle and slowly become morally better. That's what Vishal's idea of *karma* is supposed to be doing: teaching us to do a little better in each subsequent lifetime. But look at human history—there is no evidence of that happening. I don't know how many thousands of generations of humans there have been in total, but I lived through trench warfare in France, and I see no signs that this generation is morally superior to every preceding generation.'

'So the alternative is . . . ?'

'Immortality without reincarnation. As the Bible says, "It is appointed unto men once to die, but after this the judgment".'

'That sounds even grimmer,' I complained. 'But we can leave that for another time—the rain really has stopped. We should get back to the village.'

SIXTEEN

~

Getting back to the village was certainly what we tried to do. But things didn't work out quite as we intended.

I stepped out of the shelter of the spreading branches of the box tree. The rain had stopped completely. It hadn't just eased off, it had stopped. Not a drop was falling. The problem was those thick storm clouds still filled the sky from horizon to horizon. The sun had set and the moon was buried somewhere in the clouds. Not a single star was visible. The night was as dark as a dungeon.

'Which way back to the road?' I mused out loud. 'We need to retrace our steps.'

'You are my guide,' said Jack. 'Lead on, young Morris.'

So I led on. In, as it turned out, entirely the wrong direction. What made me so confident I have no idea. Some people, I know, are born with an inner compass that always points them in the right direction. I am the exact opposite: no sense of direction at all (turn me around three times in the kitchen and I can't find the door). I have about as much sense of how to track through the English countryside in the dark as a penguin has of doing algebra. So where my certainty came from I have no idea.

'I'm sure this is the way we came,' I announced, displaying a gift for creative fiction at short notice.

Jack may have been doubtful, but if so he kept his doubts to himself and set off beside me trudging across the damp moors. So deep was the darkness that I could see nothing of my companion. I only knew he was there by the steady splosh of his footfalls on the sodden field.

After about ten minutes—or perhaps fifteen, or possibly even twenty, my sense of time being in the same non-functioning category as my sense of direction—I discovered a low stone wall. When I say 'discovered', what I mean is I collided with it, making a loud 'harrumph' sound and almost falling over as I did so.

'Careful, Jack,' I said, 'there's a stone wall here'—thus earning myself five points in the Extremely Obvious category. I earned another five by announcing, 'We'll need to climb over it.'

Jack courteously did as I suggested, then he stopped and looked at me. I could faintly see his smiling face in the dim, red glow from his pipe. The more uncomfortable circumstances became, the happier Jack seemed to be.

However, he did lay a hand on my shoulder and say, 'Are you quite sure this is the way we should be going?'

'Well . . .' I admitted, 'we do seem to have been plodding on for rather a long time.'

'Surely we should have hit the road by now?'

'If we were going in the right direction, yes, we should have. And that leads me to confidently announce that we are now thoroughly lost. Where we are in relation to the road and the village I haven't a clue.'

'That does pose a bit of a problem, young Morris. What do you suggest?'

'The ground beneath my feet seems to be rising up a slope in that direction,' I said, pointing with an arm invisible in the darkness at an equally invisible horizon. 'I suggest we keep going up the slope. If we get high enough we might spot a light from a farmhouse . . . or something.'

'I do have the feeling,' said Jack, 'that we are competing in Lewis Carroll's caucus race—but your proposal is as good as any, so lead on.'

Once again I led on. But this time without any of the confidence I felt when we left the box tree.

Perhaps five minutes later we reached what might have been, judging from the ground beneath our feet and the faint breeze we could now feel, the top of a ridge.

'Down there,' said Jack, once we had caught our breath. 'Below us and a little to our left, behind those trees—is that a light from a window?'

'I believe you're right, Jack. Come on, let's head straight towards it.'

So we did. Keeping that dim light from a curtained window in view meant climbing over another low stone wall, clambering down a steep grassy slope and pushing through occasional bushes and brambles, but we kept on track.

As we drew closer, the clouds parted a little and at least half of the moon appeared. The dim light was enough for our dark-adapted eyes to make out the shape of a small cottage looming ahead of us in the darkness. We hurried in that direction.

'That's too small to be a farmhouse,' I puffed. 'I had no idea there was an isolated cottage out here on the moors.'

'Since we have no idea where "here" is, your ignorance of its existence is hardly surprising,' suggested my companion. 'Besides which we seem to be at the bottom of a deep, narrow fold in the hills—this place is probably invisible from anywhere up on the moorlands, even in broad daylight.'

A low picket fence surrounded the cottage. We found the

gate and swung it open. As we did so, sounds could be heard from inside. There were low voices and the sound of people moving. Then came an anguished cry followed by a heavy crash and a thump. Jack ran ahead of me up the path and knocked vigorously on the cottage door.

The sounds within ceased. Jack knocked again, but silence was the only response. As he knocked a third time, I began to grope my way around the rough stone walls of the cottage. I got to the curtained window we had seen from the ridge top, but the curtains were drawn to the very edges of the sash. There was no gap giving me a glimpse of the room within, only the dim glow seeping through the curtain fabric. I continued my circumnavigation but found no other sign of light, and no other entry point.

I rejoined Jack at the front door as he knocked yet again. The silence inside the cottage was now total.

'Hello,' Jack called. 'Is there anyone in there? We're lost on the moors—we want some directions.'

Faintly the silence was broken by shuffling sounds from inside the small cottage.

'I think someone's coming to the door,' I whispered, although why I whispered I don't know—we were not trying to hide our presence. Perhaps it was the heavy air of mystery that hung over the dark cottage that made me lower my voice.

Then came the sound of not one but several bolts being slid back, and the door creaked open a few inches. The face that confronted us was startling: it was a heavy, masculine face, as brown as walnut, with deep-set eyes and strange tattoos on the forehead and both cheeks. It was surrounded by long black hair hanging almost to the shoulders.

'Sorry to bother you, old chap,' said Jack in his hearty, confident way, 'but we've managed to get ourselves thoroughly lost.

We're looking for the road that will take us back to Plumwood village. You can't help at all, I suppose?'

A suspicious look passed over that exotic face, then the man swung the door open a few more inches and leaned out. He pointed with a gnarled and knuckly brown hand in the direction of one corner of the cottage.

'That way,' he almost grunted. 'Straight. You go straight.'

'Is it far to the road?' I asked.

'Ten minutes,' said the stranger, 'no more. You go straight.'

'If you don't mind my mentioning it,' said Jack, 'we did hear a cry and a fall as we approached your cottage. Is your friend inside all right?'

'No one here,' said the man, with a note of alarm in his voice. He stepped back and began to ease the door closed. 'No one here.'

'Are you quite sure . . .' Jack began.

The stranger thumped himself on the chest and grunted loudly, 'Just me. Just me.'

Then the door closed swiftly and firmly in our face, and we heard all those bolts being slid back into place.

SEVENTEEN

~

Getting back to Plumwood turned out to be tiresome but fairly straightforward after that. Unseen in the background, Fate was quietly ticking off all the unpleasant surprises as having been delivered on cue and was now leaving us to our own devices. The clouds broke up a little further, scattering moonlight and starlight on the landscape, and we were able to make a straight track across the fields in the direction the stranger had indicated.

Sure enough, he had put us on the right path, and we soon came to the hedge that bordered the road. We searched until we found a small gap in this and pushed our way through onto a familiar narrow country road.

As we walked back to the village—and a long, winding walk it was, for my uncanny sense of misdirection had taken us further away from Plumwood—we discussed the mystery of the isolated cottage and its strange inhabitant.

'Clearly he's a foreigner,' said Jack, 'a native from some remote place judging by those strange tattoos on his face. However, I claim no expertise in such matters.'

Then we talked about what such an exotic character might be doing in an isolated cottage on our moors. Finding him in this very English rural landscape was as disconcerting as discovering an opium den in a Women's Institute meeting hall. The man, colourful though he was, simply did not fit with the damp, dull English countryside.

We also talked about who else might have been in the cottage with him—for we had the impression there might have been someone else inside, someone who had cried out as we approached.

We concluded by tossing around theories and possibilities, with me suggesting that I raise the matter with the Dyer family at Plumwood Hall. Perhaps they knew of the cottage, or who owned it.

We parted at the gates to the Hall, Jack going on to the village, and supper and a comfortable bed at the pub, while I walked up the winding drive to the Hall. I had, I discovered, missed dinner, but Mrs Buckingham, who couldn't stand to see anyone go hungry, served me some steak and kidney pie in the kitchen. She warmed the pie first in the oven, and chatted to me cheerfully as she waddled around, laying out the things she would need for breakfast next morning.

I responded to her cheerful chatter by telling her the story of our adventures on the moors. I left out our encounter with Douglas and the bookmaker's tough as I wanted to give that episode a great deal more thought. But I talked about the rain storm, about getting lost and about the hidden cottage we came across with its strange inhabitant.

'Oh, I know who that is, sir,' said she. 'He made my blood run cold when he come up to the Hall when he first arrived.'

'Arrived from where?'

'South America, sir. They told me he come from the Amazon jungle, sir. He was the one that brought the body of Lady Pamela's brother back home. A surprisingly kind thing for him to do, I thought—him being a heathen and all.'

'This is Edmund, I take it?' She nodded. 'I've only just recently been learning about him. I've been here for the better part of a year, and I've not heard him mentioned very often before.'

'Well, it were made clear to us, sir, that Lady Pamela was so upset about her brother dying—so young, and in such a faraway place—that we were never to mention it. And, of course, the family do the same.'

At this point the steak and kidney pie was placed in front of me, and I set to work demolishing it with a knife and fork.

'So this chap in the cottage,' I mumbled through mouthfuls, 'why is he still here in England? And why is he living in a cottage on the moors?'

'Well, that cottage belongs to the Plumwood estate. Years ago Lord Bosham had a gamekeeper living there—when I first come to work at the Hall, as a mere slip of a lass that was.'

As I watched the almost circular figure of Mrs Buckingham bustling around the kitchen I found it impossible to imagine her as a 'mere slip of a lass'. It was like trying to picture Mount Everest as a slight bulge in the front yard.

'It stood empty for many years, then this heathen chappie turned up with the body of Master Edmund, and it seems he didn't want to go straight back home. Well, I dare say England is much more comfortable than some jungle. Anyway, they let him have the old gamekeeper's cottage.'

'When was this?'

'Two years ago it would have to be. Maybe a bit more than that. Anyway, this dark gentleman from the jungle come up to the house when he first arrived to stock up on things—cutlery and crockery and linen and the like. And some bits of furniture too. Well, the place had been empty a long time,'

'Does he have a name, this Amazonian native?'

'Lady Pamela called him Drax. It seems like these heathens only have one name. Just Drax and nothing more. Or so I were told.'

I asked Mrs Buckingham as many questions as I could think of, but it seemed she had told me all she knew. I thanked her for the supper and went up to bed in a very thoughtful frame of mind.

The next morning I was at my desk in the library when Keggs suddenly appeared, having apparently materialised in the silent and efficient way only butlers can, and presented me with an envelope.

'This came in the morning post, sir,' he said. Then he turned and floated away in the same frictionless way in which he arrived. The letter was postmarked London. It was from the auction house I had approached for expert advice. They had authenticated the Shakespeare quarto from the photographs I had sent, and submitted a tentative appraisal.

I hurried up to Sir William's office on the first floor and broke the good news of the prize find that had turned up in a dusty corner of his library. He was delighted and shook my hand as if I were some long lost uncle from whom he expected to inherit a small fortune. And, in effect, he just had—given the value of the quarto. However, he made it clear that he had no intention of putting the rare book on the market, but instead he wanted me to find a way to display it in the library.

Sir William insisted we have a brandy to celebrate. Although the sun was not yet over the yardarm, I accepted the offer, knowing how good Sir William's cellar was. He rang for Keggs and in due course two brandies in snifters were delivered. So there we were: drinking French brandy, in a very English oak-panelled study, with South American memorabilia on the walls. In the past I had taken those items of decoration to be merely an assortment of eccentric collectables chosen by Sir William, but I now realised that the arrows, blowpipes, spears and the rest must have some connection with the late Edmund.

I asked Sir William if the collection on his walls came from his late brother-in-law and he coughed and spluttered into his brandy.

'Oh, so you've heard about Edmund, have you?' he said when he'd recovered. 'We do try not to mention him for poor Pamela's sake. She misses him dreadfully, the poor dear.'

He took another sip to show the Napoleon the respect it deserved.

'Look here,' he said, with an anxious expression on his face, 'I don't know who mentioned Edmund to you, but it shouldn't have happened. And now that you've heard I trust that you'll be sensitive and not mention it in Pamela's hearing. Not ever.'

After assuring him I would be vigilant in the matter, I finished my brandy and left, not for the library but for the village—having put in a few moments of effort in my salaried position I wanted to return to my main employment for the moment: keeping Tom Morris out of the hands of the law on a charge of murder.

I found Jack at *The Cricketers' Arms* in Plumwood, sitting in the parlour doodling in a notebook. Although when I glanced over his shoulder I saw it wasn't doodling: in his small, neat scrawl he had compiled an account of everything we knew about the case so far.

Pulling up a chair I told Jack what I had discovered from the cook the night before.

'So it seems we were mistaken,' I concluded. 'There is no one else living in the cottage, only Drax, the South American who came from—according to Mrs Buckingham—the Amazon jungle. Whatever sounds we heard last night must just have been Drax bumping around in the cottage.'

Jack looked thoughtful for a moment, then took his fountain pen back out of his pocket and scribbled a few more lines at the end of his notes. When he had finished I asked, 'And what has all this note-taking and analysis told you?'

'That we need to get to know the victim,' Jack replied firmly. 'I have no doubt that understanding the victim, who she was, what she was and how she related to those around her, is the key to this puzzle.'

EIGHTEEN

~

In pursuit of more information about the late Connie Worth, we made our way back to Plumwood Hall, or what is known in the higher sort of literature as 'the scene of the crime'.

As we walked up the drive we noticed Sir William Dyer in consultation with his head gardener near the rose beds. Seeing us approaching he hurried across.

'Mr Lewis,' Sir William said, 'I'm glad I've run into you again. That invitation I mentioned—how would tonight be? Are you free to come to dinner at the Hall this evening?'

Jack said he was, and Sir William said good, that's settled, and went back to his conference with Franklin over curbing the appetite of the more enthusiastic aphids or whatever the problem was. Jack and I proceeded into the house to find whichever family members might be about and might be amenable to talking about the murder victim.

In the morning room we found Douglas and Stiffy sitting in sulky silence, as if they had just argued with each other and had agreed to disagree as long as they could ignore each other while doing so. Stiffy was turning over the pages of a book but appeared not to be focussed on the print, while Douglas was staring out of the window at the rolling lawns of Plumwood

Hall, with no clear intention except, perhaps, to watch the grass grow.

Jack roared 'Good morning' at his full lecture hall volume. Stiffy dropped her book and Douglas flinched as if he had been hit in the small of the back while bending over to smell the roses.

'Don't do that,' he complained as he turned around.

'Sorry to disturb your quiet and peaceful contemplation,' said Jack, 'but we need your assistance.'

'What for?' asked Stiffy suspiciously.

'To catch a murderer,' said Jack.

'If it's the murderer of the Black Widow you want,' said Stiffy coldly, 'he's standing beside you.'

Jack clapped me on the shoulder. 'There you are, Morris—even before you've been charged the jury has found you guilty. But why?' he asked abruptly, leaning forward and staring at Stiffy. 'Why do you believe him to be the guilty party?'

'He was next to Connie when she died. He had the best opportunity to poison her slice of cake. In fact, he was the only one with the opportunity.'

'And opportunity,' responded Jack, 'is all that is needed? He had the opportunity therefore he committed the murder *quod erat demonstrandum*?'

'Exactly,' she said with a sniff.

'And you saw this happen?'

'Not personally.'

'Can you tell me why this rather dull scholar would abruptly become a homicidal maniac? Perhaps Genghis Khan would do that sort of thing just to keep his hand in, but why would Tom Morris?'

I was about to object to the word 'dull' but decided I should hold my counsel for the time being.

'Why doesn't matter,' said Douglas, walking across from the window. 'I agree with Stiffy. Sorry, Tom old chap, but I can't see who else could have done it.'

'Now look what you've done to poor Morris here,' said Jack with a smile. 'He now displays an expression of glum depression that would attract comment in a Siberian salt mine. For myself, I am much more interested in motive: leaving aside the possibility of homicidal mania—the only motive that fits Morris—what reason might anyone have had for killing Connie Worth?'

A sudden and uncomfortable silence descended on the room, as if Jack has broached the forbidden topic.

'Is there nothing,' prompted Jack, 'about Mrs Worth that would have caused her to be chosen by the Homicide Victim of the Month Club?'

'*I* can tell you something about Aunt Connie,' said a voice from the doorway. I turned around. It was young Will, apparently having grown tired of his outdoor sporting activities, or perhaps having run out of moving targets. His arrival was not greeted with universal enthusiasm.

'Ah look, the pest is here,' groaned Douglas.

'Why aren't you outside somewhere,' sneered Stiffy, 'pulling wings off flies or torturing small, helpless animals?'

'I still think it was jolly odd,' persisted Will, who had clearly heard taunts along these lines often before and had long since learned to ignore them. 'Odd that she had plenty of the folding stuff when she should have been flat, stony broke.'

Jack asked why she should have been so totally impoverished.

'Because it was Uncle Charles who had all the money in that family. And when he disappeared so abruptly a couple of summers ago, Aunt Connie didn't have a bean. That was why she went and sponged off poor Aunt Judith.'

'Listen, Will,' growled Douglas threateningly. 'You should be like the hangman who's run out of customers—you should keep your trap shut.'

'I don't see why. It's not like it's some sort of secret or something.'

'Tell me,' said Jack in a polite but firm voice, 'about your Uncle Charles, Aunt Connie and Aunt Judith.'

Douglas threw his hands in the air in a gesture of resignation as he grumbled, 'You might as well keep going now, you young jackass.'

The story that young Will told—haltingly, because he was now aware of letting family skeletons out of cupboards—was a strange one. It seemed that Charles Worth had gone for a walk across the moors one summer's afternoon.

'He left through those French windows over there,' said Will, pointing at the far wall, 'his dog trotting by his side. I watched him cross the lawns and disappear among the trees. No one's seen him since.'

Pressed for details, he said that the dog's dead body was found among the heather on the moor, killed by a single blow to its head.

'Not,' I asked, 'a blow from the famous blunt instrument so beloved by mystery writers?'

Will nodded.

Douglas gave a loud, rather melodramatic sigh.

The body of Uncle Charles, Will explained, never turned up—even though a hysterical Connie had insisted he too must be dead. In the absence of a body his estate could not be distributed—even though he'd left a will in which he named his wife Connie as his only heir (they had no children).

Suddenly impoverished in this way, Connie Worth, as Will told the story, went to live with another aunt—Judith

Trelawney, the beautiful younger sister of Lady Pamela. It seems that Connie Worth appointed herself to the role of friend and companion to the younger woman.

Then Judith Trelawney also died, suddenly and violently. She and Connie were staying in a suite of rooms at a Brighton hotel when Judith fell from the balcony. It was a top floor balcony and the fall was fatal. Although the coroner decided that her death was an accident, it struck me that Connie Worth seemed to attract violence the way a magnet attracts iron filings.

Stiffy rose from her chair with the air of being bored by these family reminiscences, and left the room.

Douglas simply looked impatient.

'Right,' he snapped. 'Have you finished your storytelling now, Will?'

The younger boy shrugged his shoulders and said in a bewildered way, 'I just thought it might be relevant to the whole murder mystery business . . . sorry . . . I was just trying to be helpful.'

'And so you were, young Will,' boomed Jack. 'Very helpful indeed.'

'Oh, really?' said Douglas suspiciously. 'In what way?'

'In the change that came over Connie Worth's fortunes. Following her husband's disappearance she was so penniless she needed the charity of others, but you tell me, Will, that during her stay here at the Hall she was not short of cash.'

'She had a wad of big, white fivers,' said Will enthusiastically. 'I saw them when I was walking past her room. It was a wad large enough to choke a horse. She was stuffing them furtively' (he said this word slowly, as if he had just learned it) 'into her purse.'

'I still can't see how it can have anything at all to do with Connie's murder,' growled Douglas sullenly.

'Perhaps,' admitted Jack, 'it has nothing to do directly with the murder itself, but it's puzzling, isn't it? Both puzzling and interesting.'

NINETEEN

~

The dinner party that night was a rather strained one. Sir William tried to encourage Douglas to discuss life at Oxford with Jack, but Douglas, while polite, seemed to have nothing to say and no questions to ask. He appeared, in fact, to shrink into his shell. That, of course, didn't stop Jack from giving advice. He pressed upon Douglas the importance, given the Oxford tutorial system, of getting the set reading done during the breaks between terms.

'In between terms,' said Jack, 'you put on the polish; during the terms we put on the shine.' Douglas nodded but said nothing. 'And remember,' Jack continued, 'you don't have to work hard if you work steadily. Only innately lazy men are hard workers—they are forever trying to catch up on work they should have done.' And he went on with a good deal more wise counsel for a young student.

Sir William kept endorsing Jack's advice with nods, muttered agreements and comments of 'Did you hear that, Douglas?'

When that stream finally ran dry, Sir William asked me what I'd been doing to keep Jack amused during his time in Plumwood. I could have said, 'Trying to solve a murder mystery', but instead I talked about our walks on the moors.

'One place we got to is that ruined tower,' I said. 'I think it's called the Hunting Tower.'

'Oh, ah,' grunted Uncle Teddy from his end of the table. 'Yes, yes, the Black Tower, that's what that is. You ask the villagers. Yes, yes, ask them.'

'And what will they tell us?' asked Jack.

'That it's haunted!' hissed Uncle Teddy in a theatrical whisper as he leaned forward over his plate. 'The villagers won't go near the place at night. Not near it at all. Not even close. After dark they go out of their way to avoid it. You ask them.'

Sir William laughed and said, 'Village superstition, Uncle Teddy—that's what it is. And you know that's all it is.'

Uncle Teddy went back to his meal with a rather grumpy look on his face.

'What I call it,' said Sir William, 'is Bosham's Folly. It was built by the seventh Lord Bosham as a base for hunting parties on the moors. I understand why—they had to roam a long way from the Hall to find grouse. But even so, why he didn't build a simple hut or cottage I'll never know. That monstrosity must have taken a team of stonemasons a year to build. And the seventh Lord Bosham died shortly after it was finished. Hence, Bosham's Folly.'

'It did occur to us when we were there,' I said, 'that there'd be a superb view from the top of the tower—assuming, that is, the staircase is still intact. Unfortunately, we found the door at the base of the tower locked.'

'You can see all the way to the coast,' said Will enthusiastically. 'When I was a little squirt I used to climb to the top with that old brass telescope we found in the attic. I could see the tops of the cliffs and the fishing boats when they put out.'

'I never knew you used to climb to the top of the tower,' said Lady Pamela, with a properly dignified note of concern in her voice. 'When did this happen?'

'Years ago,' said Will. 'I was only about nine or ten at the time.'

'Nine or ten!' Lady Pamela allowed a note of horror to creep into her voice. 'Climbing those crumbling old stairs. Alone, I take it? If you'd fallen you might not have been found for hours . . . or days!'

'It was all right,' Will responded, looking slightly chastened. 'I was quite safe. That staircase is as solid as rock. It's a circular stone staircase built into the side of the stone walls. There was never any danger, honestly.'

'What surprises me,' said Sir William, 'is that you found the tower locked.'

'There's a heavy wooden door that rattled in its doorframe when I shook it,' I said, 'but—securely locked.'

'As young Will said, it was never locked in the past. Anyway,' Sir William continued, 'might you return to the tower on one of your future rambles on our moors?'

Jack and I both agreed that we might.

'In that case you should take the key to the tower,' volunteered Sir William. 'There is a key, I'm sure of that. The last time I saw it, it was hanging on the key rack in the kitchen. Mind you, that would have been a year or two ago. But it might be worth checking.'

This was my employer telling me what I should do, so naturally I agreed. Then Sir William asked where else we had got to in our walks.

'We found a cottage—a quite remote and isolated cottage,' said Jack. 'We stumbled across it entirely by accident. I would assume that in normal circumstances it would be almost invisible—from up on the moors, that is. It's in a kind of narrow valley or deep fold in the hills. We only found it because of my young friend's spectacular lack of any sense of direction.'

'It was dark,' I said in my defence. 'Pitch black. We'd been caught in a sudden rain squall and I rather lost my sense of direction, what with the rain and the dark and all, so instead of heading back towards the village I led Jack in entirely the opposite direction.'

'Still, it was a nice, brisk walk in the fresh evening air,' said Jack, with a grin on his face.

As this exchange was going on, a look passed between Sir William and Lady Pamela that I couldn't quite interpret but that seemed to be, somehow, significant.

'That's the old gamekeeper's cottage—' began Will, always eager to display his knowledge.

Lady Pamela interrupted him before he could say more. 'And what did you find at the cottage, Mr Lewis?'

'A most exotic gentleman,' Jack replied. 'He answered our persistent knocking at his front door and gave us very helpful directions to get back to the village.'

'He was certainly a colourful character,' I commented. 'Covered in tattoos.'

'I didn't know there was anyone living in the old game-keeper's cottage,' Douglas complained. Will joined in the complaint, saying he'd like to meet this chap—whoever he is.

'His name is Drax, I believe,' I said.

'That's right, Mr Morris,' said Lady Pamela. Her surface dignity was intact, but I thought I detected an almost panick-ing sense of fluster seething underneath. 'He is a native from South America.' Then addressing the whole dinner table she said, 'He brought your Uncle Edmund's body back from the upper reaches of the Amazon River. It was an extremely kind thing for him to do, and he expressed a desire to stay here for a while, so we've let him have the gamekeeper's cottage.'

'I knew nothing about this,' Douglas grumbled, with Will seconding the motion.

'You boys were both away at school at the time,' Lady Pamela explained. 'We did bring you back for Edmund's funeral, you may recall.'

'There wasn't any tattooed South American native at the funeral,' said an aggrieved Douglas.

'Drax didn't want to attend so naturally we didn't force him,' Sir William said, with the air of coming to his wife's rescue.

'Why didn't you tell us about him?' Will complained.

'There was nothing really to tell,' murmured Lady Pamela, waving her hands in the air with a delicate gesture of brushing away annoying insects.

'I remember him,' grunted Uncle Teddy. 'Dark chap. Brown as a walnut. Didn't have much to say for himself. In fact . . . I don't think I ever heard him utter a single word. Ugly looking chap, I thought.'

'I say, Douglas,' said Stiffy enthusiastically, 'let's go out to this old gamekeeper's cottage and meet this wild tattooed native. He sounds fascinating.'

'Stephanie, my dear,' said Lady Pamela firmly, 'I'm afraid I must discourage you strongly from any such action. The man doesn't feel entirely comfortable in our society. He's a very solitary man. It probably comes from living in those remote jungles all his life. He prefers to be alone, and I don't think we should violate his privacy. Don't you agree, my dear?'

'He asked to be left alone,' said Sir William from the head of the table, 'and we've respected his wishes. I would ask all of you to do the same.'

He looked around the table, and then added, 'Now I think it's time we all retired to the library—there's something I want to show you.'

TWENTY

~

Chairs were pushed back and the members of the dinner party made their way out of the dining room and into the library, wandering slowly but purposefully—like the cattle being called home across the Sands of Dee.

'I think we may say, Tom,' Sir William proclaimed as he threw open the double doors of the library of Plumwood Hall, 'that this is your realm, your little kingdom. At least it has been for many months past.'

'The only king I've resembled here,' I replied, 'was King Canute trying to hold back the rising tide of paperwork and cataloguing cards.'

I walked him over to the desk where I had done most of the work and where the thick book containing the catalogue of the contents of his library was almost complete. I began to explain the process and the results, but I was interrupted by his cries of 'Excellent! Excellent!' Clearly Sir William did not want to be overly bothered with the details. He had bought a house with a great library and now he had a catalogue of its contents. The point was to own a lot, and to have a clear record of exactly what one owned. The pleasure was in the possession.

'And now,' he said, turning to face the room, 'I have an announcement to make.'

Silence fell and the small party turned to face their host.

'In the course of his work in this library our resident scholar, Mr Tom Morris here, has made a very significant find. In a remote and, he tells me, dusty corner of the library . . .'

'. . . buried under a pile of old law books . . .' I added.

'. . . he has found a rare and valuable volume. Show them, Tom.'

I went to the sideboard and picked up the clearly very old, but otherwise unremarkable, leather-bound book lying there.

'This,' I said proudly, 'is a Shakespeare quarto. This edition of *Romeo and Juliet* is, I have now established, from the very first printing of that play. This is what is called a Q1. It came from the workshop of a printer named John Danter in 1597.'

Lady Pamela beamed. 'That's makes if very special, doesn't it? To be that early, I mean?'

Sir William just beamed back at her, so I replied, 'It certainly does.'

'There must be very few houses,' she continued, 'with so rare and important a book.' I could hear the clicking inside her brain as she wound her social standing up by several notches.

'What do you think of it, Mr Lewis?' Sir William asked.

I handed the volume to Jack, who gently opened the cover and looked at the title page: *An Excellent conceited Tragedie of Romeo and Juliet, As it hath often (with great applause) plaid publiquely.*

'This really is a jolly good find,' Jack enthused. 'It's what's called a "bad quarto" of the play.'

'Oh, dear me,' said Lady Pamela. 'Wouldn't it have been better if it had been a good quarto?' The gearwheels of social standing, she feared, might be grinding or slipping a cog.

'It only means,' explained Jack, 'that it's very early. It seems unlikely that the printer of this book was working from

Shakespeare's own copy, but rather he rushed out this volume from a prompt copy or something of the sort. It's about 800 lines shorter than the second quarto, and it contains a great more in the way of stage directions. Calling it a "bad quarto" is not a value judgment—it just refers to its important historical role in the establishment of Shakespeare's text.'

Lady Pamela breathed a sigh of relief, and began thinking about which of her friends she could boast to about this find.

The group clustered around and Jack found himself fielding a host of questions. I looked at my friend as he briefly became the centre of attention—a stocky man of medium height with a ruddy face and a balding head. In these social situations Jack was always happy to blend into the background, but he was the Oxford don here, the expert on the subject, and at this moment he was not allowed to blend. His lecture voice rolled across the room as he sketched out the story of the printing of Shakespeare in the same precisely constructed sentences he would have employed instructing undergraduates.

Then Keggs the butler arrived with a large silver tray. There were port glasses and a decanter of port. Behind him came one of the maids with another tray bearing sherry glasses and two decanters containing, respectively, sweet and dry sherry. Lady Pamela had decreed that after dinner the men were to drink port while sherry was appropriate for the ladies.

Lady Pamela began making plans for putting the quarto on display. 'We'll have to have a special glass case made,' she said, 'so that the book can be shown open. Something lockable, of course, given its value. But I must have a key so that I can come in each day and turn over a page of the book.'

Jack and I drifted over towards one of the tall windows to be followed a few minutes later by Sir William.

'How is the investigation going, Mr Lewis?' he asked.

'We've just been hearing the rather sad history of the victim of the murder, Mrs Connie Worth,' Jack replied.

'I suppose hers was a difficult life, one way and another,' Sir William agreed. 'When she married Charles we all thought she was settled and comfortable at last. Then there was the horrible business of Charles's disappearing without a trace, and with no explanation. His dog was found brutally killed on the moors, and it was assumed that Charles too had been attacked. But, as I take it you've heard, his body was never found. The police took the view that his killer, or killers, had disposed of his body off the cliffs and that it had been carried out to sea.'

'Which, I understand, created difficulties for Mrs Worth.'

'Indeed. Legally Charles was not declared to be dead. So his will could not go to probate, and Connie was suddenly penniless.'

'We were told that another of your wife's sisters came to her rescue, is that right?'

There was a pause, a hesitancy, before Sir William replied. 'Ah, yes,' he finally said, 'Judith, the youngest. She took on Connie as a companion and friend. They travelled a good deal. Until Judith died. She was a very sweet girl, was Judith—very sweet indeed.'

'How did she die? A fall, wasn't it?'

'Yes, from a hotel balcony in Brighton. Very late at night and very dark—so no one saw what happened. At one stage the police thought it might have been suicide. But there was no suicide note, as I gather is usual in such cases. And no apparent reason for suicide. So the coroner settled on death by misadventure.'

Keggs arrived at that moment with port for the three of us. Sir William offered us cigars that should probably have been banned under the law forbidding the carrying of concealed weapons.

Jack politely refused the cigar and lit his pipe. After a good deal of what actor's call 'stage business' Sir William managed to get his cigar alight, and gave a good impersonation of how his factory chimneys must function.

Then came a scream from the other side of the room. It was Lady Pamela who screamed. She was standing, rooted to the spot, pointing at Douglas's girlfriend Stiffy—who was doubled over with pain and gasping for air.

As we watched she toppled forward very slowly onto the turkey rug that covered the floor, and then lay very still.

Jack was the first to get to her side. He felt her pulse and commanded, 'We need a doctor immediately.'

'I'll call Dr Henderson,' volunteered Will, running from the room.

'It's happening again,' moaned Lady Pamela. 'It's all happening again.'

TWENTY-ONE

~

Her grim prediction turned out to be horribly accurate. Stephanie Basset, known to us as Stiffy, was dead before Dr Henderson arrived ten minutes later. He bent over her, conducted a swift, decisive examination, and then said, 'The police will have to be notified.'

There were gasps and murmurs around the room, with Lady Pamela moaning softly to herself, 'I'll never live this down . . . never.'

Within half an hour there were three policemen in the room—Detective Inspector Gideon Crispin and Detective Sergeant Henry Merrivale from Scotland Yard and the village bobby, Constable Charlie Nile, all of whom had hurried up from Plumwood in response to Dr Henderson's summons. Fifteen minutes later a red-faced, puffed Inspector Hyde bustled self-importantly into the room, having driven over from Market Plumpton.

The family and the staff of Plumwood Hall were gathered in small clusters around the large library, talking in subdued whispers or, in the case of the maids, dabbing away tears. One of the younger maids saw this as The End of Civilisation As We Know It and made her own contribution by dropping a cup and saucer—which smashed on the floor, shattering everyone's nerves in the process.

For the moment I had been left to my own devices. I hovered over my desk at one end of the library feeling puzzled and uncertain. Was this another murder? Or just a remarkable coincidence? If it was a case of murder, how did it connect to the first? Was there, indeed, a homicidal maniac loose in this small community? I had so many questions I could have popped onto one of those radio quiz shows and felt right at home.

From the far end of the room I could hear Jack's distinctive voice—a fine, sonorous, robust baritone voice with a good deal of carrying power—as he answered questions from Sergeant Merrivale about the course of events during the evening. Jack was speaking in the unhurried, clear way he always did, giving each word its due weight.

So preoccupied was I that I failed to notice the silent arrival of Inspector Crispin at my side. I think I must have jumped when he spoke—possibly setting a new Olympic record for the standing high jump.

'It was definitely cyanide again,' said the Scotland Yard man. 'Officially we have to wait for Dr Henderson's autopsy, but he assures me there can be little doubt.'

Having landed back on the spot from which I took off, and recovered my breath, I asked, 'Does that mean this is connected to the murder of Connie Worth?'

Crispin raised one eyebrow in a gesture that was almost sarcastic and had, at the very least, undertones of irony. 'How could it not be?' he asked out loud.

He seemed in no hurry to start questioning me, so I asked, 'Am I still a suspect?'

He turned his cold, steel-grey eyes on me and replied, 'I'll be frank—both of these murders are so puzzling that I'm still feeling my way through the fog. At this stage everyone is a suspect—including you, Mr Morris.'

He turned away from me and cast his eyes around the room. Then, in his quiet but commanding voice, he called out to the butler, 'Keggs, may I have a moment of your time please?'

The butler slid smoothly towards us in the manner that all butlers have—appearing to glide on some sort of anti-gravity device out of one of Mr Wells's scientific romances.

'Yes, sir?' he hooted gently, like an extremely polite ship at sea modulating its fog horn to a respectful tone. I had noticed that Inspector Hyde was always addressed as 'Inspector' and Constable Nile as 'Constable', but Keggs had apparently decided that the man from Scotland Yard was definitely a 'sir'.

'Tell me about the drinks. To begin with—who drank what?'

'All of the gentlemen drank port, sir. Lady Pamela drank sweet sherry and Miss Bassett drank dry sherry.'

'She was the only one who drank the dry sherry?'

'That is correct, sir.'

'Did she always drink dry sherry?'

'It was her normal after-dinner drink, sir. I have never known her to depart from it.'

'Was her preference for dry sherry well known?'

'Indeed it was, sir. On her first night here Lady Pamela offered her sweet sherry, and Miss Bassett announced her dislike for it. I believe the words she used were "I can't abide the stuff".'

'So each night after dinner Miss Bassett drank dry sherry?'

'Yes, sir.'

'And *only* Miss Bassett drank dry sherry?'

'Yes, sir.'

Keggs always had a ruddy, flushed complexion (he had that butler-ish port wine look). But under the inspector's questioning he had gone redder than ever and resembled nothing so much as a tomato struggling to control strong emotions.

At this point Crispin beckoned Sergeant Merrivale across and gave him instructions to have the bottle of dry sherry as well as the glass Stiffy had been drinking from taken for forensic examination.

Jack followed in Sergeant Merrivale's footsteps and cruised towards us. He was followed in turn by the pocket-sized policeman, Inspector Hyde.

'Part of a pattern, would you say?' Jack asked the Scotland Yard man.

Crispin shook his head sadly as he replied, 'We know so little at this stage. But, as you say, Mr Lewis, it seems most likely part of the same pattern.'

At that moment Inspector Hyde yapped, like a terrier after a bone, 'In that case, Crispin, why don't you arrest Morris right here and now—and stem the tide of these murders?' His petulant tone suggested a terrier with a liver condition who was having a bad day.

Taking a deep breath Inspector Crispin explained slowly and patiently that so far no motive had been discovered for me to commit either murder.

'That's where you're wrong!' snapped Hyde. Crispin said, "Go on, I'm listening", and Hyde explained that he'd run into Sir William Dyer in Market Plumpton that morning and questioned him about the case.

'While you were sitting here cooling your heels,' he added in the tone of a Napoleonic victory speech, 'I've been uncovering vital evidence—evidence of motive. Sir William told me that the first murder victim, Mrs Worth, had complained to him that she had observed Morris here attempting to purloin valuable volumes from this library—presumably to sell them for his own gain. Morris, of course, denied the charge and claimed that it was he who had found Mrs Worth trying to sneak out a rare and valuable book. The matter was, I gather, never settled, but clearly there was bad blood between Morris and the first victim.'

'The matter *was* settled,' said a voice from behind Inspector Hyde's back. It was Sir William, and he looked anything but happy. At the best of times Sir William Dyer had an unfortunate appearance—rather like a superior and especially cunning rat. At that moment he looked like a rat whose dinner had been interrupted by the irritating behaviour of one of the younger rats. 'When I mentioned that small matter in conversation this morning, Hyde, I did not expect you to put it to this entirely misleading and improper use.'

'But you said—' complained Hyde, in a whine like an out-of-tune steam whistle.

'What I meant was perfectly clear,' Sir William continued sternly. 'I was making a point about the victim's character. While I have always had the utmost confidence in Mr Morris's probity—and still have—Mrs Worth, I'm sad to say, was always short of money and not above employing dishonesty in reaching for it.'

'But you said—' Hyde repeated, sounding like one of those old folk songs in which the same refrain erupts after every second line.

'I was trying to shed some light on the character of Mrs Worth. Do you or do you not understand that?'

Hyde opened his mouth again and was clearly about to repeat his refrain when he thought better of it and kept quiet.

Inspector Crispin turned to me and said quietly, 'What did really happen, Mr Morris?'

Feeling a little embarrassed by the whole incident, I explained that I had walked into the library one day, about a month ago, to see Connie Worth slipping a small volume into her handbag.

She knew at once she had been seen and didn't resist when I reached over and took the small, leather-bound book from her hand. It was a first edition of Elizabeth Barrett Browning's *Sonnets from the Portuguese*—worth a good few pounds on the auction market.

She pretended that she just wanted to borrow it, but the surreptitious manner in which she was secreting it in her handbag while looking over her shoulder lest she be seen made it clear to me that something more permanent than borrowing was on her mind. I pretended that I needed the book for cataloguing purposes and that therefore she couldn't borrow it at the moment.

'That's right,' volunteered Sir William. 'Connie came to me and told me that story exactly in reverse—with Tom as the would-be thief and her as his discoverer. I didn't believe it for a minute—I know what Connie's like. But I called Tom in, he told the story you've just heard, and I believed him. It didn't bother him, and it didn't bother me. We all know how Connie scratches around for a few pounds here and a few pounds there. But she's family—or, rather, she *was* family—so we put up with it. I told Tom to keep an eye on her and keep anything valuable in the library under lock and key. And that was the end of the matter.' Then he turned a withering glance on Inspector Hyde and added, 'Anyone who imagines a connection between that small incident and a motive for murder has the IQ of a sea anemone.'

TWENTY-TWO

~

As Jack and I walked back towards the village later that night I asked, 'Do you believe Inspector Hyde was satisfied? Or does he still think he's found my motive for murdering Connie Worth?'

Jack chuckled quietly and said, 'What Inspector Hyde thinks is one of the great mysteries of the universe. One day they'll probably write books about him—*Great Mysteries of Our Time: including the Marie Celeste and Inspector Hyde's Brain.*'

We were walking down the long, winding drive with Plumwood Hall behind us and the bare skeletons of tall, sentry-like poplars on either side. Our way was lit by pale, silvery moonlight. Having declared the Mind of Hyde to be one of the Great Unknowables, Jack puffed on his pipe in silence.

'Speaking of great mysteries of the universe,' I said, 'where is the late Connie Worth now? In what state or condition? If there is that in every human being which survives death, has she survived death well? Or is she an unhappy soul right now?'

'From what we've heard so far, Mrs Worth seems to have been an unhappy soul during her lifetime,' said Jack thought-fully.

'True. But does death alter that for the better? Do all the ills of this life fall away at death?'

Jack sighed deeply and said, 'There are certainly some people who think that. Suicides, for example. For myself I believe that every suicide is a tragedy, but for those sad souls who choose to take their own lives, they must do so believing that death will end all their sorrows and all their woes.'

'And does it work?' I pursued. 'Does death shake off all that is bad and leave only the good? We put *Rest in Peace* on tombstones—well, do they? Rest in peace, that is?'

Jack turned to face me and chortled into his pipe stem, his face wreathed in smiles. 'I know you too well, young Morris,' he said. 'My recollection is that during our tutorials whenever you asked a direct question it was because you already had an answer bubbling away in your brain. So what is your answer this time?'

'I'll tell you, if you promise not to think me foolish.'

'The one thing I never think of you as being, young Morris, is foolish. Let's hear your ideas.'

'Well . . .' I paused reluctantly, and then plunged into it. 'I got dragged along to a spiritualist meeting once. It was Standforth who took me. He was a fellow undergraduate at Magdalen. You wouldn't have known him—he was mathematics. Anyway, he got interested. Actually, I think his girlfriend at the time was interested so he had to be. But the upshot was that Standforth insisted that I accompany him to this spiritualist meeting—something he'd promised to go to while his girlfriend was away, and report on when she got back. He didn't want to go alone, and I was curious enough to agree to tag along.'

'I think I've now heard more about your social life than I ever wanted to know, Morris. This, I take it, is leading somewhere?'

'It's leading to what happened at the spiritualist meeting.'

'Was it one of those séance events with a Ouija board or a medium? One knock for yes, two for no—that sort of nonsense?'

'Nothing like that. It was a lecture. A lady who was some sort of important figure in spiritualist circles had come up from London to lecture on the afterlife—and on the state of those who had "passed over", as she put it.'

I told Jack the story. The lady, as it happened, shared my surname, so Standforth spent the evening pretending that this 'Mrs Morris' was a relative of mine. Probably, he suggested, an aunt. That, I said, is a terrible thing to say of any woman. Aunts as a species, I pointed out, are wild creatures who normally address their nephews as 'fathead' and reduce all those around them to a nervous state known to medical science as the heebie-jeebies.

Mind you, she dressed like an aunt. This particular Mrs Morris was so fond of floral decoration on her clothing, her shoes and her millinery that she looked like a perambulating rose garden.

The lady, however, proposed an interesting theory: namely, that 'passing over' is the great escape from the burdens of this life to a more elevated and placid life on a higher plane. She talked of her discussions with those who were approaching death. They told her, at least the ones still capable of speech, that they felt a gentle warmth and saw a welcoming light.

Furthermore, this information had been confirmed in later discussions she had with the same persons some time after their 'passing over'. Clearly, dying was not, in itself, sufficient excuse for not talking to the lady from the Spiritualist Society. And the information she gathered in these chats in darkened rooms was all positive and encouraging. She assured us that good things were waiting for us.

Her advice to us was that at the moment of death we should 'go towards the light' and all would be well.

'Despite the eccentricities of the lady herself,' I concluded, 'much of what she said got me thinking. If we all have that spiritual core which is us—our energy, spirit, soul, imagination, love—then surely it makes sense to hold that shaking off the weight of physicality can be nothing but release and relief.'

Jack responded with what I had long since come to think of as his 'rhetorical guffawing'. He threw back his head and laughed heartily. 'So you think that death is like Father Christmas, do you? That everyone who dies will get gifts and be happy? Ho, ho, ho! My dear Morris, for years that tired old idea has been going around with holes in its socks and by now it's so exhausted it's about due to hand in its dinner pail.'

'What's wrong with the idea of death being good for everyone? What's wrong with everyone surviving death well? What's wrong with death being a happy release, and a great relief, for everyone?'

'Since you're putting that to me seriously, let me reply seriously. The problem arises from the need for justice. The hunger for justice lies deep within the human heart. When someone does the wrong thing, we leap in and say, "You shouldn't have done that." In those words we are appealing to a standard of justice beyond ourselves. If death is a good experience for everyone then the universe is fundamentally unjust.'

'How so?'

'Do you really believe that death meant a comforting warmth, welcoming voices and a beckoning light for Genghis Khan, Napoleon and Vlad the Impaler?'

'Well, no—there needs to be an allowance for those who have been evil.'

'What, then, would happen to those?'

'Some sort of punishment, I suppose. The spiritualist lecturer touched on the idea, but she didn't go into any details. For the most part she painted death as a good experience for the majority, but hinted at a time of suffering, weeping and wailing for the few.'

'Why only "the few"? There's the rub, Morris! There's the hidden assumption that whatever unpleasantness awaited Vlad the Impaler at the time of his death, you and I will be all right. But think for a moment about that appeal for justice that is so common among us—the "You shouldn't have done that" complaint. The standard we appeal to in those words, our personal standard of right and wrong, is one that we fail to live up to as consistently as we'd like. In our most honest moments we will speak about letting ourselves down. We will admit this, if not to others, at least privately to ourselves.'

'And the justice we all hunger for in our hearts is something we can expect to encounter at death?'

'If not at death, then when? When would those guilty of undetected murders—or any undetected crimes—logically face justice and be held accountable? I think we intuitively see death as the moment when that happens. And that is certainly what the Christian faith teaches: "It is appointed unto men once to die, but after this the judgment." And if that is what will happen at death to those guilty of gross offences, then it will happen to us also—with our long litany of smaller failures and failings. Not just "the few", Morris, but all of us.'

He paused to relight his pipe, which had gone out, and then continued, 'Judgment is what gives human beings dignity and worth. When we are treated as moral beings and held responsible for what we have done and what we have failed to do, we have dignity and value. Judgment is what makes us, and our actions, really matter.'

'That's the second time you've trotted out that rather grim quotation about judgment. I think I'd rather hear something encouraging.'

'You want an encouraging quotation? Consider this one: "Behold the Lamb of God, who takes away the sin of the world." That bears thinking about, young Morris.'

I was silent for some time thinking about the complexity of Jack's argument.

It dawned upon me, although I didn't feel like saying it out loud, that the spiritualism I'd heard about that night—with all its talk of comforting messages from the dear departed—was more about wishful thinking than the reality of an ultimately just universe in which human beings matter because they are treated responsibly.

I was about to ask Jack another question when a movement in the shadows, among the trees off to our right, caught my attention.

'Did you see that?' I asked.

Jack turned and we both peered in the direction I was pointing. What we could see were mottled layers of darkness: thin streaks of silvery moonlight, the blackness of trees and their shadows and, behind it all, the dark blue night sky with rolling banks of grey clouds. But there was clearly something else out there. We caught occasional glimpses of movement and heard the crackling of dead leaves and twigs.

Then whatever it was appeared, just for a moment, in a clearing among the trees. It looked like a man—but a man hunched down and running like an animal. Then it was gone.

'What on earth was that?' I muttered.

TWENTY-THREE

~

My question was answered at the village pub about half an hour later.

'That was the wild man of the woods, that was,' said Constable Charlie Nile, speaking like a man who'd been reading too many Tarzan comic books lately.

We were sitting in the front parlour of *The Cricketers' Arms*, each with a brandy and soda, and I'd just narrated our bizarre experience of seeing a creeping man in the shadows.

'That's what every village needs,' said Jack, with a serious expression on his face but a mischievous glint in his eye, 'its very own wild man of the woods. Mind you, not every village has one. Some villages have to make do with a panther in the woods—usually one that's escaped from a passing circus and hangs around to slaughter the occasional goat or infant.'

'I think you're pulling my leg, Mr Lewis,' said Constable Nile ponderously. 'And if you are, well, you're quite mistaken, that's all I can say.'

'Have you ever seen this "wild man of the woods" yourself?' I asked.

'Only once, at a distance, and he took off before I could get to him.'

'What do people say about him?' I continued. 'Is he a native from South America, covered in tattoos?'

'No! Of course not!' said Nile very seriously. Then he opened his eyes wide, and a light went on somewhere behind his eyeballs—it was like seeing the sun's rays break into the bedroom when you flick back the blinds in the morning. 'That's Drax you're describing, that is.'

'So you know about Drax?' said Jack, suddenly interested.

'I think most folk around here do. Not that we ever see him, of course. He keeps himself to himself. But we know Lady Pamela lets him stay in the old gamekeeper's cottage.'

'That's the isolated cottage out on the moors?' Jack prompted.

'Aye, that's it,' Nile agreed, nodding earnestly and taking a sip of his brandy and soda.

'And who lives there with him?' Jack continued, now looking very interested indeed.

'What makes you think there's someone else there?' said an astonished Nile, his eyebrows shooting up his forehead like startled caterpillars who've just heard the heavy footfalls of the gardener approaching with the insect spray.

The policeman recovered from his surprise and added, 'He's a solitary bird who lives on his own. That's a strange idea you've got there, Mr Lewis.'

Jack continued to probe, and in response the constable explained that the gossip that had come down to the village from the Hall was that Drax had been Edmund Trelawney's bearer. I knew that Trelawney was Lady Pamela's maiden name, so his words made sense to me.

Nile painted a picture of Drax as the faithful servant who carried his master's packs through the wilds of the deep Amazon jungle. When Edmund became seriously ill, Drax carried the sick man as well as the baggage back to the river.

Then he brought Edmund down the Amazon by boat hoping to get him to civilisation and medical treatment—but the Englishman died before they could reach help. The faithful Drax had contacted the family through the British embassy, and then insisted on accompanying the body home.

'That is extraordinary loyalty,' said Jack. 'Most admirable. But why has he stayed? Has there been any gossip as to why he's not returned to his own people but instead lives alone in a remote cottage on our wet and windswept moors?'

Nile found this question puzzling. 'Well, this is England, isn't it? Anyone would rather live here than in some jungle full of savage animals and deadly diseases. I suppose he'll go back eventually. But you can hardly blame him for enjoying England while he can.'

'But surely the odd thing is,' Jack persisted, 'that's he not. He's not travelling to London to see Big Ben and Tower Bridge and the Houses of Parliament. He's just sitting alone in a cottage on the moors. Would you call that enjoying England?'

Nile gave a knowing smirk. 'It all depends on the alternative, Mr Lewis. I read an article in the Sunday paper about that there Amazonian jungle. Sounded most unpleasant to me. I think this Drax has found a more comfortable spot, and he probably intends to hang on to it for a while.'

'And this Drax,' I interrupted, 'he's definitely not the wild man of woods?'

Charlie Nile laughed indulgently. 'Not a chance, Mr Morris,' he said. 'The wild man of the woods has been seen once or twice—on those nights when there's a full moon you understand—sometimes from not very far away.'

'And . . . ?' I said, wanting him to continue.

'It's definitely an Englishman. That's what they say. A fairhaired Englishman. Looking all wild and dishevelled like, but one of us . . . so to speak.'

'So how do you account for him?' said Jack, finishing his brandy and soda and leaning back in his armchair. 'How do you account for this wild man of the woods?'

'You'll just laugh at me again if I tell you,' said Nile cautiously, looking like a man whose rendition of 'The Road to Mandalay' has gone down badly at the annual village concert and who is doubtful about risking another tune.

'I promise you I won't—I'm asking you quite seriously. Now, tell me: what's your theory?'

'Well, sir, to be quite honest, I think he might be one of them tormented souls from the next life.'

'A ghost?' I asked.

'Aye, Mr Morris—a ghost. They do say as how the Black Tower is haunted. That would account for our "local phenomenon", as you'd probably call it, Mr Lewis. That would explain why the wild man of the woods only turns up rarely and is never seen by daylight.'

'Is that why the Black Tower is kept locked these days?' I asked.

Constable Nile expressed surprise. He'd grown up in the district and it was well known that the tower was never locked, he said. If we found it locked now, well, he couldn't explain that.

Jack asked how long the wild man of the woods had been making appearances. Nile said it had only been in the last eighteen months, and then he said no, I tell a lie, it must be at least two years.

Jack asked: why now? What had stirred up the ghost of a tower built in the last century and not used for many years? Why had the ghostly apparition only recently taken up roaming the woods at night as a professional activity? The constable hummed and stuttered but had no real answer to this.

Despite my interest in local folklore, I steered the village policeman back to the subject of the latest murder at Plumwood Hall.

'Inspector Crispin told us it looks like another case of cyanide poisoning,' I said.

'Did he indeed?' said Nile, with one of his caterpillar-like eyebrows making a quizzical dance across his forehead as he spoke. Jack rumbled out a comment to the effect that we were on Crispin's list of people he trusted.

'Well . . . in that case . . .' Nile said cautiously, 'I suppose there's no harm in my telling you a bit more about it. I suppose it's all right . . .'

We sat there in silent suspense waiting for Nile to definitely make up his mind as to whether this was a sharing moment or not. He eventually decided it was.

'The brass are telling us the same thing. Not that they tell us much, mind you. But I heard Dr Henderson talking about cyanide poisoning. The question then, of course, is: how was the cyanide served up to the poor girl? And from what I heard there's no doubt that it was in the sherry she drank—that glass of dry sherry. They won't know for sure until there are tests on the glass and the bottle, but both the inspectors seem to think there's not much room for doubt.'

'How did it get in there? That must be the next question,' said Jack.

'Aye, and I was talking to Sergeant Merrivale about that. He said the problem was that the bottles of sherry and port had been left standing on a small table in the hall outside the butler's pantry while dinner was served. And dinner service takes quite a long time. That being so, anyone could have got at the bottle of dry sherry and slipped in some cyanide. That's what Sergeant Merrivale thinks.'

TWENTY-FOUR

~

Jack and I continued tossing around ideas about the murders—for we were now thinking in the plural—until quite late that night. Finally we gave up. Jack went up to his room and I returned to the Hall, with an agreement that we'd meet after breakfast the next day and set out some positive steps to take in our investigation.

I slept badly. I tossed and turned all night like a sailor on a tramp steamer trying to settle into his hammock while crossing the South China Sea during a typhoon. I woke feeling like something the cat had dragged in and then had second thoughts about and discarded as inedible.

Having breakfasted on toast and coffee, and not much of either, I turned my back on my duties in the library of Plumwood Hall and set out for the village. I found Jack disposing of a large plate of sausages and scrambled eggs with enthusiasm. The difference in our appetites can be put down to the fact that he was cast as Sherlock Holmes in our little mystery while I had been given the role of Professor Moriarty, homicidal fiend.

'Jack,' I said wearily, sinking into the seat opposite him and pouring myself a large cup of tea, 'what do we do this morning? I'm counting on your giant brain to find a path that will divert me from the hangman's gallows.'

'You're in a grim mood this morning, young Morris,' he mumbled through a mouthful of breakfast. 'Sleep badly?'

I acknowledged a lack of acquaintance between myself and the Land of Nod that had been going on for some nights now.

'Be of good cheer, Morris,' said Jack, finishing his breakfast as rapidly as he finished every meal and rising from his chair. 'This morning we shall resume our conversation with the village constable. Charlie Nile was just beginning to get interesting last night when, like most country folk, he left at an early hour to toddle off to bed and get his requisite eight hours.'

We had got him talking about the murders, I remembered, and he had begun to tell us what the police team members were saying amongst themselves. I could see the value in what Jack proposed, so we left the pub and headed off in the direction of the police cottage.

We walked out into weather that was entirely out of sympathy with my inner turmoil. The skies were blue, the sun was shining, the flowers were in bloom and the birds were bellowing away at the top of their little lungs from every tree branch. That's the problem with the weather; it can never strike the right note. There I was, ready for dark storm clouds and forecasts of gales blowing in from the North Sea, and all the weather could give me was a vacuous smile. My heart was heavily overcast with expectations of low temperatures and high winds—none of which the department of meteorology had managed to mirror.

To make matters worse, the Plumwood police cottage looked like something from a postcard—it was thatched and ivy covered with a flourishing rose garden in front. It appeared that Constable Nile kept the village crime rate down with one hand while raising award-winning roses with the other.

We pushed open the wicket gate and walked up the path towards the front door. As we approached we could hear snatches of conversation drifting out of an open window. Recognising the voices as those of the two inspectors—the local man, Hyde, and Crispin from Scotland Yard—we paused to listen.

'I'll issue an arrest warrant if you won't.' The voice that was speaking was that of Hyde. I couldn't actually see the speaker but those poisonous nasal tones could belong to no one else.

I stepped over the herbaceous border onto the neatly trimmed front lawn and looked in through the open window. The two speakers were too deeply engrossed in what was clearly a debate, a clash of iron wills, to notice me. Both were seated in overstuffed armchairs. Hyde was leaning eagerly forward while Crispin was leaning back with his arms folded. On the wall behind Crispin was a framed photograph of His Majesty King George V, while behind Hyde was a glass case full of stuffed birds.

'You are being much too hasty, Hyde,' said the Scotland Yard man in measured tones. 'There is, as yet, not sufficient evidence.'

'There's been a second murder!' snapped Hyde, whose long snout was looking less like a rat on this sunny morning and rather more like a fox—a fox that has found its way into the henhouse with a knife in one hand and a fork in the other and is determined to have a feast while it's there. 'How many more murders do there have to be before you act? He needs to be safely behind bars.'

'The death of Miss Bassett is a great tragedy,' Crispin agreed. 'However, I cannot share your certainty, and I cannot act in the absence of clearer evidence.'

'There is evidence of motive,' insisted Hyde.

'Inadequate evidence. The clash between Morris and Mrs Worth was clearly an insignificant, low-voltage affair that could not, by any stretch of the imagination, motivate a murder.'

'There is evidence of opportunity.'

'Again, I can't entirely agree. There is evidence of proximity to the victim in the first murder, but no one saw Morris do anything to tamper with the dead woman's food. And there is no evidence of opportunity in the second murder.'

'Everyone had the opportunity to tamper with Miss Bassett's dry sherry.'

'Saying "everyone" fails to narrow it down to Morris. And we have no motive for Morris to be involved in the second murder.'

'As yet. Get him under lock and key and interrogate him intensely. He'll crack. He'll tell us why he did it.'

'If, indeed, he did do it.'

When iron wills clash the sparks fly. At that moment, in the cosy front sitting room of the Plumwood police cottage, there was a cascade of sparks that one might expect in the forge of a demented blacksmith.

What worried me was this stuff about 'intense interrogation'. Exactly what that involved wasn't clear, but it sounded rather like having a dentist drill into a badly infected tooth without the benefit of a local anaesthetic while being asked a lot of questions. Or, at least, something along those lines.

'What more do you want?' demanded Hyde.

'I want the method,' replied Inspector Crispin, with all the authority that came from being part of the Detective Branch of the Metropolitan Police.

'Method!' sneered Hyde in a fox-like howl. 'He'll tell us that! He'll tell us how he did it when we get him into interrogation.'

'No, Hyde—that's where you're wrong. It's up to *us* to tell *him* how he did it. Unless we can do that we have no case. Looked at as a physical problem, as a problem in logistics, it is utterly impossible for the fatal dose of cyanide to have got into that piece of cake that killed Mrs Worth. How do you imagine it was done?'

Hyde looked startled by the question. It had popped up at him like the demon king coming through the stage trapdoor in the pantomime. It was unexpected and he didn't quite know what to do with it.

Hyde was no longer sitting still. He was writhing in his chintzy armchair as if in the grip of strong emotion. He was like a schoolboy sitting for an examination in 'reeling and writhing', as Lewis Carroll would have put it. His eyes had narrowed and his teeth were bared. I expected him, at any moment, to howl like a fox at midnight—a fox on the prowl for something to sink its teeth into. And I was that 'something'.

'There'll be more murders!' howled Hyde in desperation. 'We have a killer in our midst. A warrant for his immediate arrest for murder is the only way to protect the community.'

'The members of this community can sleep safe in their beds,' replied Crispin, with an edge of irritability in his voice, 'when we have the real murderer behind bars—kept there by evidence that will stand up in a court of law.'

'We must act—and act immediately!'

'Yes, you're right. We must act to collect evidence so we arrest the right man.'

'But . . . but . . . but . . .'

'We've been back and forth over this same ground repeatedly, Hyde. I think it's time we got on with the investigation.'

Jack and I glanced at each other. We both quietly made our way out of the front garden of the police cottage and onto the village street.

'Well, what about that?' I said, once we were out of earshot of the arguing inspectors.

'I think it might be best if we avoided the company of the police for a little while,' said Jack. 'Why don't we go for a walk across the moors?'

TWENTY-FIVE

~

Rolling white clouds were scudding across the sky, turning the moors into a patchwork quilt of bright sunshine and cloud shadows with threads of purple heather woven across the whole pattern.

'Judgment,' I muttered to myself as we walked.

Jack asked if I had said something, so I repeated, more loudly, 'Judgment. That's what Hyde and Crispin are doing back there in that cottage—passing judgment on me. And if a warrant for my arrest is issued I'll have to appear in the next assizes facing judgment. And you tell me that at the end of life each of us has to face judgment.'

'Indeed I do.'

'But how can that be? For me, or anyone, to be called before a court—either an earthly or a heavenly court—and held to judgment there must be some sort of law in place. There needs to be a law, or a system of laws, that I have either broken or kept. Without such law there can be no judgment. There is no law, so whatever happens at death I cannot possibly face judgment.'

'Morris, I am mightily impressed by your argument. I'm delighted to see that you're now thinking about these things logically and carefully. Your starting point is exactly right. Unfortunately, your conclusion is totally wrong—but your starting point is excellent.' Jack was smiling broadly as he spoke, his eyes flashing with fire at the prospect of a lively battle over important ideas.

I thought carefully before I responded, 'You agree that there can be no judgment without law?'

'Precisely.'

'But you reject my conclusion that there *is* no law *therefore* there is no judgment either. Correct?'

'Indeed. So we are both singing from the same page of the hymnbook—if you'll excuse my ecclesiastical metaphor.'

'Happily. But what is the law? What law could possibly apply to all the human beings on Planet Earth? Because that's what you'd have to have—some sort of universal law. Without that, universal judgment is impossible.'

'Once again we agree. However, let me remind you that for more than two and a half thousand years philosophers have spoken of just such a law. They usually call it Natural Law.'

'That's a medieval concept!' I protested.

'It was around for more than a thousand years before Thomas Aquinas and the other medieval philosophers. What's more, it's a common sense idea that most people endorse.'

'Now that I find hard to swallow.'

'Then swallow harder—because it's the truth. Picture this: a government passes a law requiring all blue-eyed babies to be killed at birth. This strange government argues that they have abundant sociological research showing that the whole country will be happier and safer if all blue-eyed babies are strangled at birth. So they pass their law. What do you say to that?'

'That it's outrageous. That it's an immoral law.'

'Exactly! That expression you used, "an immoral law", points to the fact that there is a higher law by which all human laws are judged. That higher law—that moral sense innate in the human heart—is Natural Law. I would argue, as have many before me, that it exists because our Maker has built it into our natures. But unlike, say, the law of gravity, this is not a law of physical nature but a law of human nature.'

'Hang on, you're going too fast. You're leaping too quickly from our sense of moral outrage at evil to some law that underpins such outrage,' I protested.

We may have been striding across open moorlands, with a fresh breeze blowing around us, but Jack was back in his study at Oxford and happily in tutorial mode.

'If my speed concerns you we shall go back over those same steps more slowly.'

We walked past some philosophical cows musing in thoughtful meditation over their lunch, climbed a stile into the next meadow and then Jack resumed.

'Picture this: a friend borrows a sum of money from you and promises to pay it back in one week. At the end of the week he announces that he's not repaying the debt, and, in fact, never had any intention of repaying it. Is he breaking the Moral Law—the Natural Law?'

'Yes, of course he is.'

'We are just imagining this, but if it really happened to you, you'd be properly outraged.'

'And with good reason.'

'Now reverse the situation. You are the one borrowing the money. You need it desperately to help a sick relative. You know you'll never be able to repay it, and your friend seems to have abundant cash. So the loan is made. At the end of the week you make the announcement that you can't repay—and you'll probably never be able to repay, and you knew this when you accepted the loan and made the false promise. Same situation—but in reverse. Are you still outraged?'

'Perhaps not. In those circumstances I would have good reasons for making a promise I couldn't keep—namely, helping my sick relative. So my promise-making is dishonest, and in a sense I have misappropriated my friend's money . . . but I had good reasons for doing so.'

Jack chuckled with glee and almost rubbed his hands together as he said, 'Can you see what's happening? You haven't denied the Moral Law. You haven't said there is no such thing as Natural Moral Law. You, in fact, accept that you and your friend are both under this same higher law—higher than legislation passed by any parliament—but in your case you say you have reasons that excuse you under the Moral Law that you admit applies.'

Jack then went on to argue that it is this Natural Moral Law under which everyone must be judged after death.

'At this point Christianity and common sense coincide almost exactly. One thing the scientists tell us is that the universe is remarkably consistent—the law of gravity applies on Planet Earth, throughout our solar system and in the remotest galaxy. This consistency is the product of a consistent, intelligent Mind that lies behind it all. Hence the consistency in the physical laws that govern the universe, the biological laws that govern living bodies, and the moral laws that govern our eternal destinies.'

'Let me see if I've got this right—all human beings in the universe . . .'

'All sentient moral beings in the universe,' corrected Jack with a grin, 'if, that is, there are alien sentient moral beings on other planets.'

I smiled, knowing how fond Jack was of science fiction stories, then resumed, '. . . all of us are under a Natural Moral Law against which all of us will be judged at death. Is that it?'

'Precisely. The word the Bible uses most often for this Moral Law is "righteousness". Now I'm no Hebraist, but Adam Fox tells me that the Hebrew word translated "righteousness" is one of those picture words.'

I knew what Jack was talking about here because this subject had come up in our tutorials. There are, Jack would explain, many words which contain a hidden metaphor, or picture, out of which they have grown. His favourite example was 'sinister' which grew from a word meaning 'left-handed'. The metaphor hidden inside 'sinister' was the picture of a left-handed man who could shake your right hand while stabbing you with his left. Sinister indeed!

'So what's the picture here—in the Hebrew word for "righteousness"?'

'It's a relational picture. It pictures every human being as existing within a network, or a web, of relationships. So I am my father's son, my brother's brother, my friend's friend, my pupil's tutor and so on. Each relationship carries with it certain duties and obligations. When I get all of my relationships "right"— when I fulfil all the responsibilities of each relationship—then I am "righteous". That's the moral law I've been speaking of.'

'And this is the basis for the judgment we each face one moment after death?'

'Indeed. Only the righteous, in the terms we've just discussed, pass the judgment while all of the unrighteous fail. That is how the sheep are divided from the goats.'

'Which leaves the question—which is which? How can we know which of us is righteous in the eyes of the heavenly court and which of us is unrighteous?'

'Oh, that's easy, young Morris,' replied Jack, giving me a hearty slap on the back. 'We're all unrighteous—every one of us!'

TWENTY-SIX

~

While we had been speaking, we had, it seemed, walked over the moors in a wide arc, and I saw now that we had circled back towards Plumwood Hall. As a result we found ourselves emerging from a belt of trees and striding over the manicured lawns towards the west wing of the house.

The day remained blue and sunny. The man at the Bureau of Meteorology, who has a neat turn of phrase, had talked of a ridge of high pressure extending across most of the United Kingdom. And he had been spot on the money. The thing had not only turned up, it had rolled up its sleeves and got on with the job with an efficiency that could only be admired.

As we drew close to the terrace, Jack reminded me of Detective Inspector Crispin's rule that the way to solve a murder mystery was by understanding the victim—or, in this case, victims plural. With that in mind, Jack suggested taking a look at their rooms. If, that is, we could get into the house unobserved and do a bit of snooping around.

We crossed the terrace and entered the drawing room. It was as empty as the Gobi Desert on one of its quieter days. So was the hall beyond it, and the large staircase leading to the upper levels and the bedrooms. Jack followed in my footsteps up the stairs and along a corridor, at the end of which I threw open a bedroom door and announced that this had been Connie Worth's room.

'I'm rather surprised the police don't have this room locked up,' said Jack as we entered, closing the door quietly behind us.

'Can't explain that,' I said, speaking in a hushed voice. 'Either they think they've got everything out of the room that's here to be got, or else the locking up job was given to our friend Constable Charlie Nile—who seems to think police duties are like exam questions: only the ones that appeal to him are to be attempted.'

I stood in the middle of the room and looked around. It was an ordinary and quite plain bedroom. It seemed to have no special character, and Connie Worth had made no effort to stamp her mark on the room.

'One of the early Lord Boshams,' I remarked, 'in the Tudor period, I believe, is said to have murdered his wife in this room. With a battle-axe.'

'Did he have any special reason for doing so?' asked Jack as he began sliding open drawers.

'I believe his accountant suggested it would be cheaper than a divorce,' I replied as I flung myself upon the only wardrobe in the room. 'I say,' I added, 'I feel a bit of a heel going through a lady's things like this.'

'The lady is dead, and if her ghost could tap you on the shoulder at this moment it would probably encourage you to find out who killed her.'

'Yes, there is that, I suppose.'

We searched in silence for the next few minutes.

'Anything in particular we should be looking for?' I asked as I pushed aside the hanging clothes to see if something was hidden at the back of the wardrobe. It wasn't.

'Paper,' said Jack. 'Did she keep any records? Letters?

Receipts? A diary? Scribbled notes? Travel brochures for exotic places? Being dead she yet speaks—but only if she's left bits of paper we can find.'

'Righty-oh then,' I responded cheerfully and got on with the search.

But it turned out that Connie Worth was exceptionally neat, leaving no pieces of paper lying on the top of her dressing table or in any of the drawers or in any other place we could think to look.

After some time I stood up and said, 'If there was anything here, the police have cleaned it all out.'

'It rather looks that way, doesn't it?' Jack agreed. 'However, if she was trying to keep something hidden, where in this room might serve as a hiding place?'

Thus we entered a second phase of the search, where we lifted up the paper lining in the drawers of the dressing table—and every other conceivable hiding place—again with no results.

'What's this?' asked Jack. He'd been staring for some time at a small black and white photograph in a modest wooden frame on the dressing table.

Taking a closer look, I said, 'I believe that's a picture of Lady Pamela and Connie Worth as young women. Look—you can see the resemblance. When they were single, being sisters, they probably went around together rather a lot. Which this picture commemorates.'

'But think, Morris—think. This is the only personal decoration in the room. Apart from this one photograph the room is entirely blank—totally without character. Why this one thing?'

Jack picked up the frame and turned it over in his hands. He looked at it thoughtfully from every side for a moment, then turned it over again and carefully studied its back. He prised open the studs and lifted off the back cover. There, jammed between the back of the photograph and the frame, were two small pieces of paper. Jack took them out and gently unfolded them.

For a moment the song of the nightingale trilled in my heart: this is the vital clue, it sang, that will reveal all. The next moment the bird dropped its sheet music, hit the wrong note and the whole thing went flat. The two pieces of paper were entirely trivial, unhelpful and unimportant.

They were both receipts. One was a receipt for a delivery of meat, signed for by the cook, Mrs Buckingham. The other for a case of whisky and brandy signed for by Keggs the butler.

'Odd,' said Jack. 'And very interesting.'

'Domestic waste paper,' I groaned. 'They tell us nothing.'

'On the contrary, they tell us something very important.'

'What, exactly?'

'At the moment I'm not sure. But they ask two very tantalising questions: why did Connie Worth keep them? And why did she conceal them where they were unlikely to be seen by a maid or a casual visitor to her room?'

'I hadn't thought of that.'

'Well, think of it now. To Connie Worth these must have been more than bits of domestic ephemera—to have kept them at all, in the first place, and to have concealed them, in the second place.'

Jack slipped both pieces of paper into his pocket, and we stepped quietly out of the room. I asked Jack where to next, and he said, 'To the other victim's room.'

Stiffy Bassett's room was at the far end of the corridor, where the larger, better furnished bedrooms were found. Housing her there was part of Lady Pamela's plan to impress her and encourage her future marriage to Douglas.

On our way down that long corridor we passed an open door.

'Which room is this?' Jack asked.

'That's Sir William's study,' I said, and was alarmed to see Jack step swiftly inside.

'He doesn't like anyone just . . .' I began. But I stopped because I'd followed Jack as far as the open door and could see that the room was unoccupied. Jack wandered around looking at the decorations on the walls.

'Impressive,' he said. 'Primitive artwork from South America, bows, arrows, quivers, blowpipes, paintings of tropical orchids—an exotic collection for an Englishman's study.'

'Sent back by Edmund,' I said, speaking quickly, 'before his death in South America. Now come on, Jack. Sir William may return at any moment . . . if he finds us here . . .'

But Jack ignored me and picked up a piece of native carving painted in red and ochre. He did not look impressed. He seemed to consider it the sort of thing knocked off by some jungle native to sell to a gullible passing explorer from the souvenir counter of the local trading post.

He put the carving down and walked over to the big bow window looking down on the terrace. 'It's still deserted down there,' he said. 'I wonder where everyone is today.'

'Come on, Jack,' I repeated with some urgency. 'We can't just go barging into Sir William's study without his express invitation. He's a tough customer when he's annoyed.'

'I'm sure he is,' said Jack with a broad smile as he joined me in the corridor.

It was with a sense of relief that I led the way beyond that open study door down to the room that had been occupied by Stiffy.

Here the door was closed, but slightly ajar. I pushed on it lightly and it swung inwards—revealing Sir William Dyer, bent over Stiffy Bassett's dressing table with his back towards us.

We must have made some slight noise because he straightened up at once, and spun around to face us.

'Just giving Jack a tour of the house,' I ad libbed quickly.

Sir William gave us the sort of look Macbeth probably gave when a couple of Banquos walked into the room.

'I was . . . ,' he began, '. . . ah . . . looking for the address of poor Stephanie's family . . . should send them a condolence message . . . can't find it . . . perhaps Pamela has it . . .'

With those words he pushed past us and hurried off down the corridor.

'Well,' said Jack rubbing his chin. 'That was very interesting. What do you imagine he was really looking for?'

TWENTY-SEVEN

~

We gently eased the door closed so that we could work undisturbed, and then searched Stiffy's room as thoroughly as we could. This time with even less success than in Connie Worth's—there were no scraps of paper, not even a skerrick, to be found. Looking for something interesting in her room was like looking for a happy face among the gloomy punters trooping home after a day at Epsom.

We did find an extraordinarily generous supply of makeup, cigarettes in a silver cigarette case and a collection of the novels of Ethel M. Dell scattered carelessly over a bedside table. But nothing else.

Once again we searched for secret places where things might be hidden. But this time our search was bootless. (When I was younger I believed there was no such word as 'bootless' and the poor goof of an author who'd used it had meant to write 'fruitless'. I now know better. Later research has convinced me that in a case such as ours 'bootless' is right on the money.)

After a final rechecking of places we'd already examined I shrugged my shoulders and Jack and I left for the part of the house that was my own personal province—the library.

Jack asked to see the work I'd been doing, so I handed him the large, leather-bound book in which I'd recorded my catalogue of the collection.

He read in silence for some time and then remarked, 'This is a very careful and precise bibliography, Morris. You should think of taking up this sort of research full time. There are a lot potential areas of research in bibliography.'

'That's kind of you, Jack,' I replied, 'but I found doing this about as exciting as compiling a telephone directory for a small town in Latvia. Besides, I have other plans and ambitions.'

Jack asked me what they were, and I said I'd tell him if he promised not to laugh.

'As if I would, Morris,' said Jack earnestly. 'I take your ambitions most seriously.'

Taking my courage in both hands, I admitted that my goal was to become a writer—a novelist.

'That's a noble ambition,' said Jack. 'You should try— seriously try. When I was your age, I thought I might make a poet. In fact, I had two slim volumes of poetry published.'

'Really? I didn't know that.' I was surprised by this revelation.

'There's no reason why you should; they appeared under a pseudonym. Both volumes fell dead from the press, and I concluded that my talents did not lie in that direction. But I tell you this to encourage you to try your wings while you're young.'

'The problem, of course, is that "novelist" is not a salaried position that's advertised in *The Times* asking applicants to turn up at nine o'clock on a Monday morning and please bring references. Becoming a published novelist, I have discovered, is rather a tricky business. So, in the meantime, I have to earn a living,' I said. 'Hence this cataloguing.'

'Which is about to end, so what will you take up next, as you spend your evenings scribbling away?'

'I thought I might try a bit of school mastering. That shouldn't be too hard, and it might leave me enough free time.

I thought I might be able to teach irregular verbs and dream up complicated plots at much the same time.'

Jack patted me gently on the shoulder. Coming from Jack that was warm and enthusiastic encouragement. Then he asked to have another look at the quarto *Romeo and Juliet* I had found.

I retrieved the ancient, leather-bound volume with all the pride of a grandmother whipping out a photograph of the latest infant to grace her family line.

As he slowly turned the pages, stopping to read the occasional speech, he remarked that it was Pollard who'd coined the expression 'bad quarto' to cover several early volumes of Shakespeare—including my 1597 *Romeo and Juliet*.

He was about to launch into another of his spontaneous miniature lectures on early English printed texts when a piece of paper fluttered out of the book in his hands and floated gently to the floor.

I picked it up. 'It's a letter,' I said.

Addressed to whom, Jack asked. 'It says "Dear Judith",' I replied. Then Jack wanted to know who the author of the letter was. I turned over the single sheet of paper and at the bottom of the second page saw a signature I was familiar with.

'Well, well, well,' I said slowly.

'Don't keep me in suspense.'

'There's just a single name, "William", but I recognise the writing. I've seen that signature often—that's Sir William Dyer.'

'Is there a Judith that we know of—a Judith connected with this case?' Jack asked.

'The only Judith I can think of,' I replied, 'is Judith Trelawney—Lady Pamela's younger sister. But she's dead.'

'She might still have been the recipient. Is there a date on the letter?'

I looked at the top of the front page. 'Yes, it was written two years ago.'

'And since we've gone this far we may as well go on and read the whole letter. What does it say?'

I began to read, and I'm sure I blushed. It was a love letter. A passionate love letter. A passionate and intimate love letter. The Tom Morris who read that letter may have been an Oxford graduate, but he was a young and innocent Oxford graduate. I stopped reading and handed it over to Jack, who didn't blush at all. He read it as calmly as if it was a medieval allegory in rhymed heroic couplets. Which it wasn't. This was prose so hot I was surprised the page didn't spontaneously combust.

'Clearly this epistle was passing between two people who were already engaged in an affair,' he said at last.

'Well, such things happen.'

'Indeed, but in this case we must ask ourselves if it might be related to the murder.'

'An excellent question,' I said, looking puzzled, 'but how?'

Jack's eyes lit up and he adopted his tutorial manner. He jabbed the air with his forefinger as he made a series of logical points.

'Taking the addressee to be the only Judith we've heard of, namely, Lady Pamela's younger sister, we have an affair within the family—the sort of business that can only end unhappily. We've already heard this Judith referred to as "the beautiful younger sister", and the maids told you that Sir William was flirtatious, so an affair between the two of them is not out of the question. Sir William's primary concern in this letter is to get Judith to burn all his letters to her. Clearly his intention is that his wife will never discover what has gone on. He seeks to avoid the social, and possibly even financial, consequences of a divorce. Judith may well have burned all his other letters, but she has clearly kept this one—perhaps her sentimental attachment to it made it hard for her to destroy. Are you with me up to this point?'

'That's all entirely logical,' I said.

'Now we know this Judith died in a fall from a hotel balcony in Brighton some time ago. And we've been told that the only member of the family who was with her at the time was Connie Worth.'

'The murder victim.'

'Precisely. So could there be a connection between this letter, presumably obtained from Judith's personal belongings at the time of her death, and the murder?' said Jack, his eyes shining with the discovery.

'So Connie might have brought the letter with her when she came here from Brighton?'

'And she can have had only one reason for doing so. Given what we've been told about her character—a person known to the youngsters in the house as "The Black Widow" and "The Ice Queen"—it would have been in character for her to attempt blackmail.'

'Yes, of course!'

'Then consider the other facts we know,' Jack continued. 'She has been chronically short of money since the disappearance of her husband, but young Will saw her with a large sum in cash not long before her death. The need for money gives her a motive for blackmail, and the cash suggests she succeeded.'

'So bring this back to the murder,' I said. 'Blackmail is another crime altogether—how might it lead to these two murders?'

'It could certainly lead to the first murder,' said Jack with a knowing grin, 'since it's not unheard of for blackmailers to be murdered by their victims.'

'Logically, that would make Sir William Dyer the murderer of Connie Worth. But Jack,' I protested, 'that is physically impossible. He was never even present at the afternoon tea on the terrace where she was poisoned. He was in his room. Keggs the butler saw him there. Even I caught a glimpse of him at one stage in his window up on the first floor. Sir William may have had a motive to kill Connie, but how could he have done it?'

Jack chuckled and said, 'That's our next puzzle, isn't it?'

TWENTY-EIGHT

~

'No, no, no, no,' I protested, as I paced the library floor. 'I just can't see it. The sheer physical impossibility of Sir William Dyer getting cyanide into Connie Worth's slice of cake—and only *her* slice of cake—when he was at least fifty yards away, and he was indoors and she outdoors, makes the thing . . . well . . . what I said . . . utterly physically impossible. Which puts us at a dead end. We're right back where we started.'

'Not entirely,' said Jack. 'Where there is one blackmail victim there might be more.'

With these words Jack produced from the top pocket of his worn and tatty tweed jacket first a crumpled handkerchief and then the two slips of paper we had found in Connie Worth's room. He spread these out on the window sill—the slips of paper, not the handkerchief—and invited me to consider them.

'She was keeping these for a reason,' said Jack, 'and keeping them carefully hidden. The question is: what was that reason? Since these receipts are part of the household accounts, I propose that we talk, tactfully, to the staff—simply engage them in conversation—and see if something interesting emerges.'

With me leading the way we set off for the butler's pantry.

We found Keggs sitting at the small table in his pantry polishing some of the silverware. He was wearing white cotton gloves and using a chamois and a bottle of something called Silv-O ('It makes your silver sing', said the label in large letters).

We apologised for the interruption and Jack reminded him that his task (meaning 'his Jack's' not 'his Keggs's'—you need to follow me closely here—are you paying attention at the back of the room?) was to investigate the murders in order to clear my name. Would Keggs be happy to help by answering a few questions?

'I'm sure we all hope, sir, that Mr Morris is cleared of all police suspicions very shortly,' replied the butler in his best impersonation of Jack's rich Oxbridge accent.

'Thank you, Keggs. Now—we know about the people on the terrace on the day Mrs Worth died, but we were wondering about Sir William . . .'

Before these words could become a question, Keggs replied, 'He was in his study for the entire afternoon, sir. I know he was working hard there because at the end of the day he gave me quite a number of letters to post.'

'And you saw him there yourself?' Jack asked.

'Yes, sir, I took him afternoon tea shortly before service began on the terrace.'

'Was that the last time you saw him?'

'No, sir. When I brought him his tea he asked me for a glass of brandy—the good brandy he keeps in the gun room, not the brandy for visitors kept in the decanter in the drawing room. As soon as service was finished on the terrace, I fetched the brandy and took it up to Sir William in his study. In fact, I was standing beside him, sir, when we heard the scream from the terrace and ran to the window to see what was happening.'

This painted an odd picture. I had never seen Keggs run in the many months I had known him: the words 'run' and 'Keggs' did not seem to belong in the same sentence. Perhaps what he meant was that he glided a little more swiftly than usual.

'You were at the window together?' I asked.

'Indeed, Mr Morris. I was standing right beside Sir William when Mrs Worth collapsed, more or less into your arms.'

I turned to Jack and nodded. My nod was intended to speak volumes. Something along the lines of 'You see what I mean—utterly physically impossible . . . so cross Sir William off your list of suspects.' I managed to put all of that into a nod.

Jack must have taken that in—he takes in everything as fast as lightning—but he pursued his cross-examination of the butler.

'Now, Keggs,' he said, 'we have reason to believe that Mrs Worth might have been guilty of blackmail.'

Keggs's face took on an expression that was a careful amalgam of total astonishment and the impassive, blank look of the good servant. There was also a faint hint of disapproval at the guests gossiping about the household with the servants. He could pack as much into a facial expression as I could into a nod. It's a gift, I suppose.

'Does this come as a surprise?' Jack pursued.

'I'm quite sure, sir, there's been no hint of any such thing in the servants' quarters.' Now the disapproval was in the icy tone of voice as well as the face.

This, I thought, was not going to get us anywhere, so I thanked Keggs for his time and steered Jack out of the butler's pantry and into the kitchen.

Mrs Buckingham was sitting at the big table in the middle of the kitchen with a cup of tea. She looked more than ever like a round, sweet bun, with raisins for eyes. Except that she was smiling at us and drinking a cup of tea, which is not really like a bun at all, I suppose. So forget the whole bun thing.

'Just giving me feet a rest,' she said. 'I've been baking all morning.'

'Mrs Buckingham,' asked Jack, 'do you mind if we take you back once more to the day of the murder?'

'Oh, that do give me the shivers, that really do, sir. But if it will help I'm happy to talk to you.'

'Did Sir William come to your kitchen any time that day?' Jack asked.

'Now let me think. Yes, I do believe he called in during the morning. He came to get a key, I think. Yes, I'm sure that's it. A lot of the keys are on that board beside the door.' She nodded at the board in question.

I walked over to it and looked for the key Sir William had told us about—the key to the Hunting Tower. There was a peg with a small paper label saying 'Hunting Tower', but the peg was empty. I was disappointed. I had intended to pocket the key to be prepared for when Jack and I took our next walk in that direction.

'Do you know where the key to the Hunting Tower is, Mrs Buckingham?'

'I haven't the faintest, dearie,' she said taking another large, and very loud, sip of tea. 'It's been missing for ages.' Then she picked up a piece of shortbread, dunked it into her tea and began to chew on the soggy result.

'So on the day of the murder,' Jack resumed, 'Sir William visited the kitchen in the morning?'

Mrs Buckingham nodded her round head and blinked her round eyes.

'Did he return later in the day?'

'No, dearie, I'm quite certain he didn't.'

'He wasn't here,' Jack pursued, 'after the cake—the dark fruit cake you baked for afternoon tea—came out of the oven?'

'Oh no, not then. I'm certain he wasn't here then.'

I gave Jack another knowing look and another nod—just confirming the removal of Sir William's name from the list of possible suspects. There was no way known to man he could have interfered with that cake.

Jack thanked Mrs Buckingham for her time and we were about to leave when Keggs entered, levitating across the floor in his usual slow, stately fashion, bearing a tray loaded with the newly polished silverware.

Seeing him, Jack said, 'Keggs, I almost forgot—we found these today.' He produced with a flourish the two receipts we'd found in Connie Worth's room.

Keggs looked at the two slips of paper, blinked rapidly, and then his face went bright red, something I would have thought impossible for an impassive butler. But he really did go red—so red that any passing fire engine would have recognised him as a brother in arms.

Keggs coughed politely, sounding rather like an elderly cat with a fishbone caught in its throat, and held out his hand.

'If I may have those back, please, sir. They appear to be receipts missing from the household accounts. I have no idea how they could have gone astray.'

Jack handed over the slips of paper and we left the kitchen.

As we walked through the drawing room towards the front door of Plumwood Hall, I glanced sideways at Jack and I was surprised: he had a broad grin on his face.

TWENTY-NINE

~

A moment later the gravel of the driveway was crunching beneath our feet. The high pressure ridge across most of the United Kingdom was still doing its stuff—the sky was blue, the breeze was gentle, the birds were singing, insects all over the place were buzzing away with joy and a cocker spaniel was lying on the lawn, in the sun, snoring loudly.

Then a dark cloud loomed—not in the sky but in the driveway ahead. It was a dark, storm-threatening, rain-bearing cloud by the name of Inspector Matthew Hyde of the county constabulary. As always, he was glaring at me as if I was one of his local villagers who had failed to abate a smoking chimney.

This man I regarded as my mortal enemy. I was quite certain that his nightly prayer as he knelt at the foot of his bed was that I would end up dangling uncomfortably at the end of a hangman's rope—and that he would be there to see it.

I glared back at him, hoping my glare would convey the message that I regarded him as a slug in the salad of civilisation.

Jack, however, hailed this fiend in human form in a happy and hearty manner.

'Inspector Hyde,' he bellowed cheerfully, 'you're just what I'm looking for.'

'And what might that be, Mr Lewis?' asked Hyde, the

suspicious weasel side of his character at once coming to the fore.

'A policeman,' Jack announced. 'They say you can never find a policeman when you want one. Well, here you—living disproof of the familiar cliché. I am in want of a policeman and, lo and behold, you appear on the spot.'

This sort of banter only deepened Hyde's suspicions. He glared at Jack, he glared at me, then he glanced around as if looking for a trap.

'As you say, I'm here, Mr Lewis,' he said, lowering his eyelids and staring narrowly at Jack. 'So what can I do for you?'

'It's more a matter of what I can do for you. Morris and I have uncovered what appears to be an important clue in the case of the cyanide murders.'

Inspector Hyde folded his arms, rocked back on his heels and asked for the full details. Jack supplied them: the letter tumbling out of the old book, the addressee of the passionate love letter, the signature I recognised and the possibility of blackmail it suggested.

Hyde held out his hand and demanded, 'The letter, if you don't mind, Mr Lewis.'

Jack handed it over. The policeman read it slowly, his eyes opening wider and wider as he came across one declaration of intimate passion after another. Having turned it over and read to the bottom of the second page he immediately turned it back and read it all again—as if he couldn't quite believe it the first time and had to make sure he hadn't missed anything.

His face told us his first reaction: this was a document that should be censored by the Lord Chamberlain and would, in due course, be banned in Boston.

'The signature is incomplete,' he said at length. 'It's just the one name. Are you quite sure this is Sir William Dyer's signature, Mr Morris?'

I told him I was quite sure and suggested he obtain a specimen signature for comparison. He said he would.

'Now, as to the addressee,' he continued. 'Again there's only one name. But you suggest this must be Judith Trelawney, Lady Pamela's younger sister—now deceased.'

We agreed that, yes, that was what we were suggesting.

'Have you any proof of this?' Hyde demanded.

Jack admitted that we did not, and suggested that the county police force might attempt some investigation. Hyde growled in response, and read the letter a third time. Then he closed his eyes, rocked back on his heels again and appeared to drop into a catatonic coma.

Jack and I watched this performance with interest. When Inspector Hyde finally regained consciousness, he said, 'Now, this suggestion of yours that this letter implies blackmail—surely that's a leap too far?'

'How else,' Jack asked, 'can you account for its being hidden—presumably by someone who thought they'd found a safe place for it where it could lie undetected until they retrieved it?'

'Perhaps.' Hyde was doubtful. 'If this really is Sir William Dyer's handwriting, might he have placed the letter where you found it himself?'

'Unlikely for several reasons,' said Jack, fixing Hyde with the steely stare he usually fastened on lazy, unthinking students in tutorials. 'In the first place, if Sir William had got his hands on this document, he would have destroyed it. As you saw, in this letter he asks Judith to burn all his correspondence that might reveal their affair. He had no reason to keep this one incriminating piece of evidence. Second, if for some unimaginable reason he decided to keep it, surely he would put it under lock and key in his own study, not in a book in the library when anyone might stumble across it. And thirdly, he knew that this particular volume, the 1597 *Romeo and Juliet* quarto, was being studied by my young friend, Mr Morris. Upon learning of that, he would have immediately removed the letter from its hiding place. He didn't, because he didn't put it there.'

The inspector's brain slowly clanked into gear and processed this argument. There was a good deal of grinding and crunching of mental gears before he asked, 'If he didn't hide it there, then who did?'

'There are two possibilities,' said Jack, ticking them off on his fingers. 'Either Mrs Connie Worth in her role as the blackmailer, or else a third party.'

'So Mrs Worth might have hidden the letter there before she was murdered?' asked the policeman, like a slow boy repeating a rote lesson.

'That's one possibility,' said Jack patiently, 'but the other is more likely.'

Inspector Hyde asked Jack to explain, so he did. 'We have heard from young Will that the impoverished Mrs Worth had come into cash before she was poisoned. That implies that the blackmail had been paid. And a businessman as canny as Sir William would not cough up the cash without receiving what he was paying for.'

I chipped in to suggest that it might have been only a first instalment, in which case the document might not yet have passed from the blackmailer to the blackmailee.

Jack agreed this was very likely and then added, 'The next possibility is that the letter was uncovered in Mrs Worth's room after her death by a third party. This third party, looking for a safe and secret place to conceal the letter, chose the old book in the library.'

'Hang about, hang about,' protested Inspector Hyde, shaking his head as he tried to keep up with the speed of Jack's thinking. Nature appeared to have equipped the good inspector with about as much brain as would comfortably fit in a small aspirin bottle. 'Why would there be a third party involved?' he asked.

Jack responded to this question with one of his own: 'Why would a blackmailer have only one victim? And if Mrs Worth had other victims, one of them might have seized the opportunity of her sudden death to quickly search her room to recover incriminating items. In the process that person found this letter, saw its potential, took it and hid it.'

Inspector Hyde looked doubtful. 'That's a long chain of supposition there, Mr Lewis,' he said.

Then he cheered up considerably. A cunning smile spread slowly across his face as he said, 'Of course, that third party might have been Mr Morris here. Perhaps he was the other blackmail victim. That provides the missing motive for his murder of Mrs Worth.'

Inspector Hyde was almost rubbing his hands together in glee as he chuckled unpleasantly to himself and walked away down the drive towards the Hall.

THIRTY

~

I watched him disappear with mixed feelings of astonishment and hollow fear. 'I can't believe it,' I said. 'Anything that happens he twists around to support his suspicions of me!'

'Relax, old chap,' said Jack. 'Very shortly even Inspector Hyde's deepest and darkest suspicions will be washed away by a tidal wave of facts. In the meantime, you mustn't be too worried by what he says. The inspector's pronouncements are like much modern poetry—they bear a passing resemblance to the English language but don't actually mean anything.'

I must have still looked worried because Jack immediately continued, 'Come along, Morris, let's take a walk across the moors. A good, brisk walk will do you a power of good.'

The suggestion was a good one, so I raised no objection. We set off at once striding across the lawn and within minutes we had passed through a spinney of still bare trees, climbed over a stile and were setting out across the heather-covered moors.

Naturally as we walked my mind trotted back into those grim subjects of death and judgment that had been haunting me ever since Inspector Hyde first fixed me with his gimlet eye.

I remarked to Jack that as far as Hyde was concerned my judgment was well and truly over—I had been tried by a jury of one and found guilty. All that was still in abeyance, as far as Hyde was concerned, was my punishment.

'And you connect this, I take it,' said Jack, 'with our earlier discussion?'

'Well, if death is followed by judgment, as you insist,' I replied, 'it surely follows that we must understand something of the potential rewards and punishments that follow.'

'Indeed, and in order to do that we need to think clearly about death itself.'

I asked him to explain, and he responded with a question. 'How would you explain or define death, young Morris?'

'The end of life,' I suggested.

'However,' Jack protested, 'that suffers from being circular, doesn't it? "What is death?" The end of life. "What is life?" That which ends in death. If life and death are both defined in terms of each other, we fail to get at the inner nature of either.'

'Well, does this get us any closer?' I suggested, closing my eyes for a moment to concentrate on an appropriate formulation of words. '"The final cessation of the vital functions of a plant or animal." How's that?'

'Much better. Of course, we still haven't really got to the heart of the matter until we've unpacked the notion of "vital functions". But there's a good deal in what you say.'

This expression was the highest praise Jack ever employed in his tutorials. However, I had no time to feel a glow of satisfaction because, still having my eyes closed in concentration, at that point I fell headlong over a tussock of grass.

Jack lent me a hand and pulled me back to my feet. As I brushed down my clothes I asked, 'Do you have a better definition?'

'There is one idea I've done a good deal of thinking about, although I'm still wrestling with it. Does it help if we think about death as *separation*?'

He paused as we both clambered over a low dry-stone wall, and then resumed, 'Death most certainly is separation in many ways, so does that notion get to the core of the idea? I think it might. For a start death is separation between loved ones. The death of my mother from cancer when I was a child was a painful separation. The more recent death of my father was less painful, as it was not unexpected and came at the end of a long life. But it still cuts us off from each other—as long as I am in this world, the separation remains.'

'What about the other aspects of death?' I asked.

'They too may be different aspects of separation. For instance, it's still normal to think of the moment of death as the moment of separation between the soul and the body. Everyone from Plato to mediums conducting séances to millions of Christians over the ages has seen death in terms of that separation—the soul, the consciousness, leaves the body.'

After another pause, in which his brain was clearly whirling, he said, 'Even the kind of physical dissolution you were hinting at with your definition of death, young Morris, could be described as a body dissolving, or separating, into its component elements. Death as *separation*.'

At this point we reached the top of a low hill. In the distance we could see, stark against the horizon, the ruins of the Hunting Tower.

'Let's head for that,' I said. 'The key was missing from the board behind the kitchen door, so perhaps the door to the tower is now unlocked.'

As we started down the slope of the first of the intervening valleys, Jack said, 'But there is a deeper and more profound understanding of death as separation: namely, separation from God. That's what Christians regard as spiritual death.'

'But what about those people who choose to live their lives in this world ignoring God—wanting to be independent, wanting to be separated from God?'

'The Christian would say such people have chosen spiritual death. The alternative is to choose re-connection—spiritual life. And that's what's reflected in the judgments, the rewards and punishments, after death.'

'So you suggest that at death the separation, or connection, chosen in life comes into effect?'

'There is certainly a division, a separation, that appears at death. Jesus describes the judgment as consisting of separating, or dividing, the "sheep" from the "goats".'

'The good from the evil?'

'Or better still: the forgiven from the unforgiven.'

I had to think about this for a while. Eventually I said, 'So you're suggesting that the rewards and punishments that follow our post-mortem judgment are connected to this notion of separation, or its opposite—connection.'

'It seems a reasonable supposition to me that all the language of hell that we encounter—picturing a fire that is never quenched, a bottomless pit, an outer darkness and so on—is metaphor. It's picture language suited to our level of under-standing. The most literal statement of hell that we get comes from Jesus, who, incidentally, speaks of hell more often than any other figure in the Bible.'

'What literal statement is that?'

'When he says that the punishment at judgment is pronounced in these words: "Depart from me, for I never knew you." Those are words of banishment, of exile. If I'm right in reading those words as a literal judgment, as words of condem-nation, then people in this life, this world, who have chosen separation from God, in the next life, the next world, are treated as adults and given exactly what they've chosen—complete, total and ultimate separation from God, and his people, forever. Banishment. Exile.'

We walked in silence for a while, and then I asked, 'If you had to choose your own metaphorical or poetic language to describe the punishment of hell as you understand it, what sort of word picture would you paint?'

He thought for a moment before he replied, 'Perhaps one of those bleak, dreary northern industrial towns where the local industries have died and the place is deserted and empty. On a rainy Sunday afternoon. Dingy lodging houses, small shops that have all closed, old newspapers blowing down the street—that sort of thing. But I stress that's just a metaphor for the real thing: an awful, isolating separation.'

'You make it sound as if the people who choose separation from God are choosing an eternity of loneliness—a bit like choosing an eternity in solitary confinement. That certainly sounds like sheer hell to me,' I added with a humourless laugh.

'I'm sure,' said Jack, 'there are many metaphors that could be used to convey the same basic idea: namely, that the eternal judgment that follows death is entirely just.'

'I'm not sure that follows,' I protested.

'W. S. Gilbert insisted that the punishment must fit the crime,' said Jack. 'Well, in this case the punishment not only fits the crime, the punishment *is* the crime. The punishment for choosing to be separated from God *is* to be separated from God, cut off from the Creator—and, incidentally, from the life and love and purpose of the universe—forever. What you choose in the way you live is what you get. What could be fairer than that?'

THIRTY-ONE

~

The last of the shallow valleys, little more than dips in the rolling moorlands, between us and the ruins of the Hunting Tower was heavily wooded. As Jack and I entered the belt of trees, we saw movement ahead of us in the shadows.

As we'd been walking the conversation had so gripped my attention I had failed to notice the change in the weather. The high pressure ridge had knocked off after a busy day's work and dark clouds had rolled across the sky in its place.

The result was a deepening purple gloom, made still blacker by the thick pattern of tree trunks filling the small hollow. And in the twilight it was difficult to see anything, let alone the mysterious cause of the shadowy movements somewhere among those bare, skeletal trees of early spring.

I laid a hand on Jack's arm and pointed ahead to where I thought I saw, or possibly heard, the movement. We both stood still and listened. Then there came the quiet crunching of leaves underfoot, accompanied by a dim shifting of shadows against shadows.

'Is it an animal?' I asked. 'A deer?'

'Or is it,' asked Jack with a gleeful grin on his face, 'the wild man of the woods?'

The sound of our voices alerted whoever, or whatever, it was to our presence. Against the dim tree trunks, the dark patch of the moving figure dropped into a crouching position and then stayed very still.

'Now that didn't look anything like a deer,' I said.

'And we are, remember, in the vicinity of the Dark Tower,' said Jack, clearly enjoying the moment, 'the source, according Constable Charlie Nile, of the spectre of the creeping man.'

With those words Jack began striding boldly forward. This provoked a flurry of movement ahead of us in the purple twilight. There was a crashing in the undergrowth, and then a crouching shadow was fleeing from us—across the thickly wooded copse of old trees and up the slope on the far side.

It was like a moment out of the one of those Sexton Blake serials in *Union Jack*, my favourite weekly story paper when I was a boy. And I was not about to miss out on the adventure.

I took off in pursuit. Despite my rapid ducking and dodging in the darkness, I managed to collect a heavy blow on the side of the head from a tree branch that I failed to negotiate with sufficient clearance. As I staggered, Jack was by my side.

'I'm all right,' I insisted, and resumed the pursuit.

As I cleared the trees, the creeping man became visible sprinting in a strange, crouching, loping run towards the ruins of the old tower. At times he seemed to be proceeding almost on all fours.

'Hey!' I shouted. 'Stop there! We just want to talk to you.'

These words inspired a yet greater burst of speed, and the wild man of the woods reached the ridge top while Jack and I were still staggering up the slope.

At the peak we paused to catch our breath.

Before us, but still some distance away, stood the ruined tower. Its jagged and broken battlements stood out against the purple storm clouds like a set of rotting teeth. As we watched, the hunched shadow appeared at the base of the tower. Again it was creeping like an animal, almost down on all fours. The thing, or person, or whatever it was, tried to pull open the door.

But the door refused to budge. Once again it rattled in its frame, just as it had done for me. It appeared to still be locked.

Then the shadowy figure stood to its full height, grasped the door handle and wrenched with an almost superhuman strength. With a scream of splintering timber the door flew open and then hung limply on its hinges.

Jack and I resumed running—or, to be honest, jogging in a puffed manner—towards the tower. At the moment when the door crashed open, the shadowy figure turned around and saw us. His reaction was swift: he turned and ran. Somehow his strength seemed to be not in the least diminished, and he disappeared in a low, loping run so quickly that there was no chance of our catching him.

By the time we had reached the ruined tower on its hilltop the mysterious figure was nowhere to be seen.

'Did you . . . see what he did . . . with this door?' I gasped, my lungs still aching for air.

Jack made no attempt to answer immediately but stood catching his breath for a minute.

'I grant you,' he said at length, 'it was quite astonishing. Warnie knew a chap in his old regiment once, a weightlifter, who could do remarkable things, but nothing quite like that.' As he spoke he reached over and touched the newly splintered edge of the lintel where the lock had been torn from the frame by sheer brute strength.

At least, I pointed out, the absence of the key was no longer a problem.

'That's what everyone needs when a locked door stands in

the way,' said Jack with a loud guffaw, 'your friendly, neighbourhood wild man of the woods. Better than any locksmith.'

Still feeling a little puffed, I flopped down on a block of stone at the entrance to the tower.

'You suggested a walk,' I said. 'Well, we ended up getting something rather more vigorous than that.'

'To an old rugger blue like you, Morris,' said Jack cheerfully, 'that sort of run should be no more than a walk in the park.'

'Except that I'm no longer as fit as I once was,' I replied ruefully.

Jack lit his pipe and puffed in silence for a few moments. Then he said, 'Well, the door stands open, young Morris. It is an open invitation. Shall we do as you once suggested and explore the tower?'

I pronounced this to be a good idea and stood to my feet. I was thinking in terms of getting to the top of the tower—young Will had said it was once possible—and looking at the panorama of the landscape. If there was a spectacular thunderstorm sweeping in from the coast it might be a stunning view.

I pulled back the now sagging door, and the first thing I was struck by was the sound—the buzz of countless insects, perhaps flies or bluebottles. As I stepped in through the doorway, the second thing I became aware of was the smell. I staggered back.

'We can't go in there, Jack,' I said, coughing to clear my lungs. 'The stench is horrible.'

Jack walked over and stood in the doorway, puffing furiously on his pipe to surround his head with rich tobacco smoke and so keep out the overpowering smell. He stood peering into the darkness at the base of the tower.

After a moment he came back to my side. 'We'll have to go and fetch the police,' he said. 'There's a dead body in there.'

I took a deep breath, clapped my handkerchief over my mouth and stepped into the stone building. Sprawled across the ground floor of the tower was a body. It had been there for some considerable time. Much of the flesh was gone and the bones exposed. Flies and bluebottles were crawling over the flesh that was left.

The bottom half of the face had been reduced to bony skeleton—turning the teeth and jaw into a hideous grin, an appalling death mask.

As I watched, a large grey rat crawled out of the shadows and over the chest of the corpse. It raised its head for a moment and its red, venomous eyes stared into mine. Then it decided I wasn't a threat, so it lowered its head and began to chew on the rotting flesh.

I staggered outside to the fresh air and vomited on the grass.

THIRTY-TWO

~

Jack made sure I was all right, then he followed my example and stood just inside the doorway to the tower—staring grimly at the horror within.

When he rejoined me he asked again, 'Are you sure you're all right now?'

'Fine, fine,' I gasped.

'Then let's head back to Plumwood as quickly as we can. We have to report this to the police.'

'Can we just leave him—it—here?'

'He's been here on his own for long enough; another hour or so will make little difference. We can try to push the broken door back into place if you wish, but it's unlikely anyone will be along this way during the short time we're absent.'

We set off at once at a rapid walk.

We spoke little on that return journey. We stopped at a bubbling brook so I could rinse out my mouth, which still had a foul taste in it, and then kept on striding in a direct line towards the village.

The high street—to be honest, the only street—in Plumwood Village was deserted when we arrived. It was mid-afternoon and the weather was threatening, so all sensible folk were indoors. A brown dog sat under the shelter of the seat at the bus stop and watched us pass—like all dogs, keeping a careful eye on the behaviour of anyone who chose to walk down his street.

We found Constable Charlie Nile at the police cottage at the far end of the village. He was having afternoon tea when we knocked on his door, and he hospitably invited us to join him in a pot of tea with scones and jam. Our grim faces told him this was not a social call.

In a few words Jack sketched out the horror we had found in the Black Tower. Constable Nile pulled on the jacket of his uniform and grabbed his helmet from the hat stand.

'The Scotland Yard chappies are at the pub. At least I think they are.' He was clearly flustered. 'I saw them arrive back there about half an hour ago.'

We found Inspector Crispin and Sergeant Merrivale seated at a small table in the snug at *The Cricketers' Arms*. They had an official looking file spread out on the table and the sergeant had his notebook out.

Once again Jack told our tale of horror. Crispin made a few inquiries and Constable Nile explained that the spot was only accessible on foot, so the inspector and his sergeant grabbed their hats, donned their macs and followed us out of the village and onto the walking path that led across the moors. Before we left, Sergeant Merrivale hurried up to his room and returned with a small leather case. This he carried with him.

As we walked we filled the others in on the history of the Black Tower, or Hunting Tower, and on how we had found it locked so recently. Then we told the story of the 'wild man of the woods' and the startling way he wrenched open that heavy locked door by sheer brute force.

At this point Nile chipped in and told the visiting policemen everything that was known about this 'wild man'—which was precious little.

As we spoke we walked briskly, and before long we were back at the ruined tower. Jack and I stood back and allowed the policemen to enter—we had seen quite enough of the horror within for one day.

Charlie Nile staggered back out again quickly enough. He sat down heavily on the grass, pulled off his helmet and fanned his face with it. Such grisly horrors were not what he had expected when he signed on the dotted line to become a village constable.

Then Sergeant Merrivale came out and unpacked the small leather case he had been carrying. It contained photographic equipment. He set the camera on its tripod, attached the flash gun and returned to the tower and the decayed corpse. Soon a series of brilliant flashes from within told us that he had started making his photographic record.

Inspector Crispin came out, checked that Constable Nile had recovered and sent him back to the village with careful instructions.

'We need Dr Henderson out here as quickly as possible. And you'd better phone through to Market Plumpton and inform Inspector Hyde. We'll need some of his uniformed men out here to help move the body and to search the area.'

Constable Nile set off at a commendable pace back towards the village. Crispin asked us to stay where we were for the time being, and returned to the tower to conduct a further inspection of the body and the scene.

When he returned he was carrying a leather wallet.

'From the pocket of the dead man,' he said, holding it up. Using only his fingertips, he cautiously prised the stiff leather of the wallet open and, to our horror, a large, white maggot flopped out. That brought back the shock Jack and I had both felt when we saw that decayed, half-eaten corpse.

Seeing what was clearly written on our faces Inspector Crispin said, 'Yes, it's an unpleasant business. But sometimes we need a strong stomach in our line of work.' Then he began a delicate examination of the contents of the wallet. These he laid out on a flat rock as he removed them from the leather folds.

There were a few coins and a large, white five-pound note. A receipt of some sort with faded printing. And then a driver's licence emerged. This Crispin unfolded with great care so that it would not tear or disintegrate.

'Ah, this appears to give us the name of our victim,' he said, squinting at the faded lettering on the licence. 'If this is, indeed, his licence, he was a certain Charles David Worth.'

'I think you might find, inspector,' I said, 'that this man is the long-missing husband of the first murder victim, Connie Worth.'

'Now that, Mr Morris,' replied the Scotland Yard man, 'makes this death even more interesting.'

'How did he die?' Jack asked.

'There are no external wounds and no obvious signs of violence. So the short answer is—we don't know yet. It may be a death by natural causes, or it may be . . .'

His unspoken thought hung heavily in the air.

'How long has he been dead?' I asked.

'Hard to say, sir. That's a question for Dr Henderson, or for the police surgeon at Market Plumpton. Do you know when he went missing?'

I thought for a moment and replied, 'I think it must have been over a year ago. I'm pretty sure that's what I was told. Sorry I can't be more precise.'

'That would fit in with the state of decomposition.'

Then Crispin asked us about our visits to the Hunting Tower or Black Tower or whatever it should be called. In clear, crisp words, Jack told about our first visit when we found it locked, and then went over the events of today once more.

I looked up and saw, in the distance, struggling up the slope towards us, Constable Nile and Dr Henderson.

'Was anything found with the body?' Jack asked.

'Underneath the body there was a walking stick, a long, straight stick such as hiker's use, and a flask which seems to contain whisky.'

A puffed and red-faced Constable Nile panted up to our side. 'Here's the doctor, sir,' he wheezed, addressing Inspector Crispin, 'and Inspector Hyde is on his way with some uniformed constables from Market Plumpton. I've told Fred Rose at *The Cricketers' Arms* to direct them up here when they come.'

Crispin led Dr Henderson into the tower and left him there to make his preliminary investigation. Sergeant Merrivale came out and packed away his photographic equipment. After a very short space of time he was followed by Dr Henderson and the inspector.

'All I can do is pronounce life extinct,' the doctor was saying. 'For anything more than that you'll have to wait until I get him on the slab. In the absence of broken bones or obvious injuries, I can do no more.'

Then Crispin turned to us and said, 'You're free to go, gentlemen. Thank you for being so patient with us.'

I turned to leave, but Jack had one last question. 'If this is not death by natural causes,' he said, 'I take it that you'll consider the possibility that—'

Crispin interrupted him. 'Yes, I will—the possibility that this is the first in the series of murders that have happened here. The one that began the wave of deaths.'

THIRTY-THREE

~

It was late the following morning before we saw Inspector Crispin again.

I was keen to finish up at Plumwood Hall and leave the place forever. I had arrived at this country mansion looking upon it as a useful stopping off place on my way to writing the Great English Novel—or, at least, something passably publishable. But instead of a comfortable, well-paying way station, it now felt like one of those crumbling castles in Transylvania that any passing tourist would be well advised to leave off the itinerary.

So I spent the morning in the library working at what were almost the last stages of my task of cataloguing the whole collection.

Then I went into the village to have a pint with Jack at the pub. We were engaged in this pleasant task when Inspector Crispin arrived, this time without his faithful bulldog, Sergeant Merrivale, by his side. This surprised me as I had regarded those two as being more or less joined at the hip. Presumably Merrivale had been let off the leash and was doggedly policing elsewhere at the moment.

Crispin joined us in the snug and set a manila folder down on the table before us.

'This will interest you,' he said with a gleam in his eye that gave him a resemblance to the sales assistant in the jewellery shop as he plonks down a real sparkler in front of the customer. 'My sergeant would not approve of my sharing this information with you, but I'm not too proud to confess to being baffled—and I welcome input from the best brains in the vicinity.'

Jack beamed and asked what the information was.

'The preliminary autopsy report. To be confirmed by an analysis of what remains of the flesh, but the police surgeon in Market Plumpton and Dr Henderson, who carried out the post-mortem jointly, seem pretty confident they know the cause of death.'

'Which was?' I asked.

Crispin didn't reply immediately; instead he resumed his narrative. 'It appears,' he said, 'that there are certain tell-tale signs in the way the organs are damaged that were still visible—or visible enough for both doctors to leap to the same conclusion at much the same moment. As I say, the laboratory analysis will confirm it, but we can take the agreement of both medical men as a starting point in our thinking. The contents of the flask of whisky are also being analysed.'

Jack smiled over the stem of his pipe, which he was in the process of lighting, and said, 'And are you about to tell us what they are agreed about?'

'Poison,' said the Scotland Yard man, leaning back in his chair and waving to the landlord to bring him a pint.

'That makes three poisonings in this same district,' I said.

'Indeed, Mr Morris,' said the inspector. 'I counted them several times and got to the same number.'

Ignoring his good-natured ribbing, I said, 'So are they all linked? Was the murder of Charles Worth the first in this whole chain of murders?'

Crispin took a long sip from his pint of lager and wiped the foam from his upper lip.

'There is a slight problem,' he said.

'I take it, my dear inspector,' said Jack, 'that in this case the wrong poison was used?'

'Precisely,' the policeman agreed. 'Charles Worth died from a massive dose of arsenic—not cyanide.'

'So we either have a killer who changed poisons or two killers,' Jack said.

'And that's as far as we've got,' sighed Crispin, leaning back in his chair.

'But surely you've taken the next step,' Jack pursued, with a smile. 'Surely you've reconstructed the crime—the murder of Charles Worth—as a thought experiment.' That was one of Jack's favourite expressions that he often trotted out in tutorials. He could chew on a thought experiment with as much pleasure as a terrier could chew on a large bone.

Jack continued, 'We know he went for a walk on the day he died. He set off across the moors in the general direction of the tower where he was found, with his dog by his side. The dog was later found battered to death, and until yesterday the fate of Mr Worth was a mystery. Now we know he has lain dead all this time, locked inside the tower. Upon those known facts, how would you reconstruct the crime, inspector?'

'I'd much prefer to hear your reconstruction, Mr Lewis. When you run that particular thought experiment in your head, what is the outcome?'

'Very well, then,' said Jack cheerfully, 'if you insist. In such a poisonous attack the first question to ask is Cicero's famous question, *cui bono*? We have already been told that under his will the financial benefit—apparently a substantial financial benefit—would go to his wife. So it was in the interests of

Connie Worth for her husband to die and for his body to be found. The first happened, the second didn't.'

'Ah, yes,' said Inspector Crispin, 'that makes it interesting, doesn't it? How do you imagine that may have come about?'

'If Connie Worth had, indeed, poisoned her husband's whisky flask, my guess would be that she herself was also out on the moors that day—not too far behind her husband.'

'You've lost me,' I protested. 'Why would she do that?'

'To retrieve the whisky flask from her husband's dead body as soon as he collapsed,' Jack replied. 'Her plan may then have been to leave the body to be discovered by someone else while she disposed of the incriminating poisoned flask.'

'That's exactly how I imagined it,' said the inspector, looking as pleased as punch. 'I'm delighted to hear you confirm my suspicions. So, if that was the plan—what went wrong?'

'I'm no expert in these matters,' said Jack, 'but I've heard that arsenic is not a quick acting poison. That being so, Mr Charles Worth may have begun to realise that something was wrong, but by the time he did so he was too sick—and too far out on the moors—to make it back to the house.'

Jack puffed in silence on his pipe for a moment and then continued. 'What if he caught sight of his wife? What if Connie Worth drew near to the fatally ill man, near enough for him to see her, and perhaps in the circumstances—let's assume she had given him the flask or had filled it for him—he suspected her of poisoning him.'

I tried to picture the scene: the fatally ill Charles Worth catching sight of his wife and suddenly understanding that she must have poisoned him. If they had stood there, on those remote moors, eye to eye, it must have been one of those rather moist domestic moments that make a man see the woman he has married in an entirely new light.

'If,' Jack resumed, 'in that confrontation, he set his dog on Connie Worth, she would have had to fight the animal off with whatever weapon she had ready to hand—a good, stout stick or something of that sort. While this is going on, Charles Worth flees, reaches the tower and locks himself inside. Whether his dying mind thought he was protecting himself from Connie or whether he was thinking clearly enough to want to prevent his body being found and Connie reaping the benefit . . . well, we can't know.'

'That entire scenario,' said Inspector Crispin, 'strikes me as being entirely plausible. So what happens then? Mrs Worth has disposed of her husband but has missed out on inheriting his wealth because neither she nor anyone else knows where his body is. What then?'

'We know what happened then,' I said. 'She started sponging on her family. She went to live with her cousin Judith Trelawney—Lady Pamela's younger sister.'

'And that,' said the Scotland Yard man, 'brings this letter into play.' With a flourish he produced from his pocket the letter Jack and I had discovered the day before hidden in the pages of *Romeo and Juliet* in the library.

'We know,' said Jack, 'the letter must have been obtained from Judith Trelawney, for it was she who had it. And we know that Connie Worth was with Judith Trelawney at the time of her death. We may, therefore, reasonably assume that it was Connie Worth who took that letter and who used it to blackmail its sender, Sir William Dyer.'

'Wait on, wait on!' I interrupted. 'What if Judith Trelawney's death is part of all this?'

'Carry on, young man,' said the inspector.

'Well, there they are—these two women—in a hotel in Brighton, sharing a suite of rooms on the top floor. Somehow

Connie Worth must have become aware of the letter—otherwise how did she know to take it after Judith Trelawney's death? How that happened we can never know. Did she secretly search through her cousin's possessions? Did Judith come to trust Connie and tell her about the affair and show her the one remaining letter she'd kept—her one keepsake that she couldn't bring herself to destroy? I suppose either of those things is possible.'

Both Jack and the policeman listened but didn't say a word, so I kept talking. Not that I needed any encouragement—I now had up a head of steam and my imagination was racing at a hundred miles an hour.

'So, supposing all that,' I continued excitedly, 'might Judith Trelawney's death also have been murder? However Connie Worth got that letter, once she had it she had another source of income—a potentially substantial source of income, given Sir William's wealth. Did Judith Trelawney discover what Connie was up to and object? Instead of falling from that hotel room balcony, was she pushed? Was she another victim of Connie Worth's greed?'

I paused, took a deep breath and finished off the last of my tankard of beer.

There was a long, thoughtful silence. Finally Jack said, 'You paint a very black picture of Connie Worth's character, young Morris. Unfortunately, it's quite a convincing picture. If, for the moment, we accept your sketch of her murderous blackmailing nature, we have to ask ourselves this question: who else was she blackmailing?'

THIRTY-FOUR

~

That proved to be a question that kept us talking all through lunch. We reached no definite conclusion, but I had the impression that Jack was keeping his own counsel, and I would have given more than a penny to know his thoughts.

That afternoon I spent, once again, in the library at Plumwood Hall, working on what I knew would be the last pages of the catalogue. That night I excused myself from dinner at the Hall in order to dine with Jack at the village pub.

Alfred Rose, the landlord of *The Cricketers' Arms*, did us proud: roast beef and Yorkshire pudding. Not a patch on Mrs Buckingham's, of course, but still an excellent meal.

Then we retired to the armchairs in the snug with a brandy and soda each, and Jack lit up his pipe.

'What I can't be certain about,' I said, 'is that it will all happen.'

'From that cryptic remark, young Morris, I presume you have thrown the switch from Connie Worth, blackmailer and murderer, to another topic?'

'Yes, sorry, I should have said. I'm back to the "D" topic again.'

Jack smiled and said, 'You refer there, in your coy manner, to death, I take it?'

'Yes. I can understand the logic of immortality—and even of an immortality that begins with judgment. I can see how that judgment could be reflected in either separation or connection—either welcome or exile—for the "sheep" or the "goats" respectively. I can see how that whole concept is coherent. But how can there be any certainty that it will happen? And how can you be so certain that when it does we'll all be found to be "unrighteous", to use your bone-chilling word?'

'Now that's an entire bundle of questions. In fact, Morris, you're doing what I recall you doing in tutorials—firing a machine gun load of questions all at once. So let's unbundle them a bit. The first part of the question was: can we be certain? Well, I think we can be certain that this world, this universe, is a reasonable place.'

Jack paused to relight his pipe, then resumed, 'Those scientists you love to quote have told us that much. They've told us that the universe is regular and reasonable—that if you ask the universe the same question in the same way on two different days, it will give you the same answer. The universe is regular, it's reasonable. And reasonableness is the product of a Mind.'

Jack never rushed his words. He had a deliberate, almost slow way of rolling out his sentences in that rich voice of his—a manner that always carried me along with him, step by step.

'That reasonableness,' he continued, 'is clearly universal. That means it applies to the non-physical realm as well as the physical. Those unseen things—your mind, or spirit, or self-awareness, or soul—are governed by the same reasonableness as the physical world we see around us.'

'So you say that physical regularity and reasonableness apply in the physical realm and therefore regularity and reasonableness apply also in the unseen realm?'

'Precisely. But we know there is this one difference: that unseen things, such as ideas, don't decay and dissipate in the way physical things do. Plato's ideas are just as alive today as they were in ancient Athens—while Plato's body has been buried and has decayed, and the stones on which he walked are weathered and crumbling.'

Jack took a sip from his brandy and soda. 'There is a pattern of continuation in the unseen world just as there is a pattern of decay and dissipation in the seen world. And this pattern of the continuation of the unseen is entirely reasonable since every human life here on earth promises more than it attains, aspires beyond its grasp and longs for that which is unattainable in the earthly realm.'

I nodded as I said, 'And that continuation, beyond physical death, gives meaning to our lives?'

'In *Alice in Wonderland* the King of Hearts, when he looks at a document in the trial scene, says, "If there is no meaning in it, that saves a world of trouble, as we needn't try to find any." Our lives *are* meaningless unless they continue and thus fulfil the potential that only begins to emerge in this life, in this world.'

'What you say,' I remarked, 'reminds me of the way astronomers seem to work these days.'

Jack chuckled, 'You've been reading those popular science articles in the Sunday supplements again, haven't you?'

I ignored this dig and continued, 'Astronomers, so I read, often discover *unseen* heavenly bodies by noticing the perturbations in the obits, the movements, of those heavenly bodies they *can* see. Similarly, the longings, the incompleteness, in the earthly lives we *can* see are the perturbations, the disturbances, that act as evidence of a larger *unseen* existence beyond this earthly life. I think I can see the sense in that—if I think about it long enough and hard enough.'

There was a long silence with Jack's eyes glittering at me intelligently, waiting for me to absorb all these heavy ideas, grasp them and make sense of them. He could see that the wheels in my head were clattering away busily trying to process all these big concepts.

At length he said, 'God, the Great Mind behind the universe, is not a lunatic artist who starts a million portraits and finishes none of them. He's not a lunatic writer who starts a million novels and finishes none. The rest of our story, the rest of the picture, is coming for each one of us. We are already on the road towards that.'

'Which means . . . ?'

'Death is not an end—it is an incident. The road we are on now continues ever, ever on—as Tollers would say—down from the door where it began. At death our lives don't end, they change.'

'Meaning that immortality is what we have now?'

'Precisely. We are already in possession of immortality—but not of eternal life. That is the change that is wrought by death: the "sheep" and the "goats" find death to be a junction point where they are separated. The "sheep" to eternal life, permanent connection, and the "goats" to eternal death, permanent separation.'

'And which is which depends on a judgment that pronounces us either "righteous" or "unrighteous"—or so you said. But what is worse, you said earlier that each of us deserves to be pronounced "unrighteous", which makes us all goats and none of us sheep!'

'Or it would,' said Jack, 'if there were not an intervention.'

I asked him to explain.

'Christ is God's intervention in this world: the great invasion of this world from the unseen realm beyond. And this

189

intervention could best be called a rescue mission. Christ came to create a new track for us to travel on—leading us off the goat track and into the way of the sheep.'

'Hang on, get back to this ugly word "unrighteous", please.'

'Very well. None of us succeeds in fulfilling all the obligations of all our relationships. And that is true of each one of us. I pose this question: Morris, has any other person ever hurt you—either knowingly or unknowingly—in the course of your life?'

'Well, of course. That sort of thing happens to everyone.'

'That's unrighteousness in action. And then there's the reverse of that question: have you, Morris, ever hurt anyone else—either knowingly or unknowingly—in the course of your life? There's no need to say anything, old chap, since the only honest answer is "yes". Again, that's unrighteousness in action; that's us failing to get our relationships right.'

'Well, none of us is perfect,' I protested.

'That's my point: all of us are unrighteous. All of us are guilty of separation from God, and that broken relationship means that we fail in our other relationships with each other. That's what I mean by us being "unrighteous" and deserving of eternal death, not eternal life—permanent isolation and separation rather than a living, loving connectedness.'

'So everything is hopeless then?'

'It would be. Except, as I say, for God's intervention. In his death on the Cross, Christ was intervening on our behalf.'

Jack paused for a moment, and then, in his deep, warm voice, said quietly, 'Do you remember his famous cry at the time of his death? He called out, "My God, my God, why hast thou forsaken me?" Can you hear what's happening there? That is Christ going through that final, total, ultimate separation that *is* death and hell. We deserve that—he didn't. If we were ever that cut off, that isolated from God we would remain that cut off forever. But Christ was and is the Son of the Living God, and he went through death and hell on our behalf and came out triumphantly on the other side. That's the Great Intervention that means we goats can be transformed into sheep.'

THIRTY-FIVE

~

That night I found it hard to sleep. I lay in bed restless and sleepless. I could feel the ants of anxiety crawling up and down my spine—as if they had decided to have a party on my torso, invite all their friends and family, and do a lot of dancing on my nerve ends.

So it was that I lay awake late into the night, seeing the pale blue moonlight flood into my room where I had left the curtains drawn back, feeling a gentle night breeze wafting in through the open window, hearing the distant hoot of an owl and trying to pick out patterns in the oak beams as I stared listlessly at the ceiling.

Finally, some time after midnight, I was starting to drift away when I was startled into wakefulness by the sound of voices beneath my open window. What, I asked myself, was someone—or two someones, by the sound of it—doing on the manicured lawns of Plumwood Hall at . . . and here I looked at my bedside clock . . . at one o'clock in the morning?

Not able to answer my own question, I slipped out of bed and went to the open window, leaned forward and looked down. The lights were on in the drawing room below, and the curtains must have been open because light was spilling in golden bands across the terrace as far as the edge of the lawn. There was a dark figure standing in the shadows just beyond the light under the old ash tree.

And, I now realised, there was someone standing on the terrace in front of the open French windows.

Leaning a little further forward I got the shock of my life. It was Lady Pamela! I don't know what I expected. Perhaps the youngsters, Douglas and Will, out on night escapades, or perhaps Sir William roused from his bed with some emergency message from his biscuit factory, if biscuit factories have emergencies ('Sir! Sir! The strawberry cream is leaking into the vanilla nougat!'). But I certainly didn't expect the lady of the house.

Lady Pamela was rugged up in a quilted dressing gown of a rather fetching shade of mauve, and she appeared to be talking, in hushed tones, to the shadowy figure in the darkness at the edge of the lawn. Why wasn't she raising the alarm? Why hadn't she roused the whole house? Why hadn't she alerted everyone to the presence of this, I presumed, intruder? And why was I asking myself all these questions? Why didn't I just look and listen? So, I did.

She took a step further forward and gestured impatiently for her interlocutor to step closer. Presumably she wanted to keep their voices as quiet as possible. Slipping out of the blackness under the ash tree and into the pale, yellow light thrown by the drawing room candelabra was . . . it took me a moment to register the identity. It was Drax! What was the South American native doing conferring with Lady Pamela in the middle of the night? Was he threatening her in some way?

But no, that appeared not to be the case. Their heads were almost together now and they were talking in hushed tones. I couldn't make out any of the words; I could only hear the low murmur of the conversation. Rather like an audience watching those actors who huddle at the edge of the stage in crowd scenes muttering 'rhubarb, rhubarb' to each other—all I could hear was sound, not words.

There was no sense, however, of antagonism in their colloquy. Neither of them appeared to be particularly happy. Well, who would be at one o'clock on a cool spring morning? But their tones and their gestures suggested some sort of mutual concern rather than antagonism.

Then Lady Pamela seemed to make up her mind. She stepped back into the drawing room and returned a moment later carrying an electric torch and tying a scarf over her head. Then she looked back over her shoulder, once again retreated to the drawing room, and this time the lights went out. But there was a full moon and I could see clearly as she stepped back onto the terrace and turned on her torch, and she and Drax walked off side by side towards the stand of trees that bordered the lawn.

Well, this was a fine pickle. What ought I to do? I mean, Lady Pamela was a middle-aged lady and she was in the company of a wild-looking native in the dark of night. Could I in good conscience let her walk off alone, with no one to keep an eye on her? No, I decided, I could not. I thought for a moment of rousing Sir William, but decided there wasn't time.

Instead, I went to my wardrobe and hastily put on a pair of trousers and a heavy overcoat. I pulled some boots onto my feet and hurried, as quietly as my boots would allow, down the stairs to the drawing room. The light there was, as I had noticed, now off—but the French windows facing the terrace were still standing open.

I hurried outside, across the terrace and onto the lawn. Drax and Lady Pamela were now completely out of sight. My hurried dressing had taken longer than I had imagined. I took some tentative steps towards the distant stand of trees—the way I had seen them heading—and then hesitated. Where were they now?

Almost as soon as the question entered my head the answer was provided. I caught a glimpse of the dim gleam of an electric torch, bouncing in a walking pattern, beyond the trees. I set off at a good pace in that direction.

For the next little while I was engaged in tracking those two through the shrubbery and then across the moors. Now, I must admit I have no special skills as a tracker. As a boy I used to read those stories in *Chums* about intrepid trackers in the backwoods of Canada who could follow fugitives through wild country for miles and miles—tracing a faint footprint here, a snapped twig there. Even with the light of a full moon there was no question of my looking for such tell-tale signs. So I had to keep the bobbing torch in view at all times.

But I didn't want to get too close. I didn't want to be seen. If you had asked me why I felt it was important to keep my presence a secret, I don't think I could have given you an intelligent answer—except that I realised I was now behaving as oddly as the pair in front of me, and I didn't want to have to explain, to my employer or anyone else, why I was traipsing across the moors, half-dressed and half-pyjamaed, at that hour of the morning. So I hung back. But I was always ready to rush forward to Lady Pamela's defence should anything happen to threaten her safety.

We trudged on, with Drax and Lady Pamela setting a good brisk pace ahead of me, until the Hall had completely disappeared below the horizon behind us and we were pushing our way through the prickly heather that filled the wilder parts of the moorland.

Then the two ahead of me plunged down the slope of a narrow valley and passed into a thick copse of trees. I hurried to get closer in case I lost them entirely. When I reached the edge of the trees, they were just emerging on the other side, and I realised, from the nearness of their voices, that they had come to a halt.

For a long moment I stopped still. Then I began to edge forward as silently as I could. And, of course, I couldn't. I hadn't gone far before a large twig cracked noisily under my boots.

'What was that?' said Lady Pamela on the far side of the trees.

Since Drax didn't answer, she asked again, 'Did you hear anything?'

The pale beam of the electric torch swept in my direction and I huddled as low as I could behind the narrow trunks of the nearest trees. The light failed to pick me out.

Drax said something I couldn't make out, and Lady Pamela replied, 'Yes, I'm sure you're right—it was probably a badger.'

To my relief they turned away and went on.

But not far. Only a few yards further ahead they stopped again. They were standing in dark shadow, penetrated by none of the pale blue moonlight, and I heard the rattle of keys.

Suddenly I knew exactly where we were: at the remote, isolated moorland cottage occupied by Drax—the cottage Jack and I had stumbled across two days earlier. The wall of dark shadow blocking the moonlight was the front wall of the cottage.

I heard a door creak open, and then—nothing. It seemed the two had gone inside. That made it safe for me to move again, so I crept forward.

Emerging from the trees I saw the looming black shape that was the cottage. And I was right—the door was now closed, and Drax and Lady Pamela were nowhere to be seen.

I slipped forward over the tangled, overgrown grass that

surrounded the building until I reached the wall. Then I groped my way along it until I came to a window sill. There was the faintest glimmer of light coming from around the edges of the window, but the curtains were tightly drawn and no matter where I moved around that window I could not catch the smallest glimpse of what was inside.

But I could hear voices—very faintly. I put my ear to the glass and tried to pick up some words. At first I could hear only muffled murmurs. I listened for a long time, trying to make up my mind as to whether I should do something or not. Had Lady Pamela been abducted? Was she now being held in the cottage against her will? There was no sign of it as she had clearly walked off with Drax of her own free will.

Then the noises from inside the cottage changed and I could clearly make out the sound of sobbing—but it was not a woman's voice. It was a man's voice, a baritone, sobbing pathetically. Again I asked myself if the time had come for me to intervene. I leaned against the wall of the cottage for I don't know how long, feeling as uncertain and as indecisive as Hamlet on one of his vaguer days.

Before I could make up my mind to become the noble rescuer, the door of the cottage opened again and Lady Pamela appeared. Drax was behind her holding a candle. The two conferred again in hushed tones, then Lady Pamela bid him farewell.

'You did the right thing coming to fetch me,' she said. The expression in her face was decidedly glum. She was definitely down among the wines and spirits. It was probably the sort of expression Napoleon wore as they were cleaning up the loose ends after the Battle of Waterloo.

Then Lady Pamela turned around and strode off purposefully in the direction of the distant Plumwood Hall.

I watched her electric torch click on and the faint beam bob away into the darkness. Drax stood in the doorway watching her go. Then he closed the door and I heard bolts and bars sliding into place.

Suddenly it occurred to me that if I didn't follow Lady Pamela I would quickly become completely lost on those moonlit moors. I took off as rapidly as I dared and followed in her footsteps. Happily I picked up the distant torch beam and was able to follow at a safe distance all the way the back to the Hall.

When I finally climbed back into my welcome bed, the bedside clock told me it was now a little after three o'clock in the morning. That, I thought, was the strangest two hours of my life. If I were a poet instead of a novelist, I thought, I would definitely turn that into a poem. Then I fell asleep.

THIRTY-SIX

~

After breakfast the next morning I hurried down to the village to report my strange night-time adventures to Jack. I found him sitting in the sun on a wooden bench in front of *The Cricketers' Arms* contentedly puffing on his after-breakfast pipe and serenely contemplating the purpose of life. Or possibly—since I knew how his mind worked—he was thinking about the use of prepositions in Milton's shorter poems. Whatever it was, it had clearly put him in a sunny mood.

'You'll never guess what happened to me last night,' I said, flopping down onto the bench beside him, feeling rather like a music hall comedian who has just learned a new joke and is keen to launch the ripsnorter on an audience.

'Never? In that case,' said Jack cheerfully, 'I won't attempt to guess—you can tell me.'

I began to do so. I laid on the colour to make the tale as vivid as possible. Perhaps I was labouring the atmospherics and taking too long to get to the heart of the matter, because I'd only got to the point of me leaning out of my bedroom window when we were interrupted.

The white-haired old apothecary, Arthur Williamson, came puffing up the street, red-faced and looking quite alarmed. This normally calm and serene old gentleman looked as if he had pulled on his boots after breakfast only to discover that a slug had crawled into the left one overnight and was now somewhere between his toes.

However, it turned out to be rather worse than that.

'Do you gentlemen know where the police officers are?' he wheezed as he tried to catch his breath.

'Which police officers?' I asked.

'Any of them. Constable Nile will do. Or those Scotland Yard men—are they about?'

I said I hadn't seen any of them, and Jack concurred that he too had so far spotted none of the official upholders of the law that day.

'Oh dear me, dear me,' the old man flustered, flapping his hands like a seal at the zoo asking for another fish. 'I am most concerned, most concerned, and I want to alert someone, but I can't leave my shop for long. I should be back there now.'

'You tell us,' said Jack helpfully, 'then we'll find a policeman and pass it on.'

'Would you? Would you, really? Oh thank you, thank you.' The old chemist took a deep breath and then said, 'Young Ruth Eggleston has disappeared. My shop assistant. You must remember her—you both met her the day you came to my shop.'

I said yes, I remembered, and Jack said, 'What do you mean, disappeared?'

'Well, she failed to turn up for work this morning. That in itself is most unusual. She has shown herself to be a very reliable girl. Not like most of these young people today. And if she's indisposed she always sends her younger sister to tell me. This morning there was no Ruth and there was no message. And I have to go across to Market Plumpton today to collect a parcel of supplies from a pharmaceutical company—one of the chemists in Market Plumpton is holding the parcel for me. But I can't leave my shop if Ruth isn't there.'

He stopped to mop his brow with a large white handkerchief, sat down heavily on the bench beside us and then resumed, 'So I went around to her house. Ruth's mother was also concerned—a very nice woman, Ruth's mother, I've known her all her life. It seems that Ruth didn't come home last night. Her mother didn't realise this until this morning. She just assumed Ruth had come back very late and let herself in. But when she checked Ruth's bed it hadn't been slept in. So where is she? Where has she got to?'

Arthur Williamson looked left and right, up and down the village street, almost as if he expected to see his missing shop assistant pop out of one of the cottage gardens like a jack-in-the-box with a cheerful cry of 'Had you going there for a minute, didn't I?'

'Such strange things have been happening around here lately,' he continued, in the absence of the hoped for appearance. 'Very strange things. Perhaps I'm being a foolish old man, but I'm most concerned.'

'We'll find a policeman,' said Jack, patting the old man comfortingly on the shoulder. 'You get back to your shop, and we'll pass on your concerns to the proper authorities.'

'Would you? Oh, that's most kind of you, most kind indeed,' he replied. Then he rose, a little stiffly and awkwardly, from the wooden bench and waddled off down the street in the direction of his shop.

Jack and I then set off to carry out the commission we had undertaken.

We started in the pub, but were told by Alfred Rose that both Inspector Crispin and Sergeant Merrivale had left for the day. They had left early, he said, and not told him where they were going.

We then walked up the street in the direction of the police cottage. We arrived to find the village bobby, Constable Charlie Nile, just coming out of his front gate, looking, as he always did, like a clumsy but rather likeable puppy.

Jack reported Arthur Williamson's conversation, passing on the old chemist's concerns about the missing girl.

Charlie Nile seemed singularly unimpressed. 'Young people sometimes do stay out all night,' he said, with a knowing smirk as he rocked back on his heels and did his best to radiate benevolent tolerance towards the strange behaviour of the younger generation.

Jack was not happy with this.

'May I suggest, my dear Nile,' he boomed, 'that there have been two poisonings in this district in a matter of a few days. This is not the time to take the disappearance of a young woman lightly.'

Nile pushed back his helmet and scratched his head. 'Do you really think so, sir? I mean to say, if this is not just high jinks or gallivanting around then . . . do you think I should really call up district headquarters?'

Anything beyond a serious case of littering in the village street seemed to paralyse Constable Nile into indecisive inaction.

'Make the phone call,' said Jack in his hearty, forceful voice, 'there's a good chap.'

'Yes . . . yes . . . I think perhaps I'd better. Just step into the police cottage and I'll put you on the line, Mr Lewis, to pass on the details you know.'

We followed Nile into the little ivy-covered cottage. As he was dialling the number he said over his shoulder, 'I happen to know that those Scotland Yard men, Inspector Crispin and

Sergeant Merrivale, are at Market Plumpton police station this morning having a meeting with Colonel Weatherly, the Chief Constable. Oh, hello? Yes, it's Constable Nile here. Yes, from Plumwood. It seems a girl has gone missing from the village—I need one of the senior officers, please.'

There was some more uncertain to-ing and fro-ing for a while, and then the constable said, 'He wants to speak to you, sir,' and handed the phone over to Jack.

From hearing one side of the conversation I worked out that Jack was speaking to Inspector Crispin. In short, clear sentences Jack laid out the case that Mr Williamson had presented to us—Ruth Eggleston absent all night, bed not slept in and mother having no idea where she might be.

At the end of his conversation Jack handed the phone back to Constable Nile and said to me, 'Crispin agrees that it might very well be serious. He's organising a search. Bearing in mind the transparent lie she told about you buying the missing cyanide, Morris, it's not impossible that her disappearance is connected in some way with these murders.'

Nile's conversation was short, and consisted, on his part, mostly of grunted 'yes, sirs'. When he put the phone down, he said, 'They're going to make inquiries at railway stations and start a wide area search. He's told me to go from door to door in the village and ask if anyone's seen her.'

'Well, you'd better get on with it then,' boomed Jack, handing Nile his helmet, which had been lying on the hall table.

Outside in the sunshine Nile set off in one direction while Jack and I walked towards the other end of the village street.

Jack re-lit his pipe and then said, 'Now, Morris—you were in the middle, or possibly just at the beginning, of an interesting yarn. Please continue.'

'Ah, yes,' I said, 'my strange experiences of last night. This disappearance of Ruth Eggleston put that entirely out of my head. Where had I got to? Yes, that's right, the voices outside on the lawn at one o'clock in the morning. Well, what happened was . . .'

And I proceeded to tell Jack the whole story.

THIRTY-SEVEN

~

At the end of my colourful yarn Jack was quietly thoughtful for a long time. We had some time ago passed the end of the village street and kept on walking down the narrow country road with high hedges on both sides.

'Well, Jack?' I prompted when I grew tired of the silence being broken by nothing more than a lark giving an impromptu encore to its dawn chorus.

'There's one explanation that would fit your observations of last night,' he said quietly, in a kind of thoughtful rumble. 'But I don't see how it fits in with the murders. Perhaps it doesn't. Perhaps it has no connection at all.'

Then he lapsed into silence again. I was reluctant to speak, seeing that Jack's mighty brain was busy firing away on all cylinders, but I couldn't restrain myself. 'Well?' I asked, 'What about the murders? Can you see any light at the end of that particular tunnel?'

'Just possibly, young Morris,' Jack said. 'You know—I think I mentioned to you once—as an undergraduate I read philosophy as well as Greats and English. In fact, my first job was as a tutor in philosophy.'

'I didn't know that.'

'It wasn't at Magdalen—it was at University College. I mention this only because this puzzle looks rather like one of those algebraic formulas we use in formal logic. There are times when it looks like a problem in propositional calculus and sometimes rather more like predicate calculus.'

'I've never read philosophy so none of that means anything to me.'

'It doesn't need to. I'm simply saying that I see a glimmer of light—of logical light—that may make complete sense of everything. However, I need more information. There are still pieces of the puzzle missing.'

With that Jack lapsed back into ruminative silence, puffing furiously on his pipe, as if the clouds of smoke were trying to keep up with his whirling mental processes.

'Do you think Inspector Hyde is still after my head?' I asked, unable to keep my anxieties to myself.

'Probably,' said Jack. 'But there's no need to worry about Hyde.'

No need? Easy for him to say. I was the one Hyde wanted to see strung up. Was Hyde at that meeting in Market Plumpton with Crispin and the Chief Constable? Was he, even now, arguing that an arrest warrant be issued for that well-known homicidal maniac, Tom Morris?

Jack was deep in thought so I held my peace and looked around me.

The day was entirely out of keeping with my inner sense of gloom and confusion. If the weather had mirrored my soul it would have been dark and stormy. It wasn't. Showing marked insensitivity, it had swung in entirely the opposite direction.

The sun was shining, the sky was blue, birds were singing and a gentle breeze was sighing softly through the under-growth. It was the sort of morning that gets poets scribbling down notes and muttering, 'I can get something good out of this.'

But not for me. In fact, if the poet Browning had, at that moment, leaped out from behind a bush and said, 'The lark's on the wing; The snail's on the thorn: God's in His heaven—All's right with the world!' I would probably have socked him on the jaw and told him he didn't know what he was talking about.

Jack was a sensitive soul, and the moment he emerged from his deep reverie he picked up on my mood.

'Unburden yourself, young Morris,' he said cheerfully. 'You look as though you're carrying the weight of the world on your shoulders.'

Slowly, and uncertainly, I began to speak of the things that troubled me.

'Under the shadow of the scaffold,' I began, 'and don't try to reassure me, Jack, for I know how narrowly the odious Inspector Hyde is pursuing me. If the Scotland Yard man can't solve this baffling case, Hyde will, most likely, get his way. So, as I say, under the shadow of the scaffold I must face the prospect of death.'

I kicked at a stone in the road, and then resumed. 'And my problem, Jack, is that I don't like any of the options.'

Jack nodded sympathetically, so I continued. 'If the Materialist is right, at death I will be annihilated. Quite frankly, that's most unappealing. I don't want to be snuffed out like a candle—either from a hangman's noose or from old age. If the real me, the person that I am, is going to be extinguished, I can't see that my life means anything. My life would be nothing more than a brief spark in a dark vacuum. That's a most unattractive option. I quite hope that's not true.'

'In so thinking,' Jack replied, 'you stand with most of humanity. It's normal to feel the flicker of eternity—the deep desire, the longing, in the human heart for that which is greater. Last year I went to a funeral in the college chapel for a former fellow who was a pronounced atheist. He'd been a belligerent philosophical materialist all his life. And yet, at his funeral, people spoke as if he still existed. "I'm sure he's looking down on us now and smiling," I heard someone say. No one embraces annihilation, and few genuinely believe in it.'

'And you say that our longing for something more is evidence that there *is* something more?'

'Our hunger for food is evidence that food exists; our hunger for more than this life is evidence that this life is not all there is.'

'But, you see, I'm not sure I like *any* of the options. If annihilation is, thankfully, untrue, I don't like the option the spiritualists offer me either. They speak of some sort of disembodied existence. They talk about spirits drifting, unseen, around the places they occupied during their embodied lifetimes—popping into the occasional séance to pass on a message or two. Well, I'm quite fond of this body of mine, and any existence in which I'm a mere wraith, a floating, disembodied soul, seems pretty hollow.'

'The good news is that ghostly haunting is not the future that awaits us. Christian teaching is that our future can be far, far better than the unsatisfying shadowy one you've just sketched.'

'But I don't like your option either!' I protested. 'Sitting around in clouds, wearing wings, strumming on a harp—that certainly doesn't appeal to a red-blooded person like me!'

Jack threw back his head and roared with laughter. 'My dear Morris, you mustn't be led astray by medieval artists and modern cartoonists,' he hooted.

I was a little put out by this reaction, and I think my face must have shown it.

Still chuckling, Jack said, 'It's not your fault, Morris.

Popular misconceptions circulate so widely and run so deeply we can absorb them uncritically without ever seriously examining them. I suspect we absorb the clouds-wings-harp parody of eternity in childhood and never think about the subject seriously as adults.'

'Very well,' I challenged, feeling in a belligerent mood, 'give me an option for the future that is neither unpleasant nor unappealing.'

'Certainly,' the beaming Jack replied. 'The answer is found in the word resurrection. We need to understand that our individual stories make sense precisely because they are part of a much bigger story.'

He paused to relight his pipe. As he did so we turned off the road onto an even narrower country lane that curved back towards the village.

Jack took a deep breath and said, 'The big story runs something like this. God is the Loving Maker and Ruler of this world. What he made was all this.' He gestured at the rolling fields around us and the sky above us. 'In other words, a physical world inhabited by physical beings. Among those physical creatures were human beings. Those human beings had a special role to play—as God's agents or representatives, managing this world according to his directions. That was where it began. It's a picture of perfection. But then it went wrong. Or rather, we went wrong. Our primeval parents, those first human beings, rejected God's directions and went their own way.'

'You see,' I objected, 'that's the bit I don't understand. If God is perfect, and his creation was perfect, how could that sort of rebellion happen? Does God have limitations?'

'As it happens, God has one limitation: he cannot act against his own nature. When God gave the first human beings freedom, it was perfect freedom, real freedom—not fictional freedom, not pretend freedom. He made people, not puppets. And our primeval parents abused that freedom by freely choosing to reject God. For God's own people, God's own representatives and agents, to reject his rule was a major breakdown—a tear in the fabric of space and time. And through that tear in space and time, death entered.'

Jack paused to look at me. He gave me the same sort of quizzical, questioning look I had seen so often in tutorials. Seeing that I was keeping up with his argument, he continued.

'That gives us the bookends to the big story—it travels from Creation to New Creation. Human history is a story that travels through the dark valley of a corrupted, fallen world—but it's travelling towards a future in which Creation is restored.'

'But this world is a good place!' I protested.

'Quite correct, Morris,' Jack agreed. 'It is a good place. It's just not good enough. Along with the sunshine, the love and the laughter, there are pains, anxieties and tears—evidence that this world is damaged and that history is sweeping us along towards a time when the hurts will be healed. That's why the long-term promise for Christians is one in which our post-mortem existence occurs in bodies made new and whole—resurrected bodies.'

'Not that I see a lot of resurrected people walking around just yet,' I sneered cynically.

'Renewed Creation, resurrection, is the bookend at the far end of the story of human history. But its promise makes it clear that there is something more substantial planned than strumming harps in clouds.'

'Well, if that were true it would be most comforting,' I said, still feeling in a rather cynical mood. 'But in the meantime, what happens?'

'We're not told exactly,' Jack replied, quite comfortably.

'I doubt we'd understand if we were. But we can be safe in the hands of a God who loves us and made us for relationships— with himself and with each other. Remember what Jesus promised to the repentant thief on the Cross beside him: "Today shalt thou be with me in paradise." The Christian's immediate future is in safe, powerful hands. And his long-term future is restoration to a restored physical world in a new restored body.'

'That's rather a novel idea, isn't it?'

'It's in all the Christian creeds. And the idea itself is many thousands of years old. Millennia ago, poor old Job, surrounded by his comfortless comforters, said, "Though worms destroy this body, yet in my flesh shall I see God." Does resurrection in a restored, perfected physical world appeal to you as an option?'

'More than any of the alternatives,' I admitted.

THIRTY-EIGHT

~

We got back to the Plumwood pub—*The Cricketers' Arms*, Alfred Rose prop., licensed to sell beers wines and spirits—in good time for lunch. Mrs Rose offered us bread, cheese, pickles and cold ham. That particular combination of ingredients is, I'm told, called a 'ploughman's lunch'. I'm not sure how the law stands on this matter, since neither Jack nor I are ploughmen. But we were hungry enough to regard ourselves as honorary ploughmen, at least until after lunch.

We took our plates of food and pints of bitter out into the sunshine of the beer garden behind the pub. The spring weather was still in an extremely jolly mood and kept nudging us with stray sunbeams and puffs of soft breezes to join in the fun. Relax a little, it seemed to say—what can you worry about on a day like this?

Even I was finding it hard to stay glum with a pint of bitter in my hand and the sun in my face.

After a few minutes Inspector Crispin and Sergeant Merrivale arrived. Jack beckoned them to join us at our table. As the inspector walked over, he gave us a detailed weather report.

'Nice day,' he said.

Then Jack asked, 'How goes the investigation?'

'Frustratingly slowly,' the Scotland Yard man admitted as

he pulled up a chair and sat down. 'And I had to spend my morning saving your hide again, Mr Morris.'

'How so?'

'I thought my use of the word "hide" might give you a clue,' Crispin smiled.

'Oh, I see,' I mumbled. 'Inspector Hyde is still on my trail, I take it?'

'Oh, he fancies you for these murders, sir,' growled Sergeant Merrivale, with an unpleasant smile on his face. 'There's no doubt about that.'

As he spoke my heart sank. It seemed to me that so far Inspector Hyde had just been tootling around and now he intended to roll up his sleeves, spit on his hands and really get to work—the job of work in question being yours truly, Suspect Number One. If Hyde started throwing his weight around there was no telling what he might pull off. I feared the next time I saw Hyde I might have to fight him off with a blackjack.

'How is the search for Ruth Eggleston going?' Jack asked.

'No news so far,' said Crispin.

'Do you believe her disappearance might be linked to the murders?'

'I very much fear it is. That's why I've sent word to every town in the vicinity, and put every local village constable on door-to-door inquiries. I'd be delighted if she turned up and said, "What's all the fuss about?" but I fear that's unlikely to happen.'

Some silence followed as we applied ourselves to our food with the diligence it deserved. Jack as always ate quickly, and this time he saluted Mrs Rose's efforts by cleaning his plate in a matter of minutes.

When Inspector Crispin had caught up, he said, 'Now, Mr Lewis—I respect that deductive, detective mind of yours.

No doubt at some time in the near future there will be tourist coaches bringing goggle-eyed visitors to your door just to catch a glimpse of your mighty brain.'

Jack roared with laughter. 'They'll have to wait until I've finished with it,' he said. 'Then it can be pickled in formaldehyde and put on display in a local museum.'

'But right now,' Crispin persisted, 'I want you to apply it to this baffling mystery of ours. Who poisoned Connie Worth? And how on earth did they do it? Getting cyanide into her slice of cake, and hers alone, seems plain impossible. So how was it done? And who murdered Miss Stephanie Basset? And why? What hints or suggestions can you offer, Mr Lewis?'

This question prompted a long and detailed discussion. As it got underway, Sergeant Merrivale pulled out his ubiquitous little black notebook and began jotting down the ideas the two men threw up.

Jack and the Scotland Yard detective began by going through each of the possible suspects, starting with the family members at Plumwood Hall: Sir William Dyer, Lady Pamela, the boys Douglas and Will, and strange old Uncle Teddy. Then they went on to discuss the staff: Keggs the butler, Mrs Buckingham the cook, the various maids, and the head gardener, Hugo Franklin. They then considered the villagers and their possible involvement, with a special focus on the missing girl, Ruth Eggleston.

Crispin brought the discussion back to the first victim, Connie Worth, to focus on his theory that understanding the victim was the key to the solution. And she did seem to be the thunderstorm that started this whole thing. They talked about her as the probable murderer of her husband Charles, the possible murderer of her cousin Judith Trelawney, and the likely blackmailer of Sir William Dyer. They weighed up the possible value of confronting Sir William with the blackmail question, but seemed doubtful of the value of doing so at the moment.

But the talk always came back to the method: how was a fatal dose of poison delivered to a single slice of freshly baked cake, invisibly, in front of a table full of witnesses?

Crispin scratched his head and admitted he hadn't a clue, and then asked, 'What about you, Mr Lewis?'

A little reluctantly, Jack said, 'I have a vague idea forming in my mind. It's so strange I need to think it through before I share it. This notion doesn't seem very probable but it's beginning to look possible—and it would explain everything."

And that's all he would say on the subject.

The discussion moved on to the supply and delivery of the poison. And throughout all of this, much of the talk was in cryptic hints that may have meant something to Jack and Crispin, but which I couldn't follow.

Inspector Crispin was lighting a cigarette and Jack had his pipe going when a red-faced Constable Nile came huffing and puffing into the beer garden.

'Ah, I've found you,' he gasped. 'I've been looking all over for you.'

'What's up, constable?' growled Sergeant Merrivale, flipping closed his notebook and returning it to his pocket.

'A body's been found.'

He stopped after this cryptic utterance and had to be urged to continue.

When he did, he said, 'A young woman's body. It's been spotted by some fishermen at the foot of the cliffs not far from Plumpton-on-Sea. And I've turned up nothing with my door-to-door inquiries, sir, and so I thought perhaps . . . possibly . . . it might be young Ruth.'

'The body hasn't been identified?' asked Inspector Crispin.

'It hasn't been recovered yet, sir. It's at the foot of steep cliffs, and the waves are strong, so the fishermen who spotted it haven't got to it yet.'

Crispin and Merrivale looked at each other—a dark, knowing look. Then with one accord they both rose from the table.

'We'd better go and take a look ourselves, constable,' said the Scotland Yard inspector. 'Sergeant, bring the police car around to the front of the pub. Constable Nile, you come with us.'

Crispin nodded in our direction, then the three police officers left.

'What do you make of that?' I asked, turning to Jack.

'The inspector is right,' said Jack as he slowly rose from his chair. 'We need to go and take a look for ourselves.'

'You mean us two?'

He nodded and asked, 'How can we get to Plumpton-on-Sea?'

'Well, there's a local train . . . I don't know when the next one is due.'

'Then it's off to the railway station to find out. Come along.'

As we hurried up the village street towards the station, I asked why it was important for us to be there when the body was examined.

'I have a suspicion,' said Jack earnestly, 'that this corpse *will* turn out to be Ruth Eggleston. If it is, then her death, and the manner of her death, will tell us something more about the murderer, and about how desperate the murderer is becoming.'

At the railway station we found the one and only permanent employee (the station master cum porter cum ticket collector), who told us that a train would arrive in half an hour and sold us tickets.

The local railwayman turned out to be as reliable as Bradshaw, and thirty minutes later we were steaming towards Plumpton-on-Sea.

THIRTY-NINE

~

The slow local train consisted of two carriages and a guard's van pulled by an ancient locomotive. This clanked and hissed and wheezed asthmatically, and when faced by the smallest hill seemed to pause to contemplate early retirement rather than tackle a slight upward incline. Finally, with a deep steamy sigh of relief, the little engine got us to our destination—Plumpton-on-Sea.

In golden sunshine, and with a fresh breeze blowing in from the sea, Jack and I walked down the hill from the railway station to the little town and the sea front.

The tide had retreated, leaving most of the local fishing fleet lying on the mud bank. No policemen were in sight. In fact, the sea front was deserted except for a group of men standing, in a listless way, in front of the Fishermen's Co-op.

As we walked up to them Jack, who could be at ease in any company, introduced us and asked about the body that had been found.

'Aye, Jeb saw it this morning—when he was collecting his lobster pots out beyond the wash,' said one of the older men slowly, doling out each word as if it was a gold coin and he wanted to spend it carefully.

I asked if the police had recovered the body yet.

'Oh, aye,' replied the same old man, seemingly the spokes-man for the group. Then he fell into a lengthy silent meditation on the meaning of life, the universe and everything. This seemed to exhaust him because he lowered his aging bones onto an upturned barrel before he went on, 'Two of the young chaps climbed down the cliff to where the body was. It was George's boy, Caleb, it was, and young Jeb. Aye, they climbed down and fastened a rope onto the body, so the police could pull it up to the top of the cliff, like.'

He continued in his slow, methodical way to explain the risks that George's boy, Caleb, and young Jeb had run climbing down that cliff.

'That rock crumbles, it does. Not safe at all. But the tide is rising, so you couldn't get around the base of the cliff. No one could. And there's a swell today. We saw that when we went out, didn't we, boys?'

The boys, all of whom were middle aged, nodded and muttered in agreement that there was indeed a swell and that they had indeed noticed this fact when they took their boats out that morning.

'So that means waves, you see,' continued the old man of the sea, squinting at Jack. 'Big waves. So you can't walk around the cliffs, and they had to get the body up quick like, before the waves picked it up and carried it out to sea.'

Jack managed to indicate that he was deeply interested by this detailed narrative before asking if they'd succeeded.

'Oh, aye. They did that. They brought poor wee girlie into the village and put her on a bench in the old boathouse over there. The police doctor is looking at her right now.'

Jack, who seemed to have picked up on the conversational etiquette that these fishermen expected, then chatted about the weather and asked them about the catch.

When these conversational decencies had been observed, we thanked them for their help and made our way to the old boathouse on the far side of the stone breakwater that protected the little harbour.

The door to the boathouse was standing ajar and voices were drifting out as we approached.

Inside we found Inspector Crispin, Sergeant Merrivale, Constable Nile and Dr George Henderson, the district GP. Lying on a wooden bench was the pale, battered body of poor young Ruth Eggleston. Their voices fell quiet as we entered the boathouse.

I felt a surge of mixed emotions—part sadness at the loss of so young a life and part anger at whoever had done this. I choked up a bit, and had difficulty getting my words out as I made some fatuous comment along the lines that it turned out to be Ruth after all.

'Do we know how she died?' Jack rumbled, and I could hear the faint tinge of anger in his voice.

Dr Henderson looked at Crispin as if asking for permission to speak. The inspector nodded and Henderson said, 'Not from the fall.'

He paused to draw a tarpaulin up to decently cover the corpse. Then he continued, 'There was almost no bleeding, you see. She was dead long before she went over the clifftop.'

'So it's clear, Mr Lewis,' said Crispin, 'that it's not suicide. She didn't kill herself out of remorse for that concocted farrago about the cyanide missing from the chemist's shop. It's a bit grim in here—let's get back out into the sunshine.'

We all thankfully followed his lead. Constable Nile was despatched to make a phone call to arrange for the body to be collected. Inspector Crispin turned to face the sea and took in a lungful of fresh air.

'Another murder,' he said.

'Do we know how?' I asked.

'I won't be able answer that,' replied the doctor, 'until after the autopsy. But I can say now there are no marks of violence on the body.'

Jack raised his eyebrows and nodded at Crispin who nodded back. Then Jack turned to me and explained their wordless communication. 'Most likely another poisoning,' he said.

In sombre silence the small group walked across the top end of the sloping, cobbled ramp that led down to the water towards Plumpton-on-Sea's waterfront pub. We all felt the need of a drink.

Five minutes later we were standing in the front bar parlour of *The Mermaid and Fisherman*, each with a pint of bitter in his hand.

'He's getting desperate,' said Jack, addressing his remark to Inspector Crispin.

'More than that,' the Scotland Yard man said, 'I think he's starting to panic.'

'He,' barked Sergeant Merrivale in his bulldog growl, 'or she. We haven't even settled that yet.'

'We're not getting any further forward,' Crispin agreed. 'What do we do? Wait until every suspect bar one is murdered and then arrest the last person standing?'

'Be assured, my dear inspector,' said Jack more cheerfully, 'that almost all the pieces of the puzzle are now in place. Almost all. There's one mystery my young friend Morris stumbled across last night. I believe it has no connection to the murder. Once I have assured myself of that fact, then much of the undergrowth will have been cleared away and I will see much more clearly.'

'So how do you piece together the story of Ruth Eggleston's death, Mr Lewis?' asked Sergeant Merrivale. 'What do you think happened?'

'Given the transparently false story she told us when we visited the chemist's shop,' Jack replied, 'she had some connection with the murderer. Based on that connection, and on what she did to protect the villain, it now seems fairly certain that the murderer came to see her as a threat. So last night he—or, as you say, sergeant, she—arranged to meet Miss Eggleston privately. Clearly, if this is another case of poisoning, something was consumed. Perhaps the murderer bought drinks. However it was done, Miss Eggleston was murdered. In the early hours of the morning her body was transported . . .'

'So the murderer must have a car,' Crispin interrupted.

'That seems most likely,' Jack agreed, 'and hence the body was transported to an isolated spot on the clifftop and thrown down onto the rocks below. The tide must have been falling at the time. In other circumstances the body might have been carried out to sea and her fate would have remained a mystery.'

'As it is,' Crispin responded grimly, 'we know there's someone out there we must identify and catch before there's another death.'

FORTY

~

Inspector Crispin apologised for not being able to offer us a lift in the police car. We understood that with Crispin, Merrivale, Nile and Dr Henderson there were four bulky men and a driver squeezed into a small black Austin and we had no desire to share their discomfort. Sardines well acquainted with the social confinement of a sardine tin would have complained of the lack of elbow room in that small black Austin.

We took the train.

The journey back to Plumwood was even slower than our outward trip to the coast. This time the train took the scenic route in a long curve that only after a series of stops at small rural halts would bring us back to the village.

It seemed that the same elderly locomotive that had carried us to the coast was still pulling the local branch line train, and in the interim its character had not changed. It still took a leisurely view of its task and had a relaxed attitude towards the timetable. This it seemed to regard as a mere approximation, a guess and no more, of where it ought to be and when. It was in no hurry to get back to its shed, and was prepared to linger over the journey, enjoying the bucolic scenery.

This gave us time to talk.

'Awful business,' I said, and Jack agreed.

'Does this latest death—I suppose I should call it this latest murder—give you any more pieces of the puzzle?'

'At best,' Jack replied, 'it tells me a little more about the mind of the murderer. And the more I know about the way that particular mind works, the less I like it.'

I asked Jack to explain, so he continued, 'There is an ingenious twisted darkness to that mind—a totally immoral viciousness that is unpleasant to contemplate.'

Talking about the murders was a grim and unpleasant subject, so I led our conversation in other directions.

'You said that the key to understanding what the future, ultimately, holds is found in the word resurrection?'

Jack agreed that he had said so.

'The problem,' I objected, 'is that resurrection is so fanciful. Now, I ask you, Jack, what do the inhabitants of cemeteries do? Nothing! They just lie there. And that's all that dead men have done since the dawn of history. Dead men stay dead. It's a universal truth that has never been broken. The dead have dropped out of circulation. They've stopped eating their lunches and have cancelled their magazine subscriptions. There just are no resurrection men around, Jack! It's never happened. And that makes it an impossible foundation for any sort of future hope.'

'Never?' Jack asked, raising one eyebrow.

'If it had ever happened it would be the biggest talking point in human history,' I asserted.

'It did, and it is,' Jack replied.

I told him to go on, and Jack raised the subject of the supposed resurrection of Jesus Christ from the dead.

'Just a myth!' I interrupted. 'Ancient myths are full of gods who die and are reborn. This is just another of those.'

This time Jack laughed heartily, 'I once thought exactly as

you do, young Morris. I remember one night Tollers and Dyson took me to task on just this point. Those ancient myths you speak of Tollers called "good dreams"—ideas planted by God in human cultures to prepare them for the Big Event he was always planning to pull off. And the evidence that he did pull it off is solid and well-documented historical evidence.'

'You'll never convince me of that,' I said with confidence.

'Would you like me to try?'

'I'd love you to try—but I warn you, there's little chance you'll succeed.'

Jack paused to light his pipe, and then said, 'You are familiar, of course, with church buildings?'

'Naturally. Substantial buildings, usually with crosses on them.'

'Precisely. You'll find them in every suburb, town and city.'

'What about them?'

'They shouldn't be there. Both logically and historically, they shouldn't be there. Without the resurrection of Jesus Christ from the dead, their presence is inexplicable.'

'But,' I protested, 'there are a number of major religions, so why do you say that Christian churches are surprising?'

'Because of the origin of Christianity. Judaism is the faith of a people, an identifiable ethnic grouping. Hinduism and Buddhism also have their foundations in the history of nations. So the survival and spread of these religions is hardly surprising. Islam spread by means of the military conquest of the Arabian peninsula. But Christianity had none of those advantages.'

He paused for a moment, just as he did in tutorials, for this point to sink in, then he continued, 'When Jesus was executed by the Roman authorities . . . and, by the way, that fact is undeniable.'

'How so?'

'The crucifixion of Jesus under the orders of Pontius Pilate, the Roman governor of the province of Judea, is recorded by both Christian and anti-Christian writers from the very earliest times. Roman and Jewish historians, as well as the gospel writers, record this execution. Jesus certainly died on a cross after only a few years of public life in or around AD 33.'

'I have no difficulty accepting that. But why does that make his resurrection any more likely?'

'Because the movement he started should have died with him. At the time of his death Jesus had a relatively small number of followers—probably around five hundred. Certainly not the tens of thousands following Islam, Hinduism, Buddhism or Confucianism. And those five hundred were neither rich nor powerful—for the most part they were tradesmen or minor civil servants. And when he was executed they were, understandably, terrified. Most of them fled from the scene of his execution and talked of abandoning the cause and returning to their old lives. They were defeated, disheartened, dispirited, depressed and ready to give up.'

Jack paused to relight his pipe and glance out of the window. 'However, just thirty years later these same men and women had spread the Christian message so far and so powerfully across the Roman Empire that the Emperor Nero could use them as scape-goats for the Great Fire of Rome. Thirty years, Morris—think on that number. That's about half a lifetime. Something must have happened to galvanise that small, defeated and dispirited group, something so astonishing, so life-changing, they were prepared to face martyrdom in the name of Jesus. They swept across the greatest empire the world had known up to that time and turned it on its ear. There was clearly something more than mundane human power involved there.'

He leaned forward and looked me in the eye, 'Something had turned their defeat into astonishing victory; something as amazing and life-changing as their leader, Jesus, coming back from the dead.'

'But . . . but . . . other similar groups from that time have survived,' I responded.

'Have they?' Jack asked with a smile and a glint in his eye. 'Have they? Christianity began as a movement within Judaism. At the time there were other similar movements within Judaism: the Pharisees, the Sadducees, the Zealots, the Essenes. Where are their buildings? In fact, where is the evidence they have survived at all? And the other religions of ancient Rome— Mithraism or the worship of Diana of the Ephesians—where are their temples in our cities, suburbs and towns?'

He leaned back, took a deep breath, and said, 'Without the resurrection of Jesus, the survival of Christianity and its spread around the globe—to become the largest faith on earth—is inexplicable. Logically Christianity should not exist. Its Founder was killed at an early age, crucified at a time when the Romans were crucifying thousands. Jesus Christ should be unknown to most of us—remembered only by those scholars who study the dusty, forgotten corners of ancient history. Instead of which, his is the most famous name on earth. Something of utterly astonishing power so changed his small, rag-tag bunch of followers that they changed the world. Nothing less than his resurrection from the dead explains that.'

Jack puffed his pipe in silence for a moment, then said, 'The resurrection meets Hume's criterion for a genuine, historical miracle—since the survival, and global spread, of Christianity can't be intelligently explained without it.'

I was silent for a while. I certainly couldn't deny the evidence of my eyes—the presence of Christian churches everywhere.

And I had never before thought of their existence as remarkable in any way.

'Of course,' said Jack, seeing my silence as an invitation to continue, 'there's all the other supporting evidence as well.'

'Such as?'

'Such as the failure of the authorities at the time to kill off the Christian movement at its very beginning by displaying the corpse of Jesus. They didn't because they couldn't. There was no corpse. The tomb was empty. And the hostilities between these galvanised and changed followers of Jesus and the authorities began at once. There was no crucified corpse to be put on display because the story Peter and the rest told was the literal truth.'

I looked out of the window at the fields slowly trundling by and tried to digest everything Jack had said. Finally, I conceded, 'I should investigate this further.'

'Excellent move, young Morris, excellent! Three or four years ago a book was published called *Who Moved the Stone?* It lays out all the historical evidence and is, in my view, unanswerable. But the important thing to understand is the personal consequences this truth has for your life.'

'My life? In what way?'

'If death has been conquered once—triumphantly defeated, in fact—it can be again. And the One who has already conquered death is the One who offers to take away the sting of death for you and me.'

FORTY-ONE

~

'Tonight I have a small adventure planned for us,' said Jack with a sense of glee. 'Meet me at nine o'clock on the terrace at Plumwood Hall. And bring a torch.'

We were walking down the village street from the railway station when Jack uttered these astonishing words. Jack was walking towards his dinner at the village pub and I was heading for mine in the oak-panelled dining room of Plumwood Hall, on the outskirts of the village. I say astonishing words because I had always thought of Jack as someone who found a walking holiday in the Cotswolds enough of an adventure. Now he seemed to be planning something on another scale entirely.

'What do you have in mind?' I asked, not unreasonably.

All I got in response was an enigmatic smile and the words, 'Wait and see.'

As he was about to enter the pub he turned back to ask, 'You can lay your hands in an electric torch, I take it?'

'I've seen one in the kitchen. I'm sure Mrs Buckingham will let me borrow it.'

'Excellent. And I have no doubt mine host Alfred Rose will be able to lend me one. Until nine o'clock then.'

It was late afternoon by the time I walked up the gravel drive towards the Hall. Dark banks of cloud filled the western horizon, piling up like some vast medieval castle in the sky and filling the landscape with an eerie olive and silver light. Occasional blood-red beams of the westering sun escaped from behind those cloudy towers and ramparts and somehow increased the threat that the night might end in a violent storm.

Dinner was a quiet, sombre affair. Conversation was sullen and desultory, and no one gave Mrs Buckingham's dinner the respect it deserved—pushing away only half empty plates still piled high with roast meats.

After dinner I retired to the library. I had found in the Plumwood collection a first edition of Johnson's *Rasselas* which I'd been saving up to read when I wanted to fill an hour or two. But I was restless and uneasy. Speculating on Jack's planned 'adventure', I put the book to one side and paced the library floor, wondering what he had in mind and what the next few hours might hold.

At nine o'clock I went up to my room, pulled on a pair of rubber-soled shoes and made my way, as quietly as I could, to the drawing room. The lights were off and it was empty, so I crossed the room, opened the French windows and stepped out onto the terrace.

The last of the daylight had disappeared sometime earlier, fading in a purple haze which a poet, or a depressive, might have described as the fading of all hope. I pulled the curtains closed behind me and gently shut the French windows.

The night was as black as a bat's wing at midnight. The evening was so quiet I could have heard a polite cough from a sparrow half a mile away. The air was filled with the kind of electric stillness that comes before a mighty thunderstorm. I looked up at the sky but could see nothing. The curtain of clouds blacked out even the faint glimmer of stars.

Then from the lawn just beyond the terrace I saw a brief

flash of light. I hurried towards it, squelching over the dew-wet grass to where Jack stood.

'You have your own torch?' he whispered.

I nodded. Then I realised he couldn't see me nod in that dungeon-like gloom, so I whispered my affirmative reply.

'Come along then,' he hissed. 'This way.'

When we had put some distance between ourselves and the house, I asked, 'What is this all this about? What are we up to?'

Jack, who had been walking briskly just ahead of me, stopped and turned around. 'Let's see,' he said, 'if we can solve the mystery of Drax and his cottage on the moors once and for all.'

We pushed on in silence after that, through bushes we couldn't see whose branches whipped back and struck us in the face, and over stiles that we had to clumsily feel for with our hands and feet.

There was no moon, and only faint, occasional glimpses of dim starlight when those dense clouds rolled back for a moment, like a gate swinging open in the cloudy castle above out heads. Then, just as silently as it opened, the gate would swing closed again, the cloud cover would be complete and even the feeble glitter of the starlight would vanish.

We used our torches sparingly, not wishing to be seen from the house or by any gamekeepers, or poachers for that matter, who happened to be about. We seemed to plod on endlessly into the night. A kind of mystical monotony gave our strange journey the feeling of a nightmare—as if, with every step we took, the object of our long walk retreated further away; the sort of haunting journey that happens only in dreams.

But that stumbling trek in the dark did finally end. As we reached the hollow that hid Drax's isolated cottage, the clouds parted giving a feeble glow of starlight. By then our eyes were so dark-adapted we were able to make out the faint outlines ahead of us in the dim, silvery light. The stand of pine trees between us and the cottage seemed to my fevered imagination to resemble a flock of black ravens. If those trees had taken wing and circled overhead uttering croaking cries of doom, I would not have been surprised.

Jack indicated with a gesture that we should be as quiet as possible. We picked our way through that copse making each footfall as gentle and silent as we could. At last we reached the cottage. Once again all the blinds were drawn, and only the faintest yellow gleam indicated that lamps were lit inside.

We approached the first window but were unable to see anything—the blinds covered the window panes from edge to edge. With Jack in the lead, we then slid silently along to the second window where, in an unusually careless moment, Drax had left a small kink in the blind.

Jack put his eye to the gap and looked for a long time. When he finally drew back he pressed his lips to my ear and whispered, 'Look. But don't cry out and don't say anything.'

We changed places and I pressed my eye to the window. What I saw astonished me.

I saw a man, an Englishman by the look of him, with a shock of blond hair. He had a pock-marked and scarred face. He was tied tightly to a chair, and he was sobbing. Drax was hovering over him. The prisoner looked wild-eyed at the South American native, who was, presumably, his captor. Those wide-open, pale-blue eyes swivelled franticly backwards and forwards and large drops of perspiration stood out on his forehead.

My heart was pounding, and my instinct was to thump at the cottage door, rush inside and free the prisoner. At that moment Jack laid a calming hand on my shoulder and patted me gently. Then I remembered his instructions not to cry out and not to say anything.

As I continued watching, Drax, who had been absent for a few moments, reappeared. He was carrying a bowl of soup and began feeding his prisoner slowly and carefully—spoonful by spoonful. When the soup was finished, the prisoner appeared a little calmer. He hung his head down on his chest and seemed to be visibly sobbing, although we could hear nothing.

Jack took my arm and gently pulled me away from the cottage. In that faint starlight he put his finger to his lips to indicate continued silence, then beckoned me to follow.

We retraced our steps through the trees and climbed the far side of the hollow. When Jack judged that we were far enough away, he asked, 'Well, what did you make of that?'

Following his example I kept my voice low, so I almost hissed, 'That native is holding a man prisoner! An Englishman by the look of it! Aren't we going to do something?'

'Yes, we are. I believe it's time for us to approach Lady Pamela and suggest, gently, that it would be for the best if the world knew the truth about Edmund.'

'Lady Pamela? Edmund? I don't understand.'

'Come along, back to Plumwood Hall—I'll explain on the way.'

FORTY-TWO

~

We re-entered the Hall by the drawing room French windows that I had carefully left unlocked. From there we went to the entrance hall and the foot of the main staircase. Here we encountered Keggs. He was making his last round for the night with his large bunch of keys, locking all the downstairs doors and windows. We had got back just in time.

The butler looked startled to see us. He obviously did not expect to find mud-spattered travellers staggering into the house after ten o'clock.

'Keggs,' I said, 'you remember Mr Lewis, don't you?'

He nodded his head but continued to regard us with relentless disapproval.

'It's important that Mr Lewis and I see Lady Pamela. Is she still up?'

'Her ladyship has retired to her room for the night. But her maid has not yet run her bath.'

'Well, would you let her know we're here please? And that we need to see her urgently.'

He hesitated. After a long moment he said, 'I take it this is a matter of the utmost urgency, sir?'

'You may so take it, Keggs,' I replied firmly. 'If you would please let her ladyship know.'

'Very well, sir. Perhaps you had better wait in the library. I'll tell her ladyship you're there. She will either come to you herself or send her maid.'

'She will come herself,' boomed Jack, 'if you say one word to her.'

'Sir?'

'Say *Edmund*—just that, and she will see us.'

'If you say so, sir.'

Keggs departed on his mission, and Jack and I climbed the stairs to retire to the library. In doing so we passed the door of Sir William's study, which was standing slightly ajar. In consequence we could hear voices from within.

'You'll not get another penny from me, Jackson—not another penny.' That was, unmistakably, Sir William's voice.

In reply came a strange voice, one I didn't recognise: 'You are the cruellest and most heartless businessman in the whole of England.' This was said not in an angry tone but in a sad, almost heartbroken one.

'Yes, and that's why I'm the success I am,' replied the biscuit tycoon.

Intriguing though this conversation was, it was no part of our present occupation and we moved on to the library.

We'd been there less than two minutes when Lady Pamela appeared. Her face was white—as white as Carrara marble, and it looked as hard as marble as well.

She stood just inside the library door and raised her eyebrows.

When Jack and I failed to respond to this invitation instantly, she said, 'I believe you gentlemen have something you wish to say to me?'

Just as she uttered these words the long-threatened storm began. A rolling, rumbling crash of thunder burst from the clouds and stamped in pounding footsteps like an angry giant across the fields towards Plumwood Hall. These sounds were followed in close succession by jagged flashes of lightning. Then Thor's hammer beat again against the clouds and this time the thunder sounded even louder. The next flash of lightning showed huge raindrops splashing against the library windows. These liquid pioneers were quickly drowned by their flood of followers. Soon the rain pounding and washing against the glass made conversation difficult.

Lady Pamela took several steps closer and demanded, 'Well?'

Jack's powerful voice rose above the storm with ease. 'We have just seen Edmund,' he said. 'Drax appears to be caring for him very well.'

Lady Pamela's face remained as hard as marble, and she showed no obvious emotion, but tears sprang into her eyes. She lowered herself unsteadily into a nearby armchair. Once she was seated, she seemed to collapse and sag into the leather upholstery—as if she were as boneless as a cat in front of a fire.

She opened her mouth several times to speak but no sound came. This imperious woman was looking more uncertain than I had ever seen her. Eventually she decided what she wanted to say. 'How much do you know?'

Jack dropped his authoritarian voice to a warm and sympathetic growl as he said, 'Enough. I can guess the rest.'

Lady Pamela waved impatiently at armchairs beside her own. 'Sit down, sit down,' she commanded.

We did as we were bid. A silence followed, broken ultimately by Jack, who said, 'It's a disease, I take it, that he contracted somewhere in the upper reaches of the Amazon.'

Lady Pamela nodded.

'When Drax got him downriver,' she said, 'he was still conscious, and still coherent. The first doctor who treated him spoke English and Edmund dictated a telegram to be sent to me. In that he warned me of the inevitable course of the disease.'

She looked up at the ceiling, as if preferring not to acknowledge our presence, and spoke in a quiet, but a clear and determined, voice. 'The next telegram came from the doctor telling us that Edmund's lucid moments were becoming fewer and fewer. The usual pattern of the disease was being followed: long periods of sleep, great weakness and confusion, with rare but dangerous outbursts of energy—usually violent, aggressive energy.'

She paused, so Jack and I waited.

'Then came the telegram from the doctor saying that he had exhausted his treatments, and no improvement could be expected. The condition, he said, led to lunacy followed by a rapid death.'

She took a deep breath, then said more firmly and confidently, 'I expected the next telegram would be the news of Edmund's death. Instead, to my great surprise, it came from Drax—whose English is excellent. He was offering to bring Edmund home to die. In one of his few lucid moments, Edmund had expressed that wish. The doctor was prepared to supply enough sleeping powders to keep Edmund heavily drugged for the duration of the sea voyage.

'Of course I wired him money and instructed him to proceed at once. I met Drax at Southampton myself. We had arranged an ambulance. We didn't bring Edmund back through the village. The ambulance stopped on a quiet country lane and Drax carried him to the cottage. Edmund is dying. There seems no point in damaging his reputation or distressing the family with the truth about Edmund's . . . lunacy . . . his violent outbursts . . .'

'So you pretended he was already dead?' asked Jack.

'It was the kindest thing to do all round,' insisted Lady Pamela. 'We had a decent Christian funeral for him with an empty coffin. The family mourned his passing, keeping Edmund's secret safe. And my dear brother will die here in England as he wished. When that happens, he will be buried next to the cottage where he now lives. Drax will be well rewarded for his faithfulness and care. And he will return to his people. That's all the future can hold for Edmund now.'

When she stopped speaking, the only sound was the flooding rainwater washing over the windows and walls of the old building.

There was only one table lamp switched on in the library. It cast a warm, buttery-yellow glow around us three in our armchairs. Beyond the reach of the lamp, the library disappeared in folds of dark shadows. It seemed an appropriate setting for such a sad and grim story.

'Have you had the best medical advice?' Jack asked.

'Those people in the Amazon Basin are experts in tropical diseases,' said Lady Pamela. 'If there was anything that could be done, they would have known about it and done it.'

'Still,' Jack persisted, 'the prognosis you were given has turned out not to be correct, hasn't it?'

'What do you mean?' she demanded, as haughty as ever.

'According to what that first doctor wired to you, your brother should be dead by now, shouldn't he?'

'Drax tells me he is surprised,' she admitted. 'He's never known any victim of this infection to last this long.'

'You may consider me impertinent, Lady Pamela,' said Jack in his warm, hearty voice, 'but may I make a suggestion?'

She nodded.

'Harley Street has its own share of experts in tropical medicine,' Jack said. 'I know there are medical men researching such diseases in my own university. Given his unexpected survival, might it not be wise to have the best available doctors re-examine Edmund? Might it not be wise to reassess his condition?'

Lady Pamela blinked away the tears that were once again beginning to form.

'Might there not be other treatments that have not yet been tried? To have survived this long he must have a strong constitution. That being so, perhaps it's time to tell the family the truth, to bring in new medical consultants—and to attempt a treatment, rather than just wait for his death.'

The rain had been thundering down steadily all through this conversation. Now it began to ease off. Lady Pamela rose, a little unsteadily, to her feet.

She took a few steps towards the library door, then turned and said, 'You've given me something to think about, Mr Lewis. And I thank you for that.' Then she was gone.

As I led Jack downstairs I asked him if he needed to borrow an umbrella. He insisted the rain had eased to a mere drizzle and he would be fine. Then I said I'd accompany him back to the pub—there was much we needed to talk about.

Keggs was waiting for us by the front door. We thanked him and set off briskly down the drive. I heard Keggs lock the door behind us, and I patted my pocket to make sure I was carrying my latch key as we walked swiftly towards the village street, and the light and warmth of the pub.

FORTY-THREE

~

At *The Cricketers' Arms* Mrs Rose offered us apple pie and clotted cream and a pot of tea for a late supper. We accepted enthusiastically.

Noticing Inspector Crispin and Sergeant Merrivale at their own supper across the room, I asked Jack, 'Should we pass on what we've learned about Edmund to the police? Or to anyone else?'

'Not for the moment. Let's give Lady Pamela the chance to make her own decision.'

I nodded in agreement and then went back to attacking the apple pie and clotted cream.

About three mouthfuls later another thought occurred to me. 'What did you make of that fragment of conversation we overheard coming from Sir William's study?'

Jack polished off the last spoonful of his apple pie, leaned back in his chair and lit his pipe.

'I think,' he said as he poured another cup of tea, 'that we've learned a little more about Sir William's character. Nothing surprising really, just a little more confirmation.'

'Does that count as a piece in your puzzle?'

'A small but useful piece,' Jack replied.

Ten minutes later we were instructing Alfred Rose to pass on our compliments to his wife for her home-baked apple pie when a shadow fell across our table. I looked up and saw it was the Long Arm of the Law—the shadow of Scotland Yard.

'Evening, gentlemen,' said Inspector Crispin, 'may I join you?'

Without waiting for a reply he pulled up a chair and poured himself a cup from our pot of tea. He took a sip and then took a biscuit from the plate in the middle of the small table.

'I love digestive biscuits with my tea,' he said. Then he examined the biscuit itself and added, 'and I do believe this is a Dyer's Digestive Biscuit. Your employer, Mr Morris, and the owner of the house where this mystery began.'

'If I were writing one of those mystery novels Warnie loves so much,' I said, 'I should call this *The Case of the Biscuits of Death*.'

Jack guffawed loudly. 'But really, Morris, you would be misleading your prospective reader. I'll grant you that the title has a certain ring to it, but in this case the cyanide was not in biscuits but in fruit cake and dry sherry.'

At this point Inspector Crispin helped himself to a second biscuit as he remarked quietly, 'And in the brandy.'

'Ah,' said Jack, instantly latching on to the point, 'the pathology report on Ruth Eggleston is back?'

'Exactly,' said the inspector, chasing his biscuit down with a sip of tea. 'Once again, it's cyanide poisoning. And from the stomach contents it appears she consumed the cyanide in brandy.'

'Would that be strong enough to hide the bitter almond taste?' Jack asked.

'To a young person not used to drinking brandy, it probably would,' the Scotland Yard man replied.

'If it comes to that,' I said, 'how was the bitter almond taste masked in the dry sherry? Wouldn't Stiffy Bassett have noticed something wrong with her sherry and refused to drink it?'

'Do you have a theory on that, Mr Lewis?' Crispin asked.

'What if,' said Jack, with a knowing look on his face, 'the killer put sweet sherry into the dry sherry decanter, and then added cyanide? The combination of sweet and bitter might have made it taste like poor quality dry sherry—but by the time the victim thought to make a complaint, she would have sipped just enough of it to kill her.'

'I do believe you're right, Mr Lewis,' said the inspector. 'And the fruit cake?'

'Well, many cooks include almonds in their rich, dark fruit cakes. Connie Worth may at first simply have assumed that she'd come across a bad almond—they can slip by even the most scrupulous of cooks. Once again, cyanide is swift acting and she was convulsing before she could complain.'

'That's exactly what the police have concluded, Mr Lewis,' agreed the policeman.

For a few minutes we drank our tea in thoughtful silence.

'Going back to poor Ruth Eggleston,' I said. 'Are you now convinced she falsified the record in the poisons book?'

'I am absolutely convinced, Mr Morris,' Crispin replied. 'However, I should warn you that my local colleague, Inspector Hyde, is not.'

'I can't believe that!' I protested. 'The poor girl is killed to keep her quiet and he still thinks I purchased the missing cyanide from the local chemist!'

'I'm very much afraid he does, Mr Morris. When we left him this afternoon he told us he was off to write up a report spelling out his case for your arrest. He intends to present this to the

Chief Constable, Colonel Weatherly, and press very strongly for a warrant for your arrest to be issued immediately.'

I think I must have turned pale at these words, for Jack laughed and said, 'Calm yourself, young Morris—an arrest warrant is not a death sentence. And for my good friend Inspector Crispin and me, the evidence is pointing in entirely another direction. Am I correct, inspector?'

'You are, Mr Lewis.'

'So how do you reconstruct the tragic story of young Ruth Eggleston?' Jack asked the policeman.

'She had some sort of relationship with the killer, that much is certain. Exactly what sort of relationship I'm not ready to speculate about just yet. But there must have been some sort of connection.'

'One strong enough,' Jack added, 'to motivate her to steal cyanide from the chemist's shop and then falsify the poisons book to make it appear that the missing cyanide had been sold to my friend Morris.'

'Precisely. And that must be a very strong connection. Just what it is will, no doubt, appear in due course.'

Another rumbling roll of thunder made itself heard just then—but faintly and at a distance. The storm was moving away.

Inspector Crispin reached into his top coat pocket and produced a folded sheet of foolscap paper. This he unfolded and lay on the table in front of Jack. It was covered with closely spaced typing.

'The autopsy report on Ruth Eggleston,' he explained. 'My sergeant doesn't approve of my sharing police documents with civilians. But when I'm baffled by a case, I'm not too proud to admit it, and I'm not too proud to ask for help. Read it, Mr Lewis, and tell me what you think.'

Jack picked up the sheet and read it just as rapidly as he read everything. A moment later he handed it back to the inspector and said, 'There are no surprises, are there? The killer talked her into stealing the cyanide and falsifying the poisons book. That's a key clue to the whole mystery. I believe those steps were taken early, when the killer was still laying his plans, and before Ruth Eggleston had any idea of why she was doing what she was doing.'

'And then,' said the Scotland Yard man, 'came the first death.'

'At which point,' Jack resumed, 'she must have become frightened. She tried to play her part and continue the deception over the poisons book when we visited the chemist shop. But she was clearly uncomfortable, and she must have been having doubts about what her friend had asked her to do. Sadly, instead of coming to the police, as she should have done, the foolish girl decided to tackle her friend. Perhaps she refused to believe he was capable of murder. Perhaps he was persuasive when he protested that the stolen cyanide had nothing to do with Connie Worth's murder. But as time went on, she must have found his protestations of innocence less and less convincing. I think he saw he was losing her. So he asked her to meet to talk the matter over one last time before she went to the police. Sadly, she agreed—and she walked to her death. He met her in some isolated spot, perhaps a regular meeting place of theirs. He offered her his flask of brandy—perhaps to steady her nerves, or because she was cold. She took a sip. She was sufficiently unfamiliar with brandy not to realise that the taste was all wrong. By then the cyanide was in her system. She would have died rapidly. Then the murderer disposed of her body in the manner we know he did.'

'You keep saying "he",' I objected. 'If Sergeant Merrivale

were here he'd insist on "he or she". Or are you saying that you know for certain the gender of the killer?'

Jack said, 'At this stage Sergeant Merrivale's qualification is probably still wise. But we're getting closer, aren't we, Crispin?'

'I believe we are, Mr Lewis. I believe we are.'

'Meanwhile,' I said, a little petulantly, 'Inspector Hyde is getting closer to me!'

FORTY-FOUR

~

Despite my late night I was awake early the next morning. I had slept badly, tossing in the bedclothes for much of the night with a dismal headache. Somehow the sheets and the blankets managed to creep off the bed in one direction and the counterpane in the other, while my pillow developed lumps I had never noticed before.

The best I could achieve all night was a little fitful and uncomfortable dozing. And from each doze I would wake with a fright, a cello player sawing away at the nerve endings in my brain and a persistent ringing in my ears. Then I would doze off again only to wake up cold and have to recover the bedclothes from the floor. These I made as comfortable as I could and eventually fell into a restless sleep.

When I finally awoke in the morning, I found one arm pinned under my body and riddled with pins and needles, while my feet had emerged from the blankets and were as cold as icicles.

When I tried to get up I discovered I had a crick in my neck and a headache that had just been waiting in the wings to return with a rush the moment I was vertical. My mouth, I found, was as dry as blotting paper and as rough as sandpaper. I downed the glass of water on my beside table, put on my dressing gown, grabbed a towel and made my way down the corridor to the bathroom.

Here I ran a hot bath, as hot as I thought I could stand, and sank into it with a sense of blessed relief. Once I had scrubbed, shaved and dressed in clean clothes I felt fully recovered and made my way downstairs to break my fast.

In the breakfast room Douglas and Will were helping themselves to generous servings of bacon and eggs from the sideboard. Uncle Teddy was already seated at the table, playing listlessly with a poached egg and staring at the piece of buttered toast in his hand as if he had never seen it before.

Just after I had helped myself to bacon, eggs, mushrooms and kidneys on toast, and taken my place at the table, Sir William and Lady Pamela entered the room together. But instead of going to the sideboard to load their plates with food, they stood just inside the door and surveyed us all.

Then they looked at each other, and Sir William said, 'Douglas, Will—there's someone we'd like you to meet.'

Lady Pamela stepped back into the doorway and led into the room a young man who came with her in shuffling, hesitant, reluctant steps. It was the same young man we had seen in Drax's cottage the night before. He'd been cleaned up and was wearing better clothes, but it was the same man. His blond hair was tousled, and there was fear and confusion on his scarred, pockmarked face.

'Boys,' said Lady Pamela, 'this is your Uncle Edmund.'

Douglas said, 'No—that's not Uncle Ed.'

Will said, 'But he's dead . . .'

Douglas said, 'It can't be!'

Will said, 'He looks a bit like . . .'

Douglas said, with a note of anger in his voice, 'Uncle Edmund has a headstone in the churchyard. He's buried there. This man is an imposter.'

Will said, 'I don't understand . . .'

'We'll explain,' said Sir William. And he told the story Jack and I had heard the night before from Lady Pamela.

'Your Uncle Edmund contracted a rare tropical disease in the upper Amazon. I believe it's some sort of mosquito-borne infection. It was Drax who saved his life by getting him down-river where he could receive medical attention. You can see the marks it's left on poor Edmund's face.' Sir William hesitated, so Lady Pamela took over. 'It's also affected his mind,' she said.

The boys stared, their eyes wide open in astonishment. Edmund staggered slightly and Sir William helped him to a chair. Then he turned back to his sons and resumed telling the story: 'He had the best medical care—from experts in tropical diseases. But we were told that his case was hopeless and that we should prepare ourselves for his imminent death. So we brought him back to England to die. It's what he said he wanted. His condition was pitiful, and he was dying, and the Edmund we all knew and loved was, in effect, already dead. So we thought it best to announce his death and give him a fitting farewell.'

Lady Pamela went to the sideboard and filled a plate with toast and scrambled eggs. This she placed on the table in front of Edmund. He stared at the plate as if he'd forgotten what to do with it.

'We thought,' Sir William continued, a little reluctantly, scratching his head as he spoke, 'that it wasn't fair to Edmund to reveal his true condition. We didn't want his old friends from the Explorers' Club coming here and insisting on seeing him. We didn't want anyone to see him in his unhappy state.'

The two boys had stopped eating, and were staring at their uncle with an astonishment that was slowly turning into comprehension.

'We thought he'd be dead by now,' said Lady Pamela. 'Drax

is surprised at how long he's survived. And I've now been persuaded' (she didn't say by whom) 'that, given his failure to succumb to the supposedly fatal effects of the disease, the time has come to tell the truth and bring in new medical consultants. And that's what we intend to do.'

Will got out of his chair and walked to the confused young man's side. He laid a gentle hand on his shoulder and said, 'It's good to see you again, Uncle Ed. Do you remember teaching me to use those South American weapons? I'm ever so good with them now. You can help me practise out on the terrace again—can't you, Uncle Ed?'

Sir William patted his younger son on the shoulder and said, 'It'll be quite some time before Edmund will be playing with you again, Will.' Then, after a long pause he added, 'If ever.'

Douglas looked sullen and growled quietly, 'I don't want any of my friends to know about this. If they ever heard that I had a mad uncle . . .'

'We won't be publishing Edmund's condition,' said Lady Pamela firmly, 'if that's what you're worrying about. We'll move him from the cottage here into the house. We'll quietly ask some Harley Street specialists to visit, to examine him and to recommend new treatments that haven't been tried.'

Douglas continued to look sullen.

Then a thought leaped unbidden into my head, and before I could stop it, it had escaped through my lips. 'The wild man of the woods!' I said.

Sir William heaved a deep sigh and said, 'You're perfectly correct, Mr Morris. The sightings of the so-called "wild man of the woods" happened on those rare occasions when Edmund was at his most agitated and managed to escape from Drax's protective custody.'

'What will happen to Drax?' asked Will.

'He's coming to live in the house as well,' Lady Pamela replied. 'Edmund finds comfort in his presence, so he shall continue as the principal carer. Although we may hire a trained nurse to assist him.'

'That's super,' said Will with enthusiasm. 'I want to get to know Drax better. I want to learn all about South America.'

Just then the silent Uncle Teddy spoke up. 'It's not a disease,' he said, a wild light coming into his usually vacant eyes, 'it's hereditary. There's madness in the family.'

I half expected him to tap himself on the chest and claim to be the living proof of this.

'Don't talk nonsense!' snapped Lady Pamela angrily. 'You're not Edmund's blood relative. He's from my side of the family, not yours. He has, most remarkably, survived a virulent disease, and he is now going to be given new treatments to help him recover further.'

FORTY-FIVE

~

'So,' I said to Jack later that morning, standing in the sunshine in front of *The Cricketers' Arms*, 'Edmund is a lucky young man who has survived a death sentence.'

'Postponed it,' said Jack between puffs as he got his pipe to light. Then he began walking up the hill into the sun. I fell into step beside him, knowing that he liked nothing better than to combine stimulating conversation and brisk walking.

As we turned off the village street into a country lane, he said, 'We have to be realists, not fantasists.'

I asked him what he meant.

'Simply that we must avoid the popular fantasies of our time.'

'Namely?'

'That either we shall not die, or that death is so far away we can ignore it, or that since death is inevitable we might as well live as if it will never happen. Pretence about death is the great unspoken taboo; the fantasy at the heart of our modern lives.'

'Nonsense,' I protested. 'It's normal to suppress thoughts of death since it's normal to be afraid of death.'

'Earlier generations of Englishmen didn't think so. As recently as our Victorian forebears, death was discussed,

251

written about and elaborately marked—both in ceremonies and in marble. That, I would suggest, was because they were still sufficiently influenced by the Christian foundations of our civilisation to be realists about death. Back in the eighteenth century John Wesley said something along these lines: "The world may find fault with our doctrine, but the world cannot deny that our people die well." Whatever you think of Wesley, he is looking death squarely in the face there. That is the realism our modern world flies from.'

The sun was shining and a fresh breeze was blowing. Above us a blue sky was decorated with wind-torn scraps of cloud. They looked like old posters torn by the wind from billboards and flung into the sky like untethered kites.

'So, tell me, young Morris, have you come to any conclusion in our debate on death?'

'At the very least,' I said cautiously, 'I'm persuaded that the materialist story is not the whole story. Valuable though our eyes are, they don't reveal the whole of reality. There is more to reality than our eyes can see. There really is, I now think, a realm beyond the merely material—and that very fact makes our post-mortem survival entirely reasonable.'

'Not only reasonable, but inevitable,' said Jack. 'If your mind, your self-consciousness, is a non-material thing and therefore cannot be snuffed out in the way mere matter can be snuffed out, then your survival beyond death is certain. Your physical body will one day succumb to physical death. But you, the real you, will survive. The only significant question is: how? In what state? Well, or badly?'

'And you say the people who avoid that question are the fantasists?'

'Indeed I do. Further, that the people who face it are realists.

That's what makes Christian believers the world's leading realists.'

'So Edmund has escaped from an immediate threat of death, but not from the ultimate threat of death that we all must deal with? What he has won is postponement, not ultimate survival?'

'Quite so. You see, young Morris, without knowing your current state of health, or the medical history of your family, there are two things I know about you that are absolutely true. The first is that you shall die. And the second is that you don't know when. You may survive to a great old age or you may fall under a bus tomorrow.'

'You are such a cheerful companion, Jack! You are such fun to be with,' I laughed.

Jack chortled with pleasure as he said, 'I'm simply inviting you to change sides—from the fantasists to the realists.'

'But I am comfortable being an unbeliever. Why should I change?'

'Because the question is not whether you shall survive death—you shall—but whether you'll survive it well.'

'What are the options? What might we find beyond this material world when death bids us depart?'

'Either a better world or a worse one. Our problem is that as a race of people we are not fit to inhabit a better world; we have filled the one in which we currently dwell with warfare, torture, famine, syphilis, poverty and much that is hideous and repulsive.'

'Hold hard there for a moment!' I protested. 'I'm not responsible for any of those things.'

'We've already travelled down that particular road, young Morris, and we've agreed that you are not perfect. I understand this from the inside, because I know how deeply morally imperfect I am.'

'So what conclusion do you draw?'

'For the moment let's call the better world we hope to inhabit when we shuffle off this mortal coil "paradise".'

'A common name for it.'

'Now "paradise" means, by definition, "that which is perfect". That is what makes it paradise. But if someone as imperfect as I am were admitted into its gates, it would no longer be perfect; it would no longer be paradise. So the better world I hope to inhabit beyond death ceases to be better simply because I'm there. This is clearly a problem. Something needs to be done about it.'

'I see the dilemma—so where do we find a solution?'

'It's already been found. It's the death of Jesus Christ in our place, as our substitute. On the strength of his death for us, Christ offers to forgive us and cleanse us—to wash us down, to dress us up, to make us presentable and acceptable to God as one of his people. That is the beating heart of Christian realism: "For Christ also hath once suffered for sins, the just for the unjust, that he might bring us to God." That's why Jesus could promise the repentant thief on the cross, "Today shalt thou be with me in paradise."

'So you see, young Morris, for us to enter a better world— and for it to remain better, even with us in it—we must be either perfect, or else forgiven and changed. The first is not possible, the second is.'

'Very well,' I admitted, 'if I decide I want to be a realist and do what you challenge me to do—to face death and to think about surviving death well—what is the key that opens that particular door?'

'There is only one door into the better world beyond death,

a door labelled "Forgiveness". And that door is a person—Jesus Christ. That's what he means when he says, "I am the resurrection and the life: he that believeth in me, though he were dead, yet shall he live." That's how the people I'm calling the world's leading realists understand death.'

We walked on in silence for a few moments, until I said, 'How can it possibly be that so many people—perhaps, for all I know, most people—can be fantasists about death? Why is realism not more widespread? Since death is a universal truth, why isn't realism about death universal?'

Jack gave a deep sigh and shook his head sadly, and in that rumbling voice of his he growled, 'Deceptions. The world is filled with deceptions—what Pascal calls "distractions". It's so easy to be deceived, to be distracted, by the pressures of everyday life—by everyday pleasures and everyday worries—to live for the moment and to plan no further ahead than next week or next month or next year. What people need—what you, I, what all of us need—is to be undeceived.'

'But how can I be *certain*—I mean *really* certain—about that better world that I might just possibly find on the other side of death?'

Jack smiled and gave me that look he always gave when he thought I was being unnecessarily slow on the uptake. 'In a walk through the English countryside, it's possible to be uncertain about the location of the next village, or a particular village you're looking for. But that's fine—as long as you know the road that will get you there.

'Warnie and I were out on a ramble a couple of years ago, planning to make our next stop in a town called Nesfield. Being uncertain, and fearing we were lost, we asked a local farm worker by the side of the road, "How can we get to Nesfield?" Perhaps he hadn't lived in the district long, or perhaps he'd never travelled more than a mile or two from his home village, but his answer was "I've got no idea where Nesfield is—but this is the road that gets you there." What matters about paradise, young Morris, is knowing whether or not you're on the road that gets you there.'

FORTY-SIX

~

I found Plumwood Hall in a state of disarray when I arrived back in time for lunch. The sudden reappearance of Edmund, and his settlement into the Hall, had put the place at sixes and sevens. Keggs looked distracted and maids were still rushing around getting Edmund's new living quarters ready for him.

Somewhere in the distance I could hear Sir William giving orders as a footman staggered past under a load of fresh linen. The house could not have been in more turmoil if the king had announced his imminent arrival for a brief, informal visit.

Well, I thought to myself, it's not every day that a favourite brother and uncle comes back from the dead. This, of course, set my mind back onto the lines Jack and I had been debating. Edmund had never really been dead. Jesus, on the other hand, had been certified as definitely dead by Roman soldiers who were experienced executioners. They were tough nuts unlikely to make a mistake. He'd been buried by his friends who'd also seen the dead body at close quarters. Then his grave was found empty and his followers insisted they'd been chatting to him. Rather a significant difference from Edmund's return from his non-existent grave. And rather more impressive.

In the meantime, Lady Pamela had allowed Will to take Edmund out onto the terrace to sit in the sun. Will was sitting beside his rediscovered uncle babbling away happily. Edmund did not seem to be taking any of this in, but that did not appear to bother Will, who kept on chatting. Douglas, on the other hand, I had encountered stamping sullenly down the gravel drive in the direction of the village and, I felt sure, in the direction of the village pub and a pint or two.

Feeling famished after my long morning walk I made my way to the kitchen.

'Hello, Mrs Buckingham,' I said cheerfully, 'what's happening about lunch?'

'Well may you ask, Mr Morris,' she replied without looking up from the ham she was slicing. 'It seems no one has the time to sit down to a proper lunch the way folk should, so I've been told to put a cold collation on the sideboard in the breakfast room.'

Then she looked up, took pity on me and added, 'Can I make you a nice ham sandwich, sir? Ham and mustard perhaps?'

I accepted her offer with alacrity. Ten minutes later I was sitting at my desk, near one of the tall windows in the library, with a ham sandwich and a cold glass of cider. Eating the last of the crusts, and brushing the crumbs off my desk, I looked up to see the odious Inspector Hyde walking down the drive towards the house.

As I watched he paused and pulled a folded piece of blue paper out of the inner pocket of his coat. This he unfolded and reread. Then, with an unpleasant smile on his face, he returned the paper to his coat and resumed walking. His eyes had the gleam of a rattlesnake that has just spotted breakfast.

That sheet of blue paper was, I was certain, the warrant for my arrest on a charge of murder. Hyde the Horrible had been hungry for that piece of paper for days now, and it seemed as if he had finally bullied poor old Colonel Weatherly, as Chief Constable, into agreeing that the warrant should be issued.

I suddenly had an empty feeling inside me. It was as if a vacuum pump had been applied to some of my major organs, with the result that from the chest to the hips I was rattling like an empty drum. They talk about having butterflies in the stomach; well, I had a large swarm of assorted winged insects knocking themselves out in my inner parts.

Leaving the library I hurried to the main hall where, on a side table, stood the only telephone in the house. The front door bell was ringing as I picked it up. I asked the local operator to connect me to *The Cricketers' Arms*.

Hearing a click at the other end, I said, 'Is that you, Rose?'

The local supplier of spiritous liquors agreed that it was.

'Is Mr Lewis there, please?'

In response Alfred Rose had to leave the phone to investigate. While he was away and the line was silent, Keggs glided gracefully to the front door and opened it, revealing the sinister form of Inspector Hyde on the doorstep.

'No, sir, I can't see him anywhere,' said Rose after picking up on his end of the line.

'Would you give him a message for me as soon as you can, please?'

The publican said he would.

'Please tell Mr Lewis that I'm about to be arrested . . . no, say that I *have* been arrested . . . and charged with murder.'

'That's outrageous, Mr Morris,' spluttered Rose over the phone. 'You're as innocent as a daisy, you are.'

'Thank you for your confidence, Mr Rose—but passing on the message is important and, I have to tell you, fairly urgent.'

He promised to get on to it at once and rang off.

I turned around to find Inspector Hyde standing by my elbow, smiling like a crocodile about to devour a native on the banks of the Nile.

'I have here a warrant for your arrest, Mr Morris,' he boomed like a railway guard making an announcement he wanted to be heard the length of the platform, 'on a charge of murder.' The volume went up ever further on those final words. Then he gave me an evil grin as his words echoed around the mansion. He may have had some doubts about whether there was enough evidence to convict me, but he was determined to embarrass me.

'You have the right to remain silent,' he continued, still under the impression that he was addressing the Albert Hall, 'but anything you do say may be taken down and used in evidence against you.'

'I'm innocent—use that in evidence against me!'

'Now, if you'd just come with me please, sir.'

'Hyde,' I said, 'you're an ass.'

'If you say so, sir, but you're still under arrest.'

'In fact, I'd say you're an ass in a million.'

'If you say so.'

'Worse than that, you're an ass in two million. Possibly in three.'

'If you say so. But you're still under arrest.'

By this time Keggs had re-entered the hallway and was staring at us.

'Is there anything I can do to assist you, Mr Morris?' he said in a dignified way. Then he made his own contribution to the situation by attempted to kill Inspector Hyde with a withering glance. It was a razor-sharp, knife-like glance that would have had most strong men buckling at the knees. But Hyde remained unwithered.

'Thank you, Keggs,' I replied. 'But I've left a message for Mr Lewis. He'll take care of things.'

'Oh, I doubt there's anything your important friend from Oxford can do for you now, sir,' cooed Hyde triumphantly. 'You will discover, sir, that the law will take its course.'

'Shall I inform cook that you won't be in for tea, sir?' asked Keggs, now giving Hyde the frost treatment by completely ignoring the policeman's presence in the building.

'That would be for the best, I think, Keggs. I anticipate that Inspector Hyde's mistake will take a little while to sort out.'

'Very good, sir,' said Keggs, as he turned and floated away, using the form of shimmering levitation known only to butlers.

'Now, Mr Morris,' said the inspector, 'will you come quietly?'

'Certainly not! I intend to make sarcastic remarks all the way from here to your odious police station.'

'Very well, sir,' grinned Hyde, his hand sliding towards his pocket, 'since you've informed me that you intend to resist arrest I shall have to handcuff you.'

'Don't pretend to be an even bigger idiot than you look, Hyde. In fact, come to think of it, no one could possibly be as big an idiot as you look. I am definitely *not* resisting arrest. I simply intend to provide a running commentary throughout his whole procedure.'

Disappointment flooded Hyde's face as he withdrew his hand from his pocket.

'In that case, sir, I'd like you to come with me now, please. I have a car waiting at the end of the drive.'

FORTY-SEVEN

~

I was sitting in a police cell. I had to keep looking around to convince myself this was all real. How had Mrs Morris's little boy come to be locked up in a police cell? And not for some bit of trivial fun, like stealing a policeman's helmet on boat race night. For murder. How had it come to this?

Well, I knew the answer, of course. The reason it had come to this bore the name of Hyde and had the face of a weasel and the heart of a skunk. That man was definitely off my Christmas card list.

This being my first police cell I took a look around. It was somewhat on the small side and was clearly in need of a decorator's touch. The bunk, the commode, the small table and the chair had all been painted in either light battleship grey or dark battleship grey. This seemed to show a lack of imagination. Or had the police station obtained a job lot of these two colours from the Amy and Navy Stores at a knock-down price?

All of the furniture was bolted to the floor. Perhaps this cell was frequently occupied by petty thieves and the fear was that unless everything was nailed down, one of these gentlemen might one day walk out with a chair, or possibly a small table, in his pocket.

I had failed to keep my promise of an ironic running commentary, and we had driven from Plumwood to Market Plumpton police station for the most part in sullen silence. Upon arrival I had been searched for dangerous implements and my fountain pen had been seized. What were they afraid of? That I would write a poison pen letter to Inspector Hyde? They also took away my tie and my shoe laces—presumably so that I could not hang myself from the light fitting.

The tie I understood, but had they taken a close look at my shoelaces? A mouse could not commit suicide with those shoe laces. Well, a very small mouse could, perhaps. But only if it was very determined.

In fact, I didn't mind not having a tie. I kept telling myself I was having an afternoon off, relaxing in an open-necked shirt. The shoe laces were another matter. Without them the shoes flopped loosely on my feet, and made scraping sounds on the concrete floor as I paced back and forth in that small cell.

I threw myself onto the bunk irritated by my own pacing, and annoyed by the scraping sound of my loose, flopping shoes. Turning my head to one side I saw where an earlier inmate had scratched a message in the wall. My first puzzlement was how this person had succeeded in conveying into the cell an implement sharp enough to make those marks. My second was to decipher what the message said.

Paint had flaked off over the years making much of the scratched message unreadable. However, picking up the words 'girl' and 'pearl' I decided it was an attempt at poetry. I tried to imagine some mute, inglorious Milton composing lyric verse to while away the hours in this inhospitable room.

The turning of a key and the loud slamming of bolts announced the arrival of a visitor. The cell door swung open to reveal the bulky frame of my old friend Constable Dixon. The two of us had met on an earlier visit to Market Plumpton.

'Dixon!' I cried. 'How delightful to see you again. How's your mother?'

'She's very well, sir. Thank you for asking.'

'And your feet?'

'Still giving me some trouble, sir, but I've found a new powder that's said to be a sovereign remedy for corns—so I'm about to try that.'

'Good luck, Dixon. I trust that your corns will vanish like the mist at sunrise.'

'You're very kind, sir.' Then he hesitated and recalled that he was here on official business. 'Ah, Inspector Hyde will see you now. If you'll just step this way please, sir.'

It was like being told that the dentist will see you now. And about as welcome.

I followed Dixon out of the cell and down a narrow corridor. He opened a door bearing the words 'Interview Room' and ushered me inside.

Inspector Hyde was already there and waiting for me. He was seated at a wooden table with the large, mute form of Sergeant Donaldson by his side. He waved me to the chair on the other side of the table, and I sat down facing him, waiting for the interrogation to begin.

There were papers spread out on the table, and Donaldson had a notebook and pencil in hand.

'Now, Mr Morris—' Hyde began, with a pretence of affability.

Before he could go any further I interrupted, 'But this is not right.'

'What's not right?'

'Don't you have to apply thumbscrews or something of that sort before you begin asking questions?'

'You will have your little jokes, won't you, Mr Morris? But I can assure you that you won't be joking by the time we've finished with you.'

'I saw an American gangster movie last month,' I said, 'in which the New York police used bright lights and rubber hoses to break down their suspect. However, since their suspect was Edward G. Robinson it didn't work; he refused to break. Then his gang raided the police station to break him out. They shot the policemen who'd used the bright lights and rubber hoses.'

Hyde took a deep breath, as if trying to be patient, then said through gritted teeth, 'That's not a scenario that's likely to be followed here, Mr Morris.'

I rocked back on my chair and grinned at him. 'You're probably right. Especially as I don't have a machine gun-armed gang waiting to break me out.'

'If we can get back to the matter in hand, sir. On the table you'll see a seating plan of the afternoon tea on the day that Mrs Connie Worth was murdered. Will you look at it please, sir, and tell me if it's accurate according to your memory?'

I made a show of carefully studying the paper from every angle before I replied, 'It looks pretty right to me. Has it been drawn to scale, I wonder? Because I think my chair should be shown a trifle closer to Mrs Worth's.'

'Thank you for that, sir,' said Hyde, speaking like a volcano trying very hard not to explode. 'You'll agree that you were seated next to Mrs Worth—closer, in fact, than anyone else present that afternoon?'

'I do concede that fact, inspector.'

'You sat on her left-hand side?'

'I did, and Uncle Teddy sat on her right. I suppose that makes us two the most likely suspects for slipping cyanide into her slice of fruit cake.'

'We have eliminated Mr Edward Dyer from our inquiries. So that leaves you, Mr Morris—and only you.'

'So how do you imagine I got the cyanide into the cake?'

'Perhaps you'd care to explain that to us yourself, sir?'

'I can't, because I didn't. And no one else saw me do anything at all suspicious. They've told you that, haven't they?'

'It's certainly true that whatever gesture or movement you employed in poisoning the cake went unnoticed.'

And so we went on—like a couple of cross-talk comedians in a second-rate music hall—for the next half an hour. At which time relief came in the form of a knock at the door.

'What is it?' barked Hyde.

Constable Dixon opened the door nervously and intruded his head and shoulders into the room.

Hyde snapped at him, like a terrier snapping at a rat, 'I told you I'm not to be disturbed.'

'It's Inspector Crispin, sir,' said the hapless Dixon, 'and he says he has a note for you from the Chief Constable.'

Hyde looked startled and wary, but said in that case Crispin should probably be admitted. He was. He said nothing, but the Scotland Yard man produced a hand-written note and handed it to Hyde.

Hyde read the note, then read it gain, then read it a third time. Then all the air seemed to go out of him and he shrank like a punctured balloon. He seemed to lose several inches in height as I watched.

For several moments we all sat, or in Crispin's case stood, like window dummies on display—none of us moving or speaking. Finally Hyde looked up at me and said, 'You're free to go.'

FORTY-EIGHT

~

Inspector Crispin and Sergeant Merrivale drove us back to Plumwood. The two police officers sat in the front seat, while Jack and I sat in the back. I was bending over tying up my newly restored shoe laces when I asked Jack, 'How did you manage it?'

'It was Inspector Crispin here you have to thank. All I did was to inform him that Hyde had swooped.'

'Well, in that case, many thanks, inspector. I owe you both my liberty and my sanity.'

Crispin chuckled. 'I don't think either were ever seriously at risk, Mr Morris.'

'So what did you do?' I asked as I looped my tie around my collar and began to construct a Windsor knot.

It seemed that instead of going to the police station to argue with Inspector Hyde he had driven directly to Colonel Weatherly's home. 'There,' he said, 'I laid out the case as Mr Lewis and I now understand it. The colonel immediately agreed that Hyde's action amounted to a waste of police time. He scribbled out a note for me, which I took to Hyde, with the result that you saw.'

Most of the rest of that trip was fairly quiet. I felt exhausted by my unhappy experience, Sergeant Merrivale was driving and concentrating on those narrow country roads, and both Jack and Crispin seemed to be deep in thought.

When the police car pulled up in front of Plumwood Hall, Sir William was crossing the lawn, walking his favourite golden retriever.

He pronounced himself glad to see me back and invited Jack to join the family for dinner that night. Jack accepted.

It was a much more agreeable affair than the night before. For a start, Edmund's return had lifted everyone's spirits, and Will was still bubbling over with enthusiasm and cheerful chatter. Edmund himself seemed more settled, and although he said little, just being back in familiar surroundings seemed to be doing him some good. He still looked pale and unwell and only nibbled at his food, but he managed to contribute the occasional brief utterance to the dinner table conversation.

Uncle Teddy was also in a high good humour, insisting on telling us tales of the early days of the family biscuit factory.

One thing Oxford does for a man is to teach him the art of small talk, so Jack kept up his end with the occasional anecdote, witty pun or Latin tag.

When dinner was over, Sir William apologised that he had work to do in his office, so Jack and I took our glasses of port and a bowl of nuts to the library and settled down among the books.

Jack, who had obviously spent much less time than I had in the collection, prowled up and down the shelves looking for treasures. I strolled down the longest of the bookcases and one volume caught my eye. It was Trotter's translation of Pascal's *Pensées*. Because Jack had referred to Pascal earlier in the day, I pulled it off the shelf and opened it at random.

I threw myself into an armchair, picked up my glass of port and began to read. I hadn't read more than a page and a half when I was startled to come across much the same point Jack had been making to me that morning.

Pascal ridiculed those who lived without any thought of life's latter end, and who let themselves be guided by their whims and pleasures without any reflection or sense of discomfort, and who only thought of making themselves happy in the moment. Pascal suggested they were hoping to abolish eternity by turning away their thoughts.

This was a bit too close to the bone for me, so I closed the book and returned it to the shelf. I needed to think about something a bit more cheerful—such as murder.

'The big puzzle,' I said to Jack as I helped myself to a handful of nuts, 'is still surely the method of the first murder. How was it done? Isn't that the issue?'

Jack turned towards me, his glasses reflecting the golden glow of the desk lamps in the library, making him look like a sparkling and particularly clever Irish pixie.

'Precisely,' he said in his rich, rumbling voice. 'That's the heart of the matter, young Morris.'

'And what about who? Whatever mysterious method was used to get cyanide into one slice of freshly baked cake—and only one—who did it? Or, as they say on the back of those yellow-jacketed thrillers Warnie reads: whodunit? Are you any closer to answering that question?'

'The pieces of the jigsaw puzzle are coming together. There are two clues drawing them together: the blackmail, and the forged poisons book at the village chemist shop.'

'I can see no connection,' I said.

'Isn't that what you asked *me* to do?' Jack asked, 'to find those connections?'

As we talked Jack kept browsing through the shelves. Taking down one highly decorated volume, he remarked that he thought it was much too late a publication to be part of this old collection.

'It is,' I agreed, 'it's 1904. But apparently some Boshams kept adding—inappropriately, I might add—to a collection that should have been left intact as a record of earlier centuries. I should really have pulled those newer volumes out and put them in a separate case.'

The book in Jack's hand was *William Tell Told Again* by P. G. Wodehouse.

'I think Warnie had a copy of this in the nursery at Little Lea—probably the same edition.' Jack's face was glowing at the memory as he spoke. Then a dark shadow passed over it. '1904 was,' he said, 'four years before mother died and everything changed for us.'

There was a long, sombre silence in the library, then Jack seemed to recover himself and said how nice it was to see the old book again, even though it clearly should not have a place in the Plumwood Hall collection.

'When I found it,' I said, 'I rather liked the opening sentence. Even though he's retelling an old story for children, it has a Wodehousian ring to it. Here, take a look at this.'

I reached out for the book, then thumbed it open and read: 'Once upon a time, more years ago than anybody can remember, before the first hotel had been built or the first Englishman had taken a photograph of Mont Blanc and brought it home to be pasted in an album and shown after tea to his envious friends, Switzerland belonged to the Emperor of Austria, to do what he liked with.'

I put down the book and said, 'Now that's the distinctive Wodehouse voice.'

But Jack was no longer paying attention to my ramblings. He had on his face an intense expression I had seen once or twice before—usually when he felt he had stumbled across a new discovery.

'William Tell,' he muttered, more to himself than me. 'Yes. It's not very probable. But it's possible. And if it's possible it's how it was done.'

'What are you going on about?'

'I need to speak to Crispin at once. Where's the telephone?'

I took Jack down to the entrance hall and pointed out the instrument. He called *The Cricketers' Arms* only to be told that the Scotland Yard man was out.

'I'm going to walk back to the pub to look for Crispin,' Jack said. 'You wait for me here; I shouldn't be long.'

FORTY-NINE

Back in the library I finished the port and nuts and waited for Jack. And waited and waited. At any minute I expected to see him walking up the drive with the two Scotland Yard officers beside him. But many slow minutes passed, then half an hour crawled by, and I became bored.

Finally I concluded they were not coming and I should not expect to see them until the next day.

It was a mild autumn night so I decided to go for a walk. There was a full moon, a large lemon moon floating in a vivid violet-blue sky filling the landscape with silvery brilliance—nocturnal but bright. It was a nice night for a walk in the soft breeze and the glowing moonlight.

Strolling through the darkened and strangely quiet house, I reached the flagged terrace by means of the French windows in the drawing room then set out across the lawn with no particular goal in mind.

Slowly I strolled in the general direction of the kitchen garden and the orchard beyond it. The garden wall was a long way from the house, and to reach it I had to cross the lawn, pass under the old ash tree and go through the rose garden. Beyond the flower beds was a slight rise crowned by the old summer house. And I decided to make that my stopping point.

I mounted the half dozen steps of the small building and dropped into one of the heavy old wooden chairs that were scattered around inside.

Just beyond the summer house, at the bottom of a gentle slope, was a small rivulet that gurgled in the night, flowing rapidly to meet the River Plum at some distant point. Through the open lattice walls I could see the bubbling stream, its many ripples catching the moonlight and reflecting it back like a thousand small bright lights twinkling on and off.

On a shelf not far from where I sat was an oil lamp, and beside it a box of matches. I rose, fiddled with the lamp, lit a match and soon had the summer house filled with a dim but cheerful yellow glow. Then I settled back in the welcoming arms of the old chair and was tempted to nod off for a few moments. In fact, I think I did.

Coming to with a start and looking up, I became aware of a dark figure on the steps, just outside the circle of light cast by the oil lamp. He was smoking a cigar, and the red glow looked like a ship's lantern gleaming in the distance over dark waves. Then the figure spoke.

'Evening, Morris.' It was Sir William. 'I saw you from my study window going for an evening stroll and I thought I'd join you.'

He climbed the steps of the summer house and sat in another of the large wooden chairs that furnished the place.

'And I brought a nightcap,' he said, holding up two glasses and a bottle of Napoleon brandy. He set these down on a small bamboo table, poured a generous helping of brandy into each of the tumblers and handed me one.

'Your good health,' he said, raising his glass and taking a sip.

For no particular reason I held my glass up and looked at the moon through it. There was a faint gathering of dust on the rim.

'This needs rinsing out,' I complained.

Sir William chuckled. 'Sorry, these glasses have been sitting in my study for some time. I should have fetched clean ones from the kitchen. Too late to rinse it now—you're not going waste that good Napoleon, are you?'

'Of course not.'

I continued to look at the lemon moon through the liquid, and if I had kept on staring I might have been inspired to turn the vision into poetry.

But Sir William was becoming irritable. 'Stop staring and drink up, old chap,' he snapped.

I raised the glass to my lips and then some instinct of self-preservation stopped me. The gathering of dust on the rim bothered me.

'I think I might go and get a clean glass,' I said.

In a moment Sir William was on his feet. 'I bring you out a glass of fine old brandy and you insult my hospitality by complaining about a little dust. Be a man, Morris! Drink up!'

Now, I don't like being bullied, not even by biscuit tycoons who have more money than good taste, and to my mind Sir William was not behaving like a gentleman. I put the untasted glass down on the bamboo table and said, 'In a moment. I'm not in a hurry.'

Sir William had risen from his chair and was standing beside me.

'As you wish,' he said. And it sounded as if he was speaking through gritted teeth. The next moment something struck the side of my head. I cried out, and fell sideways in the chair. I think I must have lost consciousness for a moment, because when my head began to clear Sir William was around on the other side of the chair and seemed to be fastening a thick leather belt around my arm—tying it to the arm of the chair.

'What's going on . . . ?' I mumbled, my words coming thickly. 'What are you doing?'

I tried to rise from the chair and found that my other arm was already strapped down. I pushed with my feet, but the old chair was so heavy it was impossible to lift it. I flopped backwards in the chair and shook my head, trying to clear it.

'A joke's a joke, old chap,' I mumbled, still having some difficulty getting my words out. 'But this is beyond the pale.'

Sir William paid no attention to my protest. Instead he picked up the glass of brandy I'd left on the bamboo table.

'Now,' he growled, 'you will drink the brandy as I ordered you to in the first place.'

'Is that what this is all about? Are you offended because I didn't drink your wretched brandy? Well, let me tell you that your reaction is not that of a gentleman.'

I was still feeling light headed. I think he must have struck me a severe blow to disorient me like that. Slowly things swam into focus, and I began to think clearly again. No one, not even an offended biscuit tycoon, straps his guests to a chair to force them to drink his brandy.

Whatever was happening, it was a good deal more sinister than that.

'What's so important about that particular glass of brandy?' I demanded.

Sir William held it up in his fingers and contemplated it for a few moments.

'Very well,' he said at length, 'I'll explain. It's probably reasonable that you should be told what's about to happen to you. And why.'

He paused and looked at me with a singular expression on his face. No doubt I had an odd expression on my face as well. But if I was wary, he was definitely sinister. Perhaps we resembled a cobra and a mongoose squaring off before they commenced battle—a battle that would be fatal for one of them.

'What's about to happen,' said Sir William slowly, breaking the heavy silence, 'is that you are about to die. From cyanide poisoning. It will look like suicide. And your suicide will be taken as a confession of guilt—a confession of murder. I'll probably type out a note to that effect on the small typewriter on your desk in the library.

'Once you're dead I'll remove those straps and leave the note here, on your lap. Inspector Hyde will feel triumphant and vindicated. Inspector Crispin will have no alternative but to return to London. Your celebrated Oxford friend will creep back to his college having failed you completely. And that will be the end of the Plumwood Village murders. The case will be closed, and those of us who have survived will go on with our lives. That is what is about to happen.'

'You're mad,' I gasped, struggling to get the words out—in fact, struggling to say anything in the face of such pathological nonsense. 'All I need to do is call out and there'll be people from the house out here in moments.'

'There's no one there. The family have gone to the cinema in Market Plumpton. They've taken Edmund there as a treat. This, as it happens, is also the servants' night off. The place is empty. And this house is quite isolated and the grounds are extensive, so you could scream your lungs out and be heard by nothing more than a fox in the woods or an owl on one of those high branches.'

'No one will believe I killed those women,' I protested. 'I have no motive.'

'You're a homicidal maniac, Mr Morris—didn't you know that? Inspector Hyde already thinks you are. Your current wave of killing was triggered by Connie Worth falsely accusing you of stealing a rare book from my library. And when you started killing, you couldn't stop. Hyde already believes that, and your death will persuade the rest of them that when you couldn't control your impulse to kill, your conscience wouldn't allow you to go on living.'

I was breathing rapidly by now and feeling it was important to keep this man talking. 'The dust on the rim of my brandy glass, that's cyanide powder?'

'Indeed it is, Mr Morris. It's the cyanide that's going to kill you.'

'So if you have the cyanide that means you must have committed all of the murders?'

'I see your Oxford-trained brain has not entirely deserted you. I am the answer to that "whodunit" question that has been troubling you.'

'You killed Connie Worth and Stephanie Basset and poor Ruth Eggleston?'

He smiled at me coldly, and a shiver ran down my spine as he replied, 'Guilty as charged, your honour. Not that anyone but you will ever know. But you might as well know, since, very shortly, you will know nothing at all . . . ever again.'

'We know, and the police know, about the blackmail, so I can see why you might have wanted to kill Connie Worth, but why the others?'

'All three of them posed threats to me and to my position. And all threats must be eliminated. That's the philosophy I've followed in business all my life.' (When he said those words, I remembered the conversation Jack and I had overheard.) 'Consequently I'm regarded as a ruthless businessman, and certainly a dangerous opponent. It was poor stupid Connie who started all this business by trying to blackmail me. She should never have done that. If she had behaved decently towards me she needn't have died, and the other two would also still be alive. It was her greed that killed her—and the Basset and Eggleston girls as well. All three died because of Connie Worth's greed. And now you will die too—a fourth victim of that odious woman.'

Trying to control my breathing, I said, 'Even if there's no one to hear my cries for help, or to come to my rescue, you still can't make me drink poison if I don't want to. For your ridiculous plan to work you need to get that stuff down my throat, and that's not about to happen.'

'Oh yes it is, Mr Morris,' Sir William said in a silken, sinister tone.

He bent over me, pushed my head against the back of the chair with one surprisingly powerful hand and raised the poisoned glass of brandy to my lips with the other.

I pressed my lips tightly closed and tried to pull away, but that heavy, high-backed old chair gave me very little room to move. I pulled on both arms, but the leather straps or belts or whatever they were held me tightly.

'You're helpless, Mr Morris,' cooed Sir William, 'so the sooner you accept that fact and do as you're told, the better.'

He pressed the glass against my face and the deadly poison of cyanide-laced brandy splashed up over my tightly sealed lips. I could feel droplets trickle down my cheeks towards my chin. Sir William bent more closely over me and I could feel his hot breath on my face.

I struggled against him, but even though I was an old Rugby blue, my muscles were useless to me—I was too confined, too tightly restricted, to be able to move or resist effectively.

The hand Sir William was using to press my forehead against the back of the chair began creeping down my face. Without releasing the pressure he positioned it so that his fingers could grasp my nostrils. The next moment I was struggling for breath.

'In a moment, Mr Morris—Tom, my old friend,' grunted Sir William, as he increased the pressure, 'in a moment your lungs will run out of oxygen. Then you will either suffocate or your mouth will open and you will gulp down the poisoned brandy. You'll find that opening your mouth will be an instinctive reaction when your lungs are aching and pleading for air. That's when you will die from cyanide poisoning.'

He was right. My lungs were begging for oxygen. My brain was shouting to me to open my mouth and gasp for life-giving air. I was close to blacking out, and about to give in and open my mouth wide when all the pressure stopped.

The hand on my head, the glass at my lips—they were gone.

'Breathe, Tom! Breathe!' said Jack from just beside me.

My lips flew apart and I hungrily gasped in a large lungful of air. I coughed and spluttered and I could feel Jack unfastening the straps that held me.

As my head slowly cleared I looked up to see Sir William in front of me, held on both sides by the strong arms of Sergeant Merrivale and Constable Nile.

Inspector Crispin was there too. He was speaking to Sir William, telling him he was under arrest.

Then Crispin turned to face me. 'I'm glad we arrived when we did, Mr Morris. Another minute and we would have been too late to save your life. You can thank your friend Mr Lewis. We were searching the house for you and Sir William and he spotted the light in the summer house.'

I looked up at Jack's friendly face and managed to croak out, 'Thanks, old chap.'

'Come along, Morris,' said Jack, placing one hand under my arm to help me up. 'Back to the house. It's all over now.'

FIFTY

~

The next hour passed in a kind of blur. I vaguely remember going back to the house and Sergeant Merrivale telephoning for a police car. Then the servants came back from their night off, and the family returned from their evening at the cinema.

I sat quietly in the background while Crispin gathered the family in the drawing room and, very diplomatically, explained the situation. Lady Pamela didn't break down and weep and wail as I had expected. Instead she seemed to stiffen and harden. Whatever turmoil she was experiencing within, she showed the world a face as cold as marble. Douglas was the one who broke down and sobbed quietly. Edmund and Uncle Teddy both looked confused. Edmund was led upstairs, with Drax taking one arm and young Will the other. Uncle Teddy sat in an armchair gently rocking back and forth and muttering anxiously about who would take care of the biscuits.

The police car arrived from Market Plumpton and Sir William was led away by his retinue of police officers.

Keggs got the household organised and summoned Lady Pamela's personal maid to take her upstairs to her room.

Jack kept glancing at me, then as the drawing room emptied told me that what I needed was a large cup of tea. He must have disappeared out to the kitchen to speak to Mrs Buckingham because he returned a short time later with a tea tray bearing a teapot, cups and saucers, sugar and milk. We took this into the library, and it was only when we both had large cups of tea in our hands that I asked Jack for a proper explanation.

He paused in thought before he replied. Then he began in that slow, steady rumble of his, just as he did in tutorials, with each word carefully weighed and used precisely.

'The significant fact for me was the character of Sir William Dyer. You'll recall one of the maids described him as a "dirty old man". What she meant was that he was lecherous. It's now plain that he was a serial adulterer and a serial seducer. I think we may safely assume he seduced a number of the prettier young maids who worked here at Plumwood Hall over the years.

'The most recent of these, tragically for her, was Ruth Eggleston. I wonder if Lady Pamela became aware of what was going on, and whether that was why the young woman had to leave the Hall and find work in the village. She, of course, imagined herself to be in love with Sir William, and he, for his part, may have told her the sort of lies she wanted to hear.

'Meanwhile, there was the one real passion of his life: Judith Trelawney, the attractive younger sister of his own wife. He was much too cautious a man to have written revealing letters unless he really was swept away by passion. And we know that in this case he did write such letters.

'The truth about Judith Trelawney's death will probably never be known. Did she accidentally fall to her death in Brighton, or was she murdered by the dark and ruthless Connie Worth? Either way, the outcome was the same—a single, compromising letter from Sir William fell into Connie Worth's hands. Her decision to use that letter for blackmail led not to the wealth she expected, but to her death.

'When this threat loomed, Sir William exploited Ruth Eggleston's romantic obsession, getting her to steal a small amount of potassium cyanide powder from the chemist's shop and cover its loss by forging an entry in the poisons book. It was seeing the connection between that forged entry and the blackmail that began my train of thought.'

Jack stopped and drained the last of his tea. Then he refilled his cup and started again.

'With Connie Worth's death, Sir William thought he was safe. But he wasn't. The attempted blackmail resumed. This time the blackmailer was Stephanie Bassett.'

'Stiffy? But if she was using that same letter to blackmail Sir William, how did she get hold of it? And what makes you think she was also attempting blackmail?' I was scratching my head at this point, trying to understand everything that had been going on under my nose, as it were, without my being aware of it.

'Some of what follows,' said Jack, 'is speculation. But there's enough evidence to suggest that the course of events ran thus. Connie Worth was not blackmailing Sir William only. She had other victims. Those receipts for purchases for the kitchen and the cellar we found in her room: they were either evidence of petty dishonesty, of inflating the household accounts, or Mrs Worth thought they were. She was either attempting, or contemplating, using them to blackmail the staff. I suspect she was also blackmailing young Douglas over his gambling debts. That would explain his bitterness towards her.

'Miss Bassett was another blackmail victim. You and I saw Stephanie Bassett in the arms of David Evans when she was supposed to be engaged to Douglas Dyer. If there was a revealing letter, either from Miss Bassett to Mr Evans or the other way around, and if Connie Worth's snooping put that letter in her hands, then Stephanie Bassett was also being blackmailed.'

Jack paused to let me take this in, and sip on his tea. Then he resumed.

'Following Connie Worth's death, Stephanie Bassett hurried to Mrs Worth's room to recover the letter with which she had herself been blackmailed. In the course of her hunt through Mrs Worth's room, she found that other letter—Sir William's letter to Judith Trelawney. Of Miss Bassett's moral standards we've seen a sufficient demonstration to know that she wouldn't hesitate to use that letter herself as a blackmail vehicle. So from Sir William's point of view she became a threat, she stepped into Connie Worth's shoes, and she too had to die.

'Of course it was Miss Bassett who hid that letter in the *Romeo and Juliet* in the library. She may have found it amusing to hide a love letter in a play about tragic love. And she believed it would be safe there—at least temporarily. Before she could retrieve it and put it somewhere safer, she was poisoned.

'Then poor Ruth Eggleston's conscience began to bother her. Sir William must have met with her secretly at night in an attempt to persuade her not to tell the police to whom she had really supplied the cyanide. When she wouldn't listen, he poisoned her and threw her body over the cliff.'

'Yes, yes,' I replied quickly. 'The "who" is now abundantly clear. I can see how Sir William had a motive to commit each of the three murders. And the "how" of murders two and three is not at all puzzling—he had ample opportunity to slip some cyanide into Stiffy's sherry and he must have persuaded young Ruth to drink some brandy laced with cyanide. But how on earth did he kill Connie Worth?'

In my agitation I stood up and began to pace up and down the library.

'He wasn't even there, remember?' I said. 'He wasn't at that afternoon tea. He was up in his study on the first floor. I caught a glimpse of him at the window, so I know he was really there. Keggs's evidence supports that. So how, from that distance, did he get cyanide into one slice, and only one slice, of freshly baked cake? Surely that's utterly impossible.'

'Not impossible,' said Jack, 'just improbable. But sometimes the improbable happens.'

'But how?' I cried, throwing my hands in the air.

'It was young Will who gave us the first clue when we met him on the terrace. He told us that Edmund, during an earlier visit before his illness, taught both him and Sir William to shoot those South American native weapons. With, he told us, deadly accuracy. And on the wall of Sir William's study is a South American blowpipe. Furthermore, remember what the chemist, Arthur Williamson, was doing when we visited him in his shop? He was working at a small pill-making hand press. He was pressing powder into small, hard little pills. That's what Sir William did, with Ruth Eggleston's help, late one night in the chemist shop when the village was asleep. He used that hand press to turn a small amount of the potassium cyanide powder into a few small, hard pills.'

'And then?' I asked.

'Then he used the blowpipe, with deadly accuracy, to fire one of those pills into the slice of cake on Connie Worth's plate. He fired from the open window of his study on the first floor. It would have only taken a moment. He had lost none of his old skill, and his aim was excellent. He fired, then returned the blowpipe to its place on his wall before Keggs arrived with his brandy. He calmly sipped his brandy waiting for Connie Worth to bite into her slice of cake—in which the small tablet of potassium cyanide was now embedded. She did, and she swallowed before she realised anything was wrong. As she began convulsing, Sir William and Keggs were standing side by side at his study window.'

'Ingenious!' I said. 'In fact, doubly so. Sir William's murder method was ingenious, and so is your solution. And this is what you told Inspector Crispin?'

'It is—inspired, I might add, by that book about William Tell. When I lifted that down from the shelf I saw the point at once.'

'The point being?'

'The ability to fire a small missile over a considerable distance with precise accuracy. That put the last piece of the puzzle in place, and I hurried off to lay the matter before the good inspector.'

Jack rose from his armchair and wandered over in the direction of my desk, still nursing his cup and saucer in his hand.

'Are you finished here?' he asked.

'Completely,' I replied. 'I could leave tomorrow.'

'Then you should. Put all this drama behind you and return to the life of deep thought and profound meditation for which you are best equipped.'

I smiled as I said, 'And what should I be meditating on?'

'Why, the subject of our recent discussions, of course. Tell me, Morris, have you ever read the service for the burial of the dead in the Book of Common Prayer?'

'Not my favourite bedtime reading, I must admit.'

'You should. It would do you a power of good. You see, dear old Thomas Cranmer wrote that service not for the dead, whose fate is sealed and settled by the time the coffin is being lowered into the ground, but for the living. The great thrust of the service is along the lines of: remember that you too shall also die. "Man that is born of woman hath but a short time to live," in Cranmer's sparkling prose; "He cometh up and is cut down like a flower." And so on.'

'Charming thoughts,' I said sarcastically.

'Important thoughts,' Jack retaliated, 'since all of us shall one day be translated from this life to the next. And if we don't spend our lives preparing for that, we are wasting our lives.'

He put his teacup down on my desk and smiled at me broadly. 'Come along, young Morris, grab your hat and coat and come with me down to the pub. Tea is all very well, but there are moments that call for a pint.'

AUTHOR'S NOTE

~

This adventure in which C. S. Lewis helps to investigate a series of three murders is entirely fictitious. However, Lewis was famous for the care and support he showed his friends—in this case his (fictional) former student and friend Tom Morris. In this tale these two, Lewis and Morris, re-encounter several (fictional) characters (mainly police officers) they had previously met in their first criminal investigation together, recorded in *C. S. Lewis and the Body in the Basement*.

This story is set less than twelve months after that earlier case. Once again we are in the middle of the Golden Age of Detective Fiction, and in the sort of country-house setting so beloved of writers such as Agatha Christie and Dorothy L. Sayers.

There are a number of period references in the book worth explaining:

- 'Eeyore' is the gloomy donkey in A. A. Milne's book *Winnie-the-Pooh* (published in 1926).
- *Boy's Own Paper* was a British story paper aimed at young and teenage boys, published weekly from 1879.
- 'Mr Marconi' refers to Guglielmo Marconi (1874–1937), often credited as the inventor of radio.

- 'Dr Havard' refers to Dr R. E. Havard (1901–1985), Lewis's GP and a member of his literary club, 'The Inklings'.
- Poirot (with his 'little grey cells') is the fictional detective created by Agatha Christie.
- 'Little Lea' was the name of the childhood home in Belfast in which C. S. Lewis grew up.
- Boxen—the writings of the very young Lewis and his brother Warren ('Warnie') about their imaginary world, *Boxen*—have now been published (in 1985).
- PPE is the shorthand way of referring to the Oxford University course that deals with philosophy, politics and economics.
- Owen Barfield (1898–1997) was a lifelong friend of C. S. Lewis.
- 'Tollers' was Lewis's way of referring to his friend J. R. R. Tolkien (author of *The Lord of the Rings*).
- 'Mr Wells' scientific romances' are the early science fiction novels of H. G. Wells, including *The Invisible Man* and *The Time Machine*.
- Jack's fondness for science fiction stories: some years after this story is set Lewis wrote his own trilogy of science fiction stories: *Out of the Silent Planet* (1938), *Perelandra* (1943) and *That Hideous Strength* (1945).
- Adam Fox was Dean of Divinity at Magdalen College during Lewis's time there. He was a member (along with Tolkien and others) of Lewis's literary group, 'The Inklings'.
- *Union Jack* was a boys' weekly story paper that published the adventures of fictional detective 'Sexton Blake'.
- *Chums* was another boys' weekly story paper published from 1892 to the Second World War. It was full of adventure stories and informative articles.
- *Bradshaw's Railway Guide* was the name of the printed

railway timetables published from the mid-19th century to the mid-20th century.

- 'Tollers and Dyson'—J. R. R. Tolkien and Hugo Dyson, two of Lewis's Oxford friends.

- 'The great Wodehouse' refers to P. G. Wodehouse, the British humourist, whose 96 books introduced to the world such beloved characters as the scatterbrained aristocrat Bertie Wooster and his unflappable butler Jeeves.

- Mary Roberts Rinehart was an early twentieth-century writer of murder mysteries, sometimes called the American Agatha Christie.

- Ethel M. Dell wrote popular British romance novels in the 1920s and '30s.

- Christmas Humphreys was a British barrister and judge who became a prominent proponent of Buddhism.

- *Who Moved the Stone?* by Frank Morrison was published in 1930. It carefully researches and analyses the evidence for the resurrection of Jesus.

- John Wesley (1703–1791) was the most widely travelled evangelical preacher of his time and the founder of Methodism.

- 1904, 'four years before our mother died'—Lewis's mother (Florence Augusta Hamilton Lewis, known a 'Flora') died from cancer in 1908. Shortly afterwards Lewis was sent by his father to an English boarding school (which he hated).